EVERETT

JENIFER RUFF

This is a work of fiction. Names, characters, places, and incidents are products of the author's imagination or are used fictitiously and are not to be construed as real. Any resemblance to actual events, locations, organizations, or person, living or dead, is entirely coincidental.

WCP

World Castle Publishing, LLC
Pensacola, Florida

Copyright © Jenifer Ruff 2014
Print ISBN: 9781629891422
eBook ISBN:9781629891439
First Edition World Castle Publishing, LLC, September 15, 2014
http://www.worldcastlepublishing.com

Licensing Notes

Cover: Karen Fuller
Editor: Eric Johnston

PROLOGUE

Everett College
March

New Hampshire was close to breaking its seasonal record of one hundred and twenty inches of snow. It had been accumulating steadily for four months. The roads inside and around campus were plowed frequently for the students and professors of Everett College. Snow and ice removal trucks had left behind a thick layer of salt brine, sand, and gravel. Brooke could feel the crunchy texture of the mix each time her running shoes touched down on the shoveled roads.

Brooke enjoyed the solitude she experienced when she transitioned from the cleared paths lined with towering walls of snow onto Stonewall Road, which was almost untouched. Very few people traveled along this isolated back road, it curved through an open valley, virtually undisturbed from one day to the next. It was plowed only occasionally because it went in the opposite direction from the chic restaurants, artsy cafes, and upscale boutiques that existed for the college students and their visiting families. Brooke ran this route in the evenings, covering the same peaceful ten-and-a-half-mile course every time. She could only manage to fit it into her schedule a few times a week because she taught an exercise class in town on most nights.

Large maple trees hovered above her, their massive branches supporting thick clumps of snow. Beyond the trees, acres of unused farmland stretched out wide to meet mountains in every direction. The top edge of a crumbling stone wall peeked out from its cover of snow. In a few weeks the snow would begin to melt. By that time, she wouldn't need to wear three layers of running gear, a hat, and gloves. There would be more daylight then and she would be able to complete her route before it was immersed in darkness.

Her breathing was barely audible, calm and rhythmic, but the air felt sharp entering her nose. Suddenly she heard a scraping, *swoosh!* behind her. Without altering her pace, she turned her head and saw the shapes of two cross country skiers approaching in the dim light. She was usually alone for her entire run on the remote country road, but she had encountered this couple before. At least one of them was bound to be a professor at Everett. They recognized Brooke and easily remembered her; the slim young woman dressed head to toe in black with a long blonde ponytail trailing from under her hat.

They smiled and said hello as they passed, their faces red from the cold and their efforts. Later, when they were back inside their home warming up in front of a fire with glasses of wine, they would say that the blonde ponytail girl was beyond foolish to be running alone at night. They would chide themselves for not telling her so when they had the chance. They were virtually in the middle of nowhere. Who knew what type of opportunistic psychopath they might encounter? Yes, it was unlikely, but not impossible. But as they slid past her, they were simply caught up in the sheer joy of strenuous exercise and recognizing the special bond they shared with Brooke because, like them, she also possessed the discipline and fortitude required to brave the extreme cold.

No one except the skiers knew she ran alone through the rural countryside in the evening. She wanted to keep it that way. Brooke preferred being alone with her thoughts, which were not wandering, but instead a regimented review of everything she remembered from the day's lectures. In each class she took meticulous notes as her professor spoke or wrote on the whiteboard. She read over her notes before the end of each day, in addition to the mental reviews she did while exercising. Eventually the class material became as familiar as lyrics to a favorite song and she could easily recall everything she had learned. On this run she was reciting the day's Immunology lecture.

If anyone else knew she was running alone in the gathering darkness beyond campus they would undoubtedly have tried to prevent her from going. The disappearance of one of her classmates a few months earlier had caused an initial panic amongst the student body. It appeared that the young woman had simply vanished at the end of the semester, the beginning of winter break. It was a chaotic time with students in various stages of departure as a historic blizzard assaulted New England and dominated the news. Because of the timing, no one was positive when or where she had gone missing from campus. Many people thought she might have wandered off drunk while celebrating the end of the term and succumbed to hypothermia in the storm, but they weren't sure. It had been three months since the mysterious incident and there was still no sign of her. Brooke couldn't help but to listen intently whenever she heard someone speculating about it.

Now everyone at Everett was strongly encouraged to walk with a "buddy" even from building to building and to call campus security for a ride if they needed to go anywhere alone at night. At first the anxiety levels were high and everyone complied with the stringent security precautions, but gradually they became more relaxed about making short trips from building to building. However, that relaxation had not by any means stretched to include running alone at night miles away from campus. That would have been advised against even before the disappearance. But fear was something Brooke had never experienced and she had always taken risks. When she exercised, she felt invincible.

The turning point on her familiar route was up ahead, represented by a rusty iron bridge. Underneath it was a large creek, frozen solid. There was a three-story drop from the bridge above, although so much snow had slid down the steep sides and on top of the ice that it filled in a large part of that distance now. Getting close to the water was extremely difficult, sharp rocks and steep terrain barring a descent. Brooke's first time there had been on a beautiful day in late fall. She had studied the patterns of water moving over and around a myriad of rocks all the while doing dozens of toe raises, first in parallel and then in turned out position. She had put forth her best effort to appreciate the moment despite the pressing feeling that she needed to get back to campus to study. That was one of the few occasions in the fall when she was simply relaxing, although attempting to relax would be a more accurate description of the event. The second time Brooke set foot on the bridge was remarkably different from the first. It was at night in December and she was alone amidst a ferocious blizzard. The storm was so powerful that it stole a once-in-a-lifetime opportunity from her. It was also the reason that she now felt compelled to run there at least once a week.

Before she completed the second half of her run, she needed to stretch, and she knew it was best to lengthen her muscles while they were warm. Stretching her muscles was just as important as other exercises for shaping them and she said so often when she was teaching.

Brooke effortlessly lifted her straightened right leg and placed her heel onto the bridge railing. Stretching her spine long to create more space between each vertebra, she placed her chest against her thigh. Reaching her gloved hand past the top of her shoe, she held still, feeling the luxurious pull of her hamstrings lengthening. After a count of twelve, she took her right leg off the railing, watching her breath spread out in the air before her, and replaced it with her other leg. Instinctively, she raised her index finger and middle finger together and was about to press them against her carotid artery under her chin to take a pulse. This was something she did habitually during her workouts to monitor her cardiovascular system. But she was wearing thick gloves and it was too cold to remove them, so she dropped her fingers without doing the count. It was easy for her to gauge her heart rate without feeling her pulse anyway. With her cheek turned sideways against her lower shin, she began to carefully scan the snow below while continuing to hold the stretch. The light was very dim, the sun almost below the horizon, blocked by the distant mountains. She stopped scanning and adjusted her gaze because she thought she caught sight of a fuchsia colored spot adjacent to the frozen creek. Her vision was exceptional, even in the present dusk, but she still wasn't positive she was seeing anything other than snow. After squinting and staring intently at the area below, she eventually decided it was just her imagination.

Nothing to see yet. Maybe next time.

She couldn't wait for the snow to melt. There was something she really wanted to see under that bridge.

Twenty-six degrees was too cold to contemplate anything for very long while standing still, so, after a quick quad stretch, she set off on the road back to Everett, determined to finish the second half of her run at a faster pace than the first so that she could hopefully feel even a little relaxed and content when she was done.

CHAPTER ONE

Eight months earlier

Everett was considered one of the most beautiful campuses in the country, its grounds brilliantly designed and well maintained. The school was founded in the late nineteenth century and boasted some of the finest examples of collegiate Gothic style architecture. Even the more recently constructed buildings: the new science labs, the athletic facilities and two additional dormitories were built to fit in seamlessly with the original architecture.

Upon arriving at her new school, Brooke went to her room to drop off all of her worldly belongings. With her father's help it had taken only two trips to move it all from his car into her dorm.

Brooke's father, Ian Walton, was a professor at Cedarhurst, the college from which she had recently transferred. Brooke knew that he would miss having her there. Certainly it was a source of pride for him to say his oldest daughter was a student at Everett, one of the top universities in the world, but it wasn't the same as having her on *his* campus. Brooke had been Cedarhurst's star student. Most of his associates knew who she was and that she could have been accepted at any college thanks to her grades, impressive extra-curricular activities, merit scholarship awards and perfect SATs. Children of faculty received free tuition at Cedarhurst, but Brooke would have received a full academic scholarship anyway, based on her high school record. So instead she was given free room and board and a small stipend. There was no question she deserved it. A few students like Brooke could raise the average admission and enrollment statistics for Cedarhurst in an extremely positive way. She was harder working than her professors had ever been, handing in papers and projects that stood out from the rest on every level. On a daily basis Ian Walton's colleagues brought him stories of Brooke's brilliance, about how she went above and beyond on every assignment, challenging their own thinking. He loved hearing it. He would miss hearing it. But he also supported her desire to transfer after all that had happened. It was a terrible tragedy and then unfortunate timing on Brooke's part. Something no young woman should have to experience. It had cost Cedarhurst its top student just as she was blazing a path to become its most esteemed graduate.

Brooke hugged her father goodbye, spent a few minutes setting up her laptop and opening bags, then changed into workout gear and headed straight to the Fitness Center. Within her first hour on campus, she was already sweating on a step mill. She was breathing hard and increasing the level to the machine's maximum pace when a petite woman with tight, curly hair approached her. It was Robin Smith, a renowned statistician with a super outgoing personality and a penchant for fitness.

"Hi. I couldn't help notice you working out and I know I've never seen you before. What type of athlete are you?" Robin assumed that Brooke was a new student on one of the school's athletic teams.

"Oh… I do just about everything," Brooke responded between controlled breaths. Other than the fact that she didn't officially play any sports. In fact she had a minor distaste for chasing a ball around; this was an accurate summarization of her exercise endeavors.

"What sort of everything?" Robin asked, looking up at Brooke with an encouraging expression.

"I love to exercise—any form of movement. I run and I teach exercise classes. At least I did. I just transferred to Everett for my junior year. This is my first day here. I have an interview set up at Resolution Fitness tomorrow, hopefully I'll be teaching classes there soon. I need a job."

"Interesting. That makes sense. You look like a professional dancer."

Robin remained standing as if she had all the time in the world, so Brooke kept talking.

"I've created my own formula for sculpting muscles. It's sort of unique and something I'm still developing."

"You need to teach some classes here. Early in the morning, or even at noon. We used to have a great instructor who taught a class for just the faculty and staff, she collected a cash payment at the door, but she graduated last year. We need someone new. I'll get my friends to come. I would love to see this formula of yours in action because it certainly appears to work. You just promise us we can end up toned like you and you'll have the room full in no time." Robin's smile was contagious, and Brooke found herself smiling back, excited.

"Okay. I can look into that. I would love to do that actually. I saw several dance studio rooms in the gym. Who would I ask about their availability?"

"Start with the fitness director. His office is just inside the main door to your left. If he's not the right person, he'll know who you should ask. Tell him Robin Smith sent you. That's me, by the way. I teach statistics. What is your major?"

"Double major in Biology and Chemistry. I'm pre-med."

"Excellent. I teach a Bio-Statistics course. It's very useful for science majors."

"I'm Brooke. Brooke Walton."

"Welcome to Everett, Brooke. See about setting up some exercise classes…that would be great." Robin walked away, leaving Brooke feeling excited about having a new project to work out.

By the end of the next day, Brooke had reserved an exercise studio in the gym for three days a week at noon, the only time it was available. Next, she created signs to advertise her method of teaching and tacked them up around the gym, on every bulletin board, in bathroom stalls, and at every location where staff convened.

***

Brooke received a note in her mailbox from Sheila Davidson, the Dean of Students for Everett's Junior Class. Apparently, Sheila liked to meet with all of the transfer students, at their convenience. Brooke walked past the administrative offices every day for the past few weeks when she traveled the route from her science labs to her dorm. She had scheduled a few minutes from her very packed schedule to drop by today after her last lab.

"I'm glad you were able to come in and talk with me for a moment. I try to meet with all of our transfer students after they've been here a few weeks. It's interesting to hear your perspectives, particularly since you have another college experience with which to compare this," Sheila said.

Brooke sat up straight and tall in a comfortable arm chair and surveyed her surroundings. This was her first time inside the Administrative Building. Like all of the buildings at Everett, it appeared to have been built with the objective of enduring beauty. Layers of mahogany molding framed the room, large antique rugs added texture, thickly framed oil paintings and drawings of campus decorated the walls. Brooke wondered if anyone had been remotely concerned with cost during the design, construction or decoration phases. Cedarhurst, which was smaller, less established and mostly for locals, had tried hard to achieve this look in a few select buildings, but didn't come close.

While Brooke studied the room, Sheila studied Brooke. She was even more dazzled by Brooke's appearance now that she was able to inspect her up close. Brooke's naturally blonde hair had underlying streaks of soft brown that matched her dark eyebrows. The symmetry of her face was near perfect and her porcelain skin added to the overall delicateness of her features. Her front tooth was slightly chipped, providing the only visible imperfection. Sheila knew first hand that Brooke was exceptionally strong, despite her slender build.

"I'm really enjoying your exercise classes," Sheila announced. "I was sore the first week, especially my glutes, but I can already feel my body tightening up."

Glutes, short for the gluteal muscles, was a word that was not part of Sheila's vocabulary until she started taking Brooke's sculpt class, a combination of yoga, Pilates, and intense ballet toning moves. At least fifteen minutes of every class was focused on working the glutes. Now she was hyper aware of how it felt to squeeze and tuck them repeatedly until they were burning from deep inside. She also knew how good they could look after enough repetitions from watching Brooke demonstrate the tiny controlled movements in class. Of course, she understood that no matter how defined your muscles were, they could not be seen or appreciated unless you were lean enough for them to show. Brooke made that pretty clear during the workouts. Which is why Sheila was making her best effort to cut down on sugary foods. It was also why she was specifically thinking about the leftover chocolate cupcakes she had seen on the table outside her office a few hours earlier. Sheila consciously blocked out thoughts of tempting desserts she didn't need and pulled her chair in closer to her desk. She raised her arm to shoulder height and wrapped her fingers around her navy cardigan-covered bicep to indicate that the tightening process was occurring there as well.

"I'm looking forward to putting my jeans on this weekend because I think they're going to be a bit looser." Sheila crossed her legs, leaned back in her leather chair and smiled. Her husband had also commented on the change in her physique. There was no doubt that positive transformation had occurred, and as long as his compliments kept flowing, she would keep attending Brooke's classes.

"It's good to hear you're enjoying the workouts," Brooke said sincerely in her soft-spoken way. During her exercise classes, she wore a microphone and instructed in the same quiet, even voice.

Sheila was one of about thirty adults who had been showing up to attend Brooke's noon time classes. She thought she would be teaching her first class to a few people, but was thrilled to count twenty-one people in attendance, including a smiling Robin Smith. Robin had loved the class, and told her this enthusiastically when it was finished, along with telling everyone else that they could thank her for giving Brooke the idea. A core group had continued to show up and spread the word to their colleagues. Several of the participants had enjoyed the class so much they had asked her where else she taught. Some were now paying the guest fee to attend the evening classes she was teaching off-campus. Resolution Fitness was making a nice chunk of extra change each time Brooke taught.

While Sheila had showered and changed into a professional looking ensemble after exercising, Brooke had power walked directly from the gym to her one o'clock biology lab, simultaneously eating a peanut butter and jelly sandwich and some trail mix she had put together at breakfast. She was still wearing her workout clothes: her signature outfit, essentially a uniform of black cropped workout pants, a fitted tank top, and a tight black zip up jacket. Her wardrobe was limited, made up almost entirely of exercise clothes. The reason she had so many of those could be attributed to her choice of outfits a few years ago when her mother happened to attend one of Brooke's most popular step classes. Mary Walton walked into the overflowing class to find her daughter in front of everyone wearing a faded gray tank top that was once bright yellow and knee-length pants so visibly frayed they looked like the bottom half of a pirate costume. She was not impressed with what she termed Brooke's "ragamuffin" look, and she couldn't understand why her incredibly naturally beautiful daughter didn't seem to care how she presented herself to the outside world. From that day on, Brooke received a new exercise outfit from her mother every Christmas and for every birthday.

"So, you're planning to apply to medical schools next year?" Sheila asked. She was glancing through Brooke's admission packet as she spoke. It was full of academic awards, accolades, and glowing recommendations, not unlike the files of all the other Everett students.

Brooke loved to talk about her plans for the future. When she was very young, she came across a Harvard study, which proved that people who wrote down their goals were more likely to achieve them. Ever since then she had made a point of documenting her goals, along with sub-goals and all the steps necessary to fulfill them. She had a detailed plan recorded in her journals, and she revisited it on a regular basis to make sure she was on track. Since elementary school, she had wanted to be a surgeon. She wanted to hold another person's life in her hands. To achieve that goal she was determined to graduate at the top of her class, summa cum laude, attend one of the top medical schools in the country, and then do her internship, residency, and fellowship at the best locations for her specialty.

Brooke knew she was different in ways she had successfully managed to hide, but when it came to school work and exercise, her overenthusiasm had always been commended. In those two areas she knew she was respected and admired and did not have to pretend to be someone other than who she was.

"Yes, I'm pre-med, so I'm taking mostly science classes....getting the Inorganic Chemistry II and Genetics taken care of this term, also Mammalian Anatomy and Macroeconomics 101."

The economics course fulfilled a requirement, as Everett expected its students to be well rounded. The rest of her course load came from the biology and chemistry departments. Her favorite class this semester was Mammalian Anatomy because the labs included several animal dissections. Undergraduate students never worked with human cadavers, so animal dissections were the best she could hope for until medical school. She loved examining the animals' insides; studying how all the different internal systems functioned together. Even the smaller components of living organisms, tissues and cells, were revealed as purposeful little machines under the powerful electron microscope.

As interesting as she found anatomy, her true passion was pathology. Brooke was fascinated with abnormalities, the transformational effects of disease, and ultimately, death. She felt a stir of excitement even thinking about it. She kept most of these feelings private; she knew they weren't completely normal. When the time came to fill out her medical school applications, she would not be describing the powerful allure of fetal abnormalities, for example, to any of the medical school admissions officers. If she explained what truly motivated her, she would most likely be deluged with recommendations for a dozen psychiatrists. She planned to write her medical school application essays about a burning desire to help people. She was certain that the admissions department expected some unique and interesting variation of that explanation and she was damn good at delivering exactly what people wanted to hear. If that wasn't the truth, she would be doing her push-ups in a prison cell right now rather than having a pleasant conversation with the Dean at Everett.

"I have Ms. Fisk for Genetics. She's excellent," Brooke announced.

"Yes, Ms. Fisk is one of everyone's favorites."

"I would love for her to be my thesis advisor," Brooke added. Her senior thesis would involve a hypothesis related to muscle response. It would be something groundbreaking. She hadn't nailed down the details yet, but she had several ideas she had been slowly developing for years outside the classroom.

A concerned look appeared on Sheila's face. "Do you know that Everett doesn't require a thesis? It's optional." She paused, looking concerned. "Brooke, you had a strong academic transcript when you transferred here. I have your files and I looked through everything after I started taking your exercise class." She smiled, but cringed inside as she recalled some of the specific information included in Brooke's transfer file. As a dean, it was perfectly acceptable for her to be familiar with students' applications, grades, and any other pertinent information that happened to fall into those files, such as, in Brooke's case, evaluations from grief counselors. Sheila had almost crossed a line she was trying to avoid. She was intent on staying away from any reference to Brooke's past at Cedarhurst and the terrible scene Brooke had encountered there. Sheila knew it was the reason Brooke had transferred. She assumed Brooke was trying to escape and forget those memories, not to be reminded of them.

"And I expect your efforts here will be just as solid..."

Without a doubt, thought Brooke. The one lesson her mother had ingrained in her psyche was that her grades meant everything.

Straight A's were Brooke's ticket for whatever she wanted out of life.

"But you're already taking an extra course and you have four labs. I also know that you're teaching exercise classes, what, seven times a week?" Sheila asked.

"Something like that," Brooke answered. In truth it averaged more like seven to ten classes a week because she could almost always count on other instructors to call her when they needed a substitute. Since Brooke always said yes, she became the first person that the other instructors asked.

"That's a lot to take on, in a very competitive environment. There's no doubt you're a hard working young lady. I just want to make sure you leave some time to enjoy yourself while you're here. It goes by so quickly you know." Sheila lifted her mug to her lips, conveying both friendship and consideration with her comment as she took a sip of tea. She was thirty-four years old. Being surrounded by the Ivy League coeds at Everett served as a constant reminder that she wasn't quite as young as she would have liked, although she much preferred her wiser self.

"Not to worry. I'm really good at managing my time. I'll fit it all in," Brooke responded with confidence. "I don't intend to miss out on anything important while I'm here." Brooke was meticulously punctual and always, always thinking ahead in her day to where she needed to be and what she needed to do next. That was one of the reasons college life agreed with her so well. Firmly scheduled times for classes, meals, work, and exercise provided a regimented structure, with open slots in between to be filled with homework and studying. That was all she needed.

Brooke shifted her gaze to the antique looking clock on the wall. There was something else she wanted to say, so badly it was like a burning itch. Something was terribly off with Mrs. MacIntyre, her chemistry professor. She didn't have her act together and she had some serious social skill issues, which, Brooke realized, may not have been relevant. The students had been quizzed on topics that were never presented during their lectures. For the first time in her academic life, Brooke was struggling, unsure of what was required to do well. She had never, ever had trouble with any of her classes before, not just because she was brilliant, but because of her hard work and focus. But her stomach grumbled softly, reminding her she needed this meeting to be brief so that she could grab a quick dinner in the dorm before she had to teach again. Then, if everything went according to plan, and she always made sure it did, she would shower before she left the gym and still have a few solid hours to study before she could concede to sleep. It was time to say good-bye to Sheila, before her schedule was compromised.

"It was so nice to speak with you, but I don't want to take up any more of your time and I need to get going, too. Thank you so much." She gave Sheila her warmest smile as she lifted her backpack off the ground and raised herself gracefully out of her seat.

"You take care of yourself. And please let me know if there's anything I can help you with while you're here. I'll see you on Friday. Work us hard, make us sore!" Sheila laughed. Then she readied herself for her next appointment, which would not be as pleasant. She was expecting a young man who was going to get his last warning about applying himself and improving his grades before he would be forced to look elsewhere to continue his college experience.

"Oh no."

Sheila remembered something just after Brooke left the room.

One of Sheila's responsibilities was to informally discuss Everett's honor code with new transfer students. Everett expected its students, teachers, staff, and administrators to adhere to the principles of honesty and integrity set forth in the honor code. With all the talk about Brooke's exercise class, she had completely forgotten to do so. Sheila chose not to call Brooke back to discuss it. Brooke had already signed a pledge to abide by the honor code, acknowledging that any form of social or academic dishonesty was a serious offense at Everett. She had also completed a required online tutorial that familiarized students with the code in its entirety. Sheila didn't feel especially concerned about her oversight, particularly not with a student like Brooke, who was already contributing in positive ways to the Everett community. Besides, Sheila firmly believed that people would do the right thing when trusted and given the chance, especially at Everett.

***

Brooke met Ethan Altman for the first time in the Blaise Bisaillon library, her favorite building aside from the fitness center. She was crazy about the library from the first moment she set foot inside. She loved the juxtaposition of its cool beauty, created by the smooth grey stone walls, and its inherent warmth. There were special touches everywhere. Bits of wisdom in ancient languages were carved above arched doorways and cozy armchairs, massive tomes were ceremoniously held open for reference, and collections with elaborately decorated spines made her feel honored to be in their presence. And all of this assembled for the sole purpose of studying, the activity that consumed more of Brooke's waking hours than anything else.

Brooke's first stop was the library's main desk, where she signed out a copy of a chemistry book that was too expensive for her to purchase. As she searched for a place to settle in, someone vacated the ideal spot, an upholstered armchair in a carpeted alcove. She quickly claimed the seat, took a deep breath and then settled in to master the chemistry material. Brooke could mentally stay focused on her studies for hours, but was challenged physically to sit still for that long. An inner compulsion forced her to move around constantly, as if her body craved movement. She began comfortably ensconced in the large chair in her normal sitting position, belly button pulled in tightly against her spine, rib cage knitted together, shoulders down her back, as she read about valence shell electron pair repulsion.

First there were subtle changes, shifting her weight from her right hip to her left, which progressed to sitting cross-legged. For an hour she progressed through her assignment, using VSEPR rules to predict the geometries of specific molecules, and a variety of yoga poses that fit in the constraints of the chair. Finally, her mind still fresh but her body restless, she saw that she was partially hidden in the alcove, and gracefully slid into a full center split on the floor in

21

front of the chair. She rested her chest on the ground, feeling the pull of the isometric stretch and the sensation of her muscles gradually relaxing. Propping the chemistry book on its edge, she continued to read.

Ethan also preferred to study in the library. It had far less distractions than the dorm and always propelled him into an academic mode. While Brooke was stretching and reading, Ethan was one floor above her, half-asleep, his tall, athletic frame slumped over a political science book. His best friend, Robert Mending, was bored and had come to the library to find Ethan because he was craving a good steak, something he needed to leave campus to obtain, and he didn't want to go alone. He knew Ethan had been at the library most of the afternoon. Robert didn't think this was necessary, not when the semester had just barely started. It was Robert's duty to keep Ethan's college experienced balanced, to prevent him from spending too much of his time studying and worrying, worrying and studying. As expected, he found Ethan in the study corral that was his home away from home, and convinced him to take a break and eat some wholesome red meat. Ethan stood up and stretched, reaching his long arms toward the ceiling, and then followed Robert down to the first floor. As they were leaving, Robert spotted something odd out of the corner of his eye. He halted, quietly extending his arm out in front of Ethan so that he stopped as well. In a side alcove he spied the slim, exceptionally toned body of a young woman in an unusual position.

"Check this out," Robert whispered to Ethan. They both headed closer to the unorthodox studier to get a better view.

As Ethan and Robert approached, Brooke swiveled around at the waist. Her body seemed to defy the limits of spinal rotation as she caught the two men grinning and staring at her. She stared back, her blue-grey eyes wide. Both Robert and Ethan felt their breath catch because she was so beautiful. She remained in her full split, twisted around backward as she settled her gaze on Ethan, choosing him perhaps because his height made him a more challenging opponent.

"Would you like to join me for a stretch?" Her voice was soft and clear, but the question was dripping with sarcasm. It was clearly meant to send them away.

Ethan shocked Robert by replacing his grin with an ultra-serious expression, walking straight over to the most captivating girl he and Robert had ever seen and silently lowering himself awkwardly in front of her. He grimaced as he assumed his best imitation of her pose. His split didn't look anything like hers, but it still hurt like hell. Brooke was so surprised, and appalled by his lack of flexibility, that neither of them spoke for a very long ten seconds as she watched him deal with his discomfort, a look of concentration on his face. Then, finally, he couldn't help it; he let out a small moan and released the stretch, dropping his bottom onto the floor without an ounce of gracefulness. They all broke out laughing so loudly that students turned to glare at them from all over the main floor.

"Hi. I'm Ethan," he said when he had caught his breath. "I haven't done that move in a long time, as in never." Brooke's smile was worth all the discomfort. Robert watched in disbelief at Ethan's good luck, before walking back to his dorm alone. He wouldn't be having steak with Ethan after all. Ethan and Brooke had dinner together in her dorm that night and he had been pursuing her politely and persistently ever since.

***

Just two weeks after they met, Brooke and Ethan were walking from the fitness center back to the dorms. Ethan held Brooke's hand while excitedly telling her he wanted to take her to a movie that night.

"This movie is supposed to be really scary. I'm hoping you get scared easily."

"I don't."

"Well, maybe this time I'll get lucky and you will. My plan is for you to be so terrified that you jump out of your seat and into my lap."

"I don't go out often," Brooke stated.

"Good thing I'm not giving you a choice."

It was difficult not to smile at Ethan's goofiness, which was very often self-deprecating. They were both laughing when Ethan looked away from Brooke and a startled look came over his face for a fleeting second. A few yards in front of them stood a sophisticated-looking woman wearing a white silk shirt, tailored charcoal suit and very fine shoes. Her brown and gold highlighted hair was pulled back from her olive skin in a tight bun, every hair smoothed perfectly in place. A large diamond stone sparkled from each ear. As her smile spread, tiny wrinkles around her dark brown eyes became visible and made her look even more attractive. She was carrying a large gleaming straw basket with leather handles.

"Ethan!" she called as she beamed at both of them.

Brooke wondered who this beautifully dressed woman could be. She didn't fit in with the other female faculty members, the majority of whom were more likely to be dressed as if hiking or even homelessness was on the agenda. And why was she so thrilled to see Ethan?

"Mom!" Ethan exclaimed as he closed the distance between them and embraced. Ethan let go of Brooke's hand to do this but then reached for it again as soon as he stepped back from his mother. After the initial surprise of seeing her, he couldn't stop smiling, but there was a hint of shyness in his demeanor.

"And this must be Brooke!" his mother announced confidently, to Brooke's amazement. "I was hoping I would get to meet you!" She enveloped Brooke in a gentle hug. Brooke placed her left hand on Mrs. Altman's back and sort of touched her lightly. Ethan still held on to her other hand, making the hugging gesture a little more difficult. Brooke's family was not the hugging kind, so she was already slightly uncomfortable, but no one else seemed to be. Brooke was surprised that Mrs. Altman knew who she was, which could only mean that Ethan had told his mother about her.

"Where's Dad?" Ethan asked.

"Oh your poor father, he was supposed to come with me but he had to do an emergency operation, it couldn't wait until Monday. I just talked to his assistant. She said he's been on his feet in the OR since seven A.M." Her expressions changed animatedly to indicate concern and then pride. It was clear to Brooke that Mrs. Altman loved Ethan's father from the way she looked when she spoke about him.

"Your father is a surgeon?" Brooke asked.

"He's the best orthopedic surgeon in the country," Mrs. Altman announced. "Surely Ethan mentioned that. I want to be home when he gets back. He's going to be so tired, I'll need to get him a drink and rub his feet. So I can't stay very long, but I had to see you and naturally I was hoping to meet Brooke. This could not have worked out better, finding you together."

"It's really nice to meet you, Mrs. Altman."

"And you, too, Brooke. What wonderful timing. But I insist that you call me Diane." She continued to beam at Brooke in a way that radiated warmth, as she discreetly studied her from head to toe.

"Okay," Brooke agreed.

"I was in the vicinity to check something out," she explained. Thin silver bracelets on her wrist clinked together as she raised her arm in a small circular gesture. "A dear friend of mine, Mrs. Horowitz, told me about an antique farmhouse that I thought might be a hoot to have, you know, so we could have a place to stay when we visit or just in case Ethan wanted to move off of campus his senior year."

Brooke was intrigued as it registered that the Altmans could consider buying a farmhouse in the same manner her parents might consider buying a new toaster oven.

"The house needed far more work than she initially thought. Honestly, it was a disaster. It needs to be completely gutted for anyone civilized to live there. So I won't be revisiting it." She laughed. It was a melodic sound.

"So here I am, just stepped on campus, and I see the two of you coming right toward me. What an attractive couple you make. And Ethan told me all about the exercise classes you teach. That explains your perfect figure. Good for you."

Brooke just smiled. What else had Ethan told her?

Along with her enthusiasm, Mrs. Altman had brought a gift, the basket she was holding. Brooke imagined it fell out of a magazine picture of beautiful people having a picnic next to a polo match. Ethan opened the lid and peered inside. It contained silverware and wineglasses, held securely against the side, crackers and cheese, and several plastic containers with salads from Ethan's favorite deli in Providence.

"Maybe the two of you can go have a picnic somewhere romantic," Diane suggested.

While Ethan was still examining the contents of the basket, someone called out his name.

"Ethan!" boomed the spirited voice of John Carlisle, Everett's lacrosse coach. Ethan's height and build were recognizable from afar.

"Oh! Look who it is!" Diane exclaimed with excitement.

Carlisle's long strides carried him quickly over to their group. As he got closer, the coach recognized Ethan's mother and greeted her by name. Mrs. Altman kissed the air about an inch from his face to the right side and then to the left. Somehow John seemed to be expecting this and handled it with ease. He acknowledged Brooke with a friendly nod.

"We could really use your son this year," he proceeded to tell her, shaking his head with a rueful grin. "We've got a strong defense, but still no one as talented as Ethan. There just aren't that many guys his size who can get the ball to midfield so quickly." John put his hand on Ethan's shoulder and continued. "I'm sorry that you can't play with us. You are missed."

"You know he would love to be back out there, John. Wouldn't you, Ethan? These things happen. That's why all of these athletes need to be serious about their academic careers, too. You never know when it can all end for you."

Brooke glanced at Ethan with a questioning look as she realized that she should have spent more time asking him questions about himself. She didn't know that he had been an All-American lacrosse player in high school. He had never mentioned that a major injury at the end of his freshman year of college had resulted in a torn anterior cruciate ligament and his second knee surgery.

Ethan continued to smile, somewhat embarrassed by all the attention. Brooke was accustomed to being center stage for at least an hour of every day when she taught her exercise classes, but at that moment, the world seemed to revolve around Ethan Altman. And Brooke became just a bit more interested in what he might have to offer.

CHAPTER TWO

Brooke had a short walk from Sheila's office to South Vernon, her dormitory. After passing through the stone archways of Middleton Hall, the student center that marked the separation between the academic and residential buildings, the perimeter of her route was bordered by large stone dormitories. Flat expanses of perfectly manicured grass filled in the interior space. Stone planters that held the last vestiges of cool weather flowers were interspersed between small trees and perfectly groomed shrubs.

The air had a slight chill, a few trees were already dropping their foliage, but most held a blazing mix of fiery hues, reds and oranges, mixed in with the green. Brooke watched warily as a young man ran backward toward her, poised to catch a Frisbee in the air. He leapt up to grab it and then turned and saw Brooke. He proceeded to exhibit the typical reaction of a young man setting eyes on her for the first time, everything else was momentarily forgotten. He flashed an admiring smile, not in any hurry to pull his Everett sweatshirt back down over his set of chiseled abs while he was in front of someone who he would love to impress. Brooke barely noticed him and kept walking. She didn't like that sort of attention.

A red-tailed hawk sailed by in her periphery and landed atop one of the benches lining the walkway. Brooke did notice its remarkable size and color, but, possibly because of a sub-conscious awareness of the Frisbee catcher, her thoughts were sharply focused on what type of abdominal work she needed to do during tonight's class. She liked every class to have at least a few unique exercises, and it was sometimes difficult to keep straight which exercises she had previously done because she was teaching so often.

As she ascended the stairs of her dorm Ethan approached her from behind, his long legs quickly covering the distance between them. He looked handsome in khaki shorts, a pink collared shirt with the sleeves rolled up and a sweater tied around his waist. As preppy as always.

"I can't believe this amazing body belongs to the girl who is my girlfriend." He spoke into her ear, his voice masculine and intelligent, as he removed her back pack from her shoulder, placed it over his own and simultaneously kissed her on the cheek.

"I love how I can brush my face against yours without getting make-up on it, since you don't wear any. Since you don't need any," he said, beaming at her.

"Ethan," she said, placing her hands on either side of his shoulders to give him a quick half-hug, as she had now become accustomed to doing. Brooke didn't mind that he was now using the term "girlfriend," although she wouldn't necessarily refer to him as her boyfriend. He was definitely a friend, and she didn't have many of those here because she was new and because she didn't invest much time in socializing. Ethan was willing to initiate everything in their relationship, which is the only reason they had one.

"Have you checked your phone today?" he asked Brooke. "I left you a message."

"I didn't. I'm sorry." She sometimes checked for messages on the way to her afternoon science labs, but today she had been hurriedly consuming her portable lunch instead.

"My mother is on her way here and she wants to take some of my friends to dinner. Tell me you can come." He gave her an endearing look.

"Oh…" Brooke's instantaneous response to almost any and every unplanned activity or invitation was no. But this time she knew immediately that she had a real excuse and actually couldn't go. She just needed a split second to remember why.

"I know you have to teach a class tonight, but do you think you could find a replacement?"

"You know I can't", she told him, amused that Ethan was the one to remind her why she couldn't go. "I'm really trying to build up this class and I've been telling people from campus to come and so I can't just not be there…that would be awful. I can't imagine anyone would come back if they can't count on me to be there when I say I'm going to be there."

"I know you're building an exercise empire. I love that. I just really want you with me. My mother wants you to come, too…but I'll explain to her that you have to teach a class. "

"Thank you so much for understanding." Brooke raised herself onto her tiptoes, her calf muscles completely extended to kiss him lightly on the lips. It seemed like the right thing to do. He still had to anticipate her action and bend down in order for her to reach him.

Ethan held the solid wood dormitory door open for Brooke. They nodded hello to the young woman working at the front desk as she looked up to greet them. Every dorm had a niche in the immediate entry way with a front desk. There was a student posted at the desk from morning until one A.M. to ensure that no one other than the dorm's residents passed the entry way unescorted. All guests needed to check in at the desk and wait for a dorm resident to come down for them. It was a job reserved for students receiving financial aid. It paid minimum wage, but at least students were able to get school work done. Brooke's friend Sarah worked there. Brooke was grateful she had her jobs teaching exercise classes. There was something unappealing about having a job that basically announced to everyone on campus that you were on financial aid. It was the same for those students whose campus job were serving and cleaning up after students in the cafeterias while the rest of the dorm's residents ate their meals. There was a stigma, although there shouldn't have been, after all, there was not a single undergraduate there who was able to pay Everett's tuition using money they themselves had earned.

The kitchen and dining area were to the left. Straight through to the back of the building was a large living room area, nicely appointed in a formal style, and big enough for a few hundred people to gather. A wide staircase with mahogany rails and carved balustrades led to the upper floors with the students' rooms. At the bottom of the staircase was the head dorm residents' apartment. Two young graduate students lived there, newlyweds Eli and Kate Newman-Shultz. In exchange for rent they were supposed to be the responsible adults in the dorm. This was a standing joke for South Vernon's residents because Eli and Kate were only a few years older than the seniors and seemed considerably less mature. As Brooke and Ethan crossed from the front desk to mount the staircase they could clearly hear Kate's voice from behind her closed door.

"You said you would do it! You told me yesterday that you would take care of it! You know you did!" Pause. "I'm so sick of you! I'm so sick of you not following through with anything! I can't count on you to do one damn thing that you say you're going to do!"

Brooke looked at Ethan and shook her head, her mouth in a tight grin. She turned and shared the same look with the young woman at the front desk, who shook her head and rolled her eyes. The sound of something slamming emanated from behind the apartment door.

"I told you. They're always fighting. I feel like I should cover my ears every time I walk past their door."

"Wow. I feel sorry for that guy," Ethan said quietly. In an effort to escape hearing their personal business, he bounded up the stairs, taking them two at a time while Brooke easily jogged her ascent next to him. The marital discord of the Newman-Shultz's faded behind them.

On the second floor, they walked halfway down the corridor before stopping at Brooke's door, diagonally across from the large bathroom on her hall. Brooke unzipped the front pocket of her backpack to take out her room key and unlock her door. It was her first year of having a dorm room all to herself and after five weeks here, she still marveled that the interior belonged completely to her. She loved the simplicity of it. Everything she needed all in one place. She had put up a few decorations to personalize the space.

Above her bed hung a giant collage of magazine photos, all of people exercising: running, skiing, rock climbing, gymnastics, and plenty of scenes of women from the New York City ballet. The pieces were chosen not for the sports they represented, but because in every picture the athletes had toned muscular physiques and their faces registered serious exertion and focus.

To the side of her laptop sat a neat stack of bills, opened with their envelopes discarded in the hallway recycling bin as soon as they were received, and a silver thermos with a large label that read DO NOT DRINK across the front. The top of her small refrigerator functioned as a side table. She didn't have a television, but there was one in the common room downstairs, and she had access to all current events on her laptop. The laptop was the most critical and necessary item she owned, along with her iPod which held all her music for teaching exercise classes. On the front of the refrigerator was a recent photograph of her siblings, Amanda, age eleven and Sydney, age ten. It was a funny picture; instead of smiling as their mother requested, they had both made awful faces for the camera. Surrounding their photograph and also attached to the desk were numerous to-do lists on yellow sticky notes.

Most of Brooke's workout clothes were in her dresser. The closet contained the rest of her wardrobe, which wasn't much; her shoes, a coat and a laundry bag full of sweaty workout clothes. Every week, for just a few hours, she had a brief feeling of accomplishment when the dirty laundry bag was empty and everything was clean. Her dirty clothes accumulated like jackrabbits because she sweated through two of everything on most days: two sports bras, two pairs of socks, two pairs of underwear, two pairs of workout pants, and two tank tops. Unfortunately, she did not have access to the laundry service that picked up clothes for some of the students and returned them clean and folded the next day, even though she needed it more than most.

"Why is your mother coming to campus?" Brooke asked. It was a two-hour drive from Ethan's Rhode Island home to Everett, and it was only two weeks ago that Brooke had met Mrs. Altman on campus.

"She's bringing a chair for my room. But I know she just misses me and she loves to see my friends," Ethan answered without a hint of embarrassment.

"So is it just the two of you going to dinner then?" asked Brooke.

"Robert and Jessica are coming."

Brooke had already met Robert, Ethan's best friend, and Jessica, Robert's girlfriend. She thought Robert was nice enough, although he had that rich guy feel about him that left her with an odd taste in her mouth, but Jessica she wasn't sure about. She had a way about her that made Brooke feel like an outsider, and not for the usual reasons that Brooke had privately come to understand and accept. No one knew about those, Brooke had seen to that by being very careful to cover her tracks for many years. But she made Brooke feel like she had done something wrong.

"What dorm do you live in?" Jessica had asked Brooke when Ethan introduced them.

"South Vernon."

"Well, I'm the president of South Vernon. How come I haven't seen you at any of the dorm meetings? Are you getting texts from me?" She was holding an extra-large coffee cup and frequently touching it to her pink lips.

"I got the texts. I think the meetings were all during times that I had to work."

"Oh. I see." Jessica seemed insulted and a little pissed off.

Brooke had received numerous texts from Jessica. They went out to everyone who lived in their dorm to announce meetings. Brooke had not been able to attend a few because of her work schedule, but there were a few she skipped because they came with little notice when her time had already been allotted to studying. As far as she knew, she hadn't missed anything critical. One had been about planning a party, which was not something Brooke cared to do and it seemed best left to the people who did care. She didn't know about the other meetings. They just weren't high on her priority list.

"I wish you could come to dinner," Ethan told her.

"I'm sorry. Remember to explain why I can't be there so your mother understands and so she won't think I'm being rude."

Brooke was really glad she had a solid excuse not to go to dinner now that she knew Robert and Jessica would be there. Ethan was nice and she had already decided it was important to make time for him; he was good for her, he would help her fit in and have a more balanced life. She didn't see why she needed to be having dinner with his mother, although his father would have been worth meeting. She was dying to talk to him ever since she discovered he was a surgeon, she had so many questions she wanted to ask. But she had absolutely no interest and no reason to spend time with Robert and Jessica.

"Don't worry about it. She'll understand." Ethan crossed the room and took a cookie from a container on top of the refrigerator. "In fact I know she'll love that you're so responsible and you have commitments. She has a thing about people who work hard."

After Ethan left, Brooke ate a quick dinner alone in the dining hall. From there she began the journey to work. It took her approximately twenty-five minutes to get from her dorm to Resolution Fitness, the only fitness center offering group classes in town. After the first week she had mastered the most efficient timing. It was a quick walk to the bus stop at the front of campus. It was literally just a stop; there was no covered shelter to protect from the elements as you waited. This was probably because it was adjacent to the giant iron gates that showcased the main entrance to Everett. A bus shelter just didn't fit with the look; it would mar their impressive beauty. The bus came by every fifteen minutes, give or take, to pick up students and travel down Ash Street, the main route through town. It was a free shuttle provided by the campus, which directly benefitted all of the store owners in town as well as the students. Brooke climbed onboard and reviewed her chemistry notes while the bus caught red lights at all four intersections. After those stops, in addition to the multiple stops for passengers, Brooke started wondering if it wouldn't be quicker to run to work. However, she knew the bus would be preferable in the winter when the temperature dropped. She was told that this part of New

Hampshire got colder than she could imagine, even coming from Connecticut. She got off the bus at its final stop on Ash Street and walked three city blocks to the gym.

After she taught her class, Brooke repeated the same twenty-five minute trip in reverse. She had showered at the gym, in part because they provided towels, one less wet dirty towel hanging around her room, and in part because it was just efficient to get it over with and then be able to get right to her school work when she returned. She rarely took the time to dry her hair. Those few minutes spent holding the blow dryer required more patience than she could summon. She simply pulled a comb through her long, wet hair and by the time she was back at the dorm it was basically dry. In a month or two it might be frozen when she got back, so she would stop washing it. It seemed there were a number of things that would be more difficult for her when the weather became colder.

She sat down at her desk, pen in hand, and opened her notebook. She planned to knock out her economics homework first. She had moved her desk from its original position against the longest wall to the end of the room, in front of her lone window. From her seat she could have watched the comings and goings on the front side of South Vernon. There was a constant flow of people entering and exiting the dorm and traveling across the quad. The sky was dark, but the ground was well lit by floodlights strategically placed around the outside of the dorm. But Brooke didn't notice any of this, she was too focused to care about what was going on outside.

"Knock, knock," said a falsely deepened voice outside her door. "I have a special delivery. It says it's for the smartest and the most beautiful girl at Everett."

Ethan was always trying to be interesting.

She hopped up from her desk and crossed the cool, bare floor in her pajamas and bare feet.

"Ethan. Hi. I just got back. How did you get up here?" she asked.

If the rules had been followed, he would not have been able to come up alone. She would have received a call from the front desk that he was waiting for her downstairs. She would have had to go down to sign him in and escort him upstairs.

"Sarah is working at the front desk. I charmed her into letting me go up. She said 'I trust you won't be stopping anywhere else on the way to Brookes' room. Y'all be good.'" Ethan's attempt to mimic Sarah's strong southern accent was actually excellent, but still comical.

Brooke would have to talk to Sarah about letting people up without calling. Including Ethan. Brooke might have pretended to be elsewhere if she'd been given the choice. But since Ethan was already here, she stepped back to let him enter her room and shut the door.

"I still have homework to do. I'm just getting started."

"I have work to do, too. I'm not staying. I just needed to give you something." Ethan proudly presented her with a beautifully wrapped box.

"What is it?"

"Open it and find out," he teased, still holding it before him.

"It's so pretty, I don't want to ruin it." Brooke took the package and fingered the gauzy ribbon tied around the sophisticated wrapping paper. It was secured in the center with a bronze "B" several inches tall that looked to be a Christmas ornament.

"You need to open it or you'll never know," he encouraged, enjoying her curiosity.

Brooke took her time carefully putting aside the ribbon and then unwrapping the paper. Opening the box revealed a soft powder blue cashmere sweater. Brooke "oohed" in surprise.

"It's so beautiful! What is it for? Why did you get this?" She looked questioningly into his eyes and then back at the gift. She lifted it out of the box. It felt amazing in her hands, finer than any fabric she had ever touched.

"It's not from me. It's from my mother. She was shopping before dinner and saw this and thought it was perfect for you. She wanted to get you a present." Ethan experienced a flash of embarrassment he had not anticipated. He began explaining his mother's actions. "She just likes to do things like that. It makes her happy. Remember she doesn't have any daughters, she doesn't get to pick out things like this for anyone in my family."

"Wow! It's so nice!" Brooke shook her head in appreciation. She held the sweater up across her torso, then touched it to her face, then hugged it back against her chest. It was so soft that she wanted to wear it and sleep in it. Aside from being cashmere, Brooke could tell from the distinctive wrapping paper that it had been purchased from a boutique across from campus. "Zoe's" was known for its high end apparel and posh environment. Brooke was familiar with it only from passing by outside.

"She likes you because I told her that you help take care of me, you know. I told her you were working on getting me to eat right and go to the gym, and she loves that you're so sort of intense. And she totally understands that you couldn't make it to dinner. And another thing…"

"What?" Brooke was listening intently. Who didn't enjoy hearing a list of reasons why they were appreciated?

"She asked how you got to your job at Resolution Fitness. I told her how you take the bus at night. She did not like the idea of you going back and forth in the dark. She was upset with me for not having you take my car. She wants you to use it so you're not waiting for the bus in town in the dark. And I've already told you I want you to use it, at least when I'm not using it…so will you please just drive my car when you have to teach there, for me, and make me happy? Because she's going to ask me the next time we talk."

The car in question was a loaded Jeep Grand Cherokee, Ethan's high school graduation present. It had replaced a sporty coupe because his parents considered an SUV with four wheel drive to be an essential item for attending college in the mountains of New Hampshire.

Brooke thought for a second. She didn't want to feel indebted to him and it seemed like such a generous offer, but maybe not to Ethan and his parents. It would certainly make her commute to work easier and shorter, providing her more time at night to study. Still it seemed odd. She had known Ethan less than two months. At home she wasn't even allowed to drive her parents ageing mini-van. It was too expensive to keep her on the insurance and since she wouldn't be home much anyway, it wasn't worth the sacrifice. But how could she say no to Ethan when she really wanted to say yes? Driving instead of taking the bus would save so much time. She leaned forward and wrapped her arms around Ethan's neck. She had done it enough times now that the gesture was almost natural. Almost.

"Yes, I will use your car if you insist. Thank you. It will make my life a lot easier. You and your mother are like my wonderful benefactors."

"Well I'm glad I can help. Really." He smiled, exposing his very white and perfect orthodontia and nodded his head for emphasis. "I know there are so many wonderful things you want to do for me, too? Right?" he said suggestively and then laughed. "Here's an extra key for the car. Just text me if you need it so I'll know. You know where I usually park."

"So you don't keep a spare key in a magnet holder under the front fender?" she joked.

"No, but would you believe that Jessica does that? She told me last year and then she was surprised when Robert and I told her how stupid it was." He laughed. "If there are no parking spots in the corner where I usually leave the car and you have to park somewhere else, text me the location so I'll know where to find it. Okay?"

"Sure." *Unbelievable*, she thought.

"So...did you miss me?"

As much as Brooke felt obligated to spend more time with Ethan, since he had just presented her with the nicest item of clothing she had ever owned along with a key to his practically brand new car, she walked him back down to the front desk and kissed him goodbye.

"Okay, I'll let you get back to the exciting world of supply and demand," he said, letting her go after attempting to prolong their gentle kiss.

Before Brooke returned to her books, she opened her dresser drawer and took another look at the beautiful cashmere sweater carefully folded and nestled on top of her well-worn shirts.

She loved it, yet it was very hard for her to comprehend why Mrs. Altman, who had met her once for a few minutes, would buy her something so special. Then she sat back down at her desk, alone in the quiet room, everything in its place, and finally got to work.

CHAPTER THREE

Amidst a wide variety of decorative pillows, Jessica woke thirty minutes earlier than intended. Not to her phone alarm, that was set to go off at eight AM, but to the voices of people having a conversation while walking down the second floor hall of the South Vernon dormitory. She straightened her arms to lift her body off her pillows and yelled loudly, "This is why I did NOT want to live in a dorm."

She was hoping to be heard by those outside her door who seemed to be doing their utmost to prevent her from sleeping. She sighed and attempted to lie back down and close her eyes. She would have preferred to spend her junior year living in a charming apartment with soundproof walls. Ideally it would also have a large walk-in closet, because the dorm closet was ridiculously miniscule. There was nowhere near enough room for even her most basic necessities. To make do, she had matching storage baskets stacked in every corner and filling her closet. Her mother's walk-in closet at home was twice as big as Jessica's whole dorm room. Trying to fit everything she needed in one room, and then live in it on top of that, was crazy! A walk-in shower would also be a must and even if it didn't have a massage head, it would at least be private so she wouldn't be forced to wear flip flops into the bathroom every day to protect her feet from unmentionable diseases and bacteria. Also necessary would be a breakfast nook with a view of a lake for coffee and studying. And, last but not least, a garage for her Volvo so it wouldn't get covered with ice that she had to scrape off her windshield on winter mornings when she needed to leave campus. She had ruined several pairs of cashmere and leather gloves last year because they were not intended for handling snow. Unfortunately for her, the apartment she desired did not exist near campus. The closest living quarters immediately beyond Everett's gates were either occupied by faculty, or were abandoned looking farmhouses. Just about every student lived in one of the dorms.

In any case, it didn't matter because her father, Foster Carroll, insisted she live on campus so that she would not miss out on the entirety of the Everett experience. He reminded her constantly how lucky she was to be there. Foster had spent four years on this same campus as a student at Everett. He was a fraternity brother in Sigma PI. That was back in the day when Everett had fraternities and sororities. After two hazing lawsuits and one incident resulting in a student being paralyzed, the Greek system had been abolished. The fraternity and sorority houses had since been remodeled into small dormitories.

As the corridor noises continued, she sighed loudly and decided that she might as well start the day. She sat up, feeling groggy and dull, and turned on the lamp next to her bed. Her espresso machine had been programmed for eight-thirty so that a demitasse with a double shot would be waiting for her when she returned from the shower. Now she was going to have to shut off the automatic program and set it for manual brew. While focusing on the coffee maker, and hoping she could remember how to change the settings, she spied the notes for her English essay spread out on her desk. A few papers had scattered to the floor. The essay was due today. She remembered with chagrin that she had gone to sleep without finishing it. She shrugged her shoulders to rid herself of the disagreeable thought of unfinished business. She had a busy day ahead of her. There was so much to do that she might have to skip her English class again anyway. She stepped out of her nightgown so that she was completely naked and walked a few steps across the room to stand on her body fat index scale. Angrily, she glared down at the numbers on the digital readout. She briefly considered taking a walk, since she was up earlier than planned and had the time to do it. She crossed the room and opened the blackout blinds she had custom ordered for her window. Bright light rushed into her room. It looked like a beautiful morning. She searched her mind for excuses not to walk. What would she wear outside that would keep her warm but still look good while she walked? Did she even have walking or running shoes? Did they match her coat? Then she concluded that she didn't feel like walking alone and by the time she got ready and then asked someone to go with her, then waited for that person to get ready, she wouldn't have enough time to walk anyway. She dismissed the entire walking idea. Instead, she put on her luxurious bathrobe and her flip-flops and headed off to the shower carrying her basket of toiletries.

She was sipping her espresso in her room with a towel wrapped around her hair when there was a tap at her door followed by an affected voice calling, "Hello. Jessica. I have something for you."

It was Brittany Harris from Beverly Hills.

Since being president of a sorority was not an option at this college, Jessica was the president of South Vernon, the most sought after accommodation on campus. It was one of Everett's original dorms but it had been completely closed for an entire summer and a semester while its architecture was preserved and its functionality was brought into the twenty first century. Jessica viewed herself as the Queen Bee of South Vernon.

Once the door bolt and chain were unlocked, Brittany extended her arm through the opening and held out a bottle of pills. Jessica accepted it graciously and closed the door. Brittany was like a worker bee keeping the queen supplied with the necessities. Brittany's incentive was the hope of spending a few weeks of the summer at Jessica's house in the Hamptons. Her offering was a container of ephedrine that conveniently served as an appetite suppressant and a stimulant. Jessica found it was just the thing she needed during exam time or for pulling all-nighters. It provided a tunnel-like focus, greatly improving her concentration. There were no exams in sight, but she figured that taking a pill today might help curb her calorie intake and help get rid of those extra pounds that her scale had, yet again, so rudely brought to her attention. The drug suited her perfectly, it made everything just a little better.

She took out one pill and then slid the unmarked bottle into her top drawer. She popped it in her mouth, along with the two anti-depressants that she took every morning, and washed them down with her espresso. Then she unwrapped and took a bite of her breakfast, a chocolate protein weight loss bar. There was a full breakfast available in the dining hall downstairs, available to her because her father had paid for the college's meal plan, but she rarely went down there to eat. She had more than enough caffeinated energy drinks in her room to last the semester.

Sighing again, dramatically, because she had so much to do, she began by turning her television to a morning talk show and sitting down on the edge of her bed. She propped one bare foot in front of her while she touched up the polish on her pedicure. She carefully stroked a thin coat of Dark Flamingo color over her toenails. Thank goodness she could multi-task. While she perfected her toenails, she began, in her thoughts, the important task of picking out an outfit. She decided on a pair of pressed twill slacks and a silk shirt and scarf. After her nails were dry, she removed her selections from their dry cleaning bags and carefully got dressed. In a few hours she had to drive into town for a special event. She had scheduled a time to deliver a box of gently used coats, hats and gloves to a local church. It was for a collection drive she had single handedly initiated and coordinated to benefit the underprivileged of New Hampshire. She had begun the effort with so much enthusiasm, sending out texts and emails and hanging up a few signs. She imagined she would need a truck in order to cart all of the donated items that would come pouring in and an assembly would be required to carry all the boxes from a truck into the church. She had planned to wear her new favorite Burberry trench coat and graciously thank everyone for their hard work. And everyone would say that it was she that they all should be thanking.

In reality, at the end of the month, everything fit neatly, with room to spare, into two large cardboard boxes. One of those boxes was full entirely of clothes that had come from Jessica's closet. She was disgusted with the lack of participation she had encountered from the other Everett students. Did they not have at least one old coat from last season that they could part with? Now that she thought about it, it was actually possible that they did not. Most of the students on campus were hardly in the running for any "best dressed" awards. Half of them wore sweatshirts every day. Ethan's new "girlfriend," for example. Brooke something or other. On each of the occasions Jessica saw her, she was wearing black exercise pants with the same Nike coat and worn sneakers.

Every single time. Whatever.

Jessica glanced at the two charity-bound boxes again and contemplated the gray fur stole lying atop the pile. She never had the chance to wear it. It was so beautiful but somehow it had gotten too small over the past year and she couldn't close the front. It must have shrunk, that was the only possibility she would consider. She took it off and tossed it back in a box.

Now that she was dressed she had time to practice some poses in the full-length mirror behind her door. The look she was aiming for would complement the words "sophisticated Ivy League socialite carving time out of her busy schedule to help others." She was expecting a photographer to capture her presentation and submit it to a newspaper. She certainly hoped so or all this work would have been for nothing. Just in case, she planned to bring her own camera so she could have someone take a picture of her presenting the checks and at the least she could submit it to the Everett school newspaper and send a copy to her mother. She knew her mother should be able to get it published in the New York Times Society Section. Then she could take a picture of the Times write-up and post it on all of her own social pages. That would be reward enough to go through all of this effort again and coordinate another collection drive. After all, the point of her efforts was to help the underprivileged whoever they may be, those who might otherwise have nothing new or beautiful to wear this year.

She turned away from the mirror and inadvertently caught sight of her English papers again. She decided to sit down on her bed, facing away from the English assignment, and check her phone messages. Why should she feel guilty about the paper? Her grades had never been fantastic. How many times had she not quite completed an assignment in the past? More than she could possibly count. Although this time she hadn't really even started. And yet she was here at Everett, wasn't she? One of the best and the brightest. So she just needed to stop worrying about it. The only thing worrying produced was forehead wrinkles. Fundraising and charity work were the type of things she needed to learn, albeit on a much, much, larger scale than this little coat drive. Analyzing the writing of the generally deranged and perverted people they seemed to be reading this year for her English class was not going to help her in the long term. Her current English course was called "Twentieth Century Authors" and it was obvious to Jessica that the professor had chosen the work of every author who was mentally unstable.

Jessica's plan was to work on Wall Street or somewhere like that where everyone dressed well. After a few years she would stop working and become the full-time wife of a philanthropist. She thought of Robert. He wasn't incredibly attractive, not like Ethan, with his all-American good looks and his chiseled chin, but he looked okay, and wealth of that magnitude was not readily available. Jessica had heard her own father comment about it. He said the Mendings had so much money he was surprised that Robert didn't have bodyguards to prevent a kidnapping for ransom situation.

She directed her attention to her phone email, deleting messages from designers and boutiques until she discovered a new email with delivery confirmation from Nordstrom's.

"Well it's about time," she proclaimed.

Her new Cole Haan brown leather dress boots with a two inch heel had finally arrived. They would provide the perfect finishing touch on the outfit she was wearing. She could put them on without changing a thing and it would work beautifully. She put her phone away, finished applying her make-up and then opened her closet, looking to the left side where her boot boxes lined the wall. She opened a large box and removed its contents. She sat back down on her bed and slid on a pair of brown leather dress boots with a one inch heel over her cashmere socks. These would do until she put on the new ones. Lastly, she positioned the silk scarf around her neck, did a final check in the mirror and then headed out to the student center to collect her package from the mailroom.

CHAPTER FOUR

Ethan was near breathless next to Brooke on the elliptical machine. This was not his idea of fun. Working out was a chore, although watching Brooke exercise in her tight workout clothes was a major turn-on.

"Don't you miss lacrosse?" Brooke asked.

"Not really," he answered honestly, sweat dripping down his forehead.

"Nothing about it? You went from training every day for years to stopping cold and you don't miss it? I think I would die if I couldn't work out."

Ethan contemplated her question. People had always assumed Ethan was an athlete because of his build. Yet he never felt comfortable identifying himself as a jock. His favorite things about lacrosse had been the pride it had brought to his parents, neither of whom was particularly athletic, through the articles in the paper and his nomination as an All-American Defender. He also loved the camaraderie of the team when everyone was happy and the shared feelings of accomplishment that came with winning tough games. But through his entire lacrosse career, the most prevalent feeling he had was anxiety. He worried that everyone would suddenly decide he wasn't that good after all, that he didn't have the skills or mental attitude it took to be a high level player. He felt like someone pretending to be something he was not, and hoping he wouldn't get found out. His insecurities dominated his feelings, no matter how well or how many times he outplayed his opponents. It was almost a relief when his final injury, the result of a single misplaced step on slippery turf, took away his opportunity to play. Thanks to his father's influence he had consultations with the top knee surgeons in the country before the best one performed the necessary operation. After months of extensive physical therapy, it was his father who strongly recommended that his college sports career should end.

"Don't you miss the exercise at least?"

"Definitely not. What are you saying?" His eyes gleamed with amusement, but inside he felt his confidence take a hit. His body wasn't as lean as it used to be when he was playing lacrosse every day. At some point his clearly visible six-pack had quietly disappeared. But he hadn't given any thought to the change in his physique until he met Brooke and felt a compelling desire to impress her.

"Just curious."

"I'm sort of glad it's over and that it wasn't my decision to make so I couldn't second guess myself. I like having more time. Less pressure."

"So what do you care about?" Brooke enunciated, her voice betraying no sign of the physical effort she was putting forth.

"I care about doing well at school. My family. And You. World Peace. Starving Children. The Steak at Del Veccias."

"Do you have siblings?"

"A brother, Michael. He just graduated from Stanford. He's going to medical school, taking a year off first." Ethan couldn't talk about Michael without feeling a surge of pride and envy. Ethan had always known what super smart and ultra-focused looked like. It looked like his father, and it looked like Michael, and now, in its most sexy and irresistible form, it looked like Brooke.

Brooke's intelligence and drive pulled on his heartstrings, and she just happened to be beautiful. Ethan didn't think a better fit existed between a living human being and all that he valued. He knew he was falling for her, hard. If she could just feel the same, it would validate him. He would gain that extra confidence that he currently lacked in spite of what he had so far achieved. His insecurities would be whooshed away into obscurity. He really needed her, and it made him very anxious that he couldn't figure out how she felt about him. She wasn't exactly falling all over him, but at least, as far as he could see, it wasn't because she was interested in anyone else.

***

Ethan entered Robert's room without knocking. It was nine P.M., the hour when Ethan and Robert had been getting together since freshman year for a study break, a beer, and to watch the "Wright Way," a conservative political talk show featuring Donovan Wright, one of Everett's most famous alumni. As Juniors, Robert and Ethan occupied rooms across the hall from each other in the Hatfield dormitory. On Sundays they nursed their hangovers together while watching the political talk shows, which they both preferred to football, on Robert's enormous 3D high-definition satellite television.

Ethan opened Robert's sub-zero beverage refrigerator, helped himself to a chilled Stella and then sat down next to Robert. Donovan Wright was just starting in with his "Daily Highlights" segment. Robert and Ethan were in the habit of following up on each of Wright's points with their own critiques. It was often necessary to pause the show to accommodate their witticisms, particularly if they were on a roll that day.

"I'm liking the tie today," Robert commented in his waspy, contemplative way.

Sitting side by side in the same position, the physical juxtaposition between the two friends was significant. Robert was of average height and thin, but not muscular, giving the overall impression of being un-athletic. He had played squash and tennis at Deerfield, and didn't enjoy either.

Donovan Wright was interviewing a radio talk show host accused of making public anti-Semitic remarks.

"How does that make you feel?" Robert asked in jest. He could get away with it because Ethan was his best friend.

"I'm so offended that I might spill my beer on your carpet. How does that make you feel?" Ethan joked.

"You mean my beer that you borrowed?" Robert corrected with a smug look.

Ethan glanced at his phone. Robert knew his friend was hoping to find a message from Brooke. He shook his head. Ethan was so whipped it was unreal.

"How is Brooke?" he asked, since he knew Ethan was thinking about her. Robert would forever picture Brooke doing that split on the library floor. First impressions were often lasting, but that one was particularly unforgettable.

"Good. She just taught a class at the gym where she works."

Robert had never seen Ethan so interested in a girl before. Ethan had talked about Brooke to his mother all through dinner the other night. Robert didn't mind so much, he found it humorous because it was so out of character, but Jessica minded. She made that clear to Robert after dinner. Robert was a little concerned for his friend. He had an inkling that Brooke might not be reciprocating Ethan's feelings to the same extent. He couldn't imagine why. Girls generally threw themselves at Ethan. Maybe Brooke was just playing hard to get.

"She's different, Robert. I feel like I need to check in on her. She keeps really busy, and to herself."

"That sounds excellent to me," Robert said. "She's low-maintenance." *Or maybe she's not all that interested in you.* "Jessica is always texting me to find out what I'm doing and then telling me where she needs me to be."

"I know. You think everyone doesn't know that? Sorry dude. It's true." Ethan laughed hard and slapped his leg. Then, with one foot on the floor and one on the ottoman, he intertwined his fingers together behind his head and leaned back into them in a stretch that further accentuated his height. "And she tells you what to wear, I've heard her; don't feel bad, I think that's normal. Maybe. Maybe it's normal. You've been together for over a year, right?"

"Yes. " And Robert wasn't sure why.

Jessica's family lived in New Jersey, in an upscale New York City suburb, but she had spent three years of boarding school at Miss White's School for Girls, a very exclusive prep school in

Connecticut. Robert had never once seen the school, but somehow, in his adolescence, he had subconsciously absorbed the suggestion that the type of girl that one should date is the type of girl who went to or came from Miss White's. He couldn't remember why, maybe they were supposed to be more promiscuous, and he didn't know where he had gotten the idea, although it most likely came from one of his overly pretentious roommates at Deerfield. It certainly did not come from his mother. She never imposed her own opinions on others. If she had, Robert would be studying fine art at the Sorbonne in Paris right now, or he would be somewhere unusual, like Hampshire College, where everyone created their own major, Theories of Middle Eastern Trash Can Art or Contemporary Matriarchal Contemplative Extinct Religions. His mother wished everyone could explore and discover what was uniquely right for them. She was the anti-Jessica in many ways.

When Robert pictured Jessica what popped into his mind was an image of her looking smug and proper, every hair in place, in a hot pink and black Lily Pulitzer dress, her nose tilted up in the air. She was condescending to almost everyone. He quickly reminded himself that she was a lot of fun when she was drunk, which he tried to facilitate whenever possible. He made a concentrated effort to conjure up only pleasant images of Jessica, like how she always smelled nice and clean. She wouldn't tell him the name of her perfume. She wanted to keep it a mystery, which he thought was sexy. What was not sexy was how she had gained a bunch of weight this year, which was really odd because he rarely saw her eat any more. Anything caffeinated–yes. Pills–yes. Food–no.

Ethan turned back to the television and Donovan Wright's next guest, a former political strategist. He laughed and slapped his knee again in response to what he considered a preposterous liberal opinion.

Robert's feelings for Jessica were an increasing source of uncertainty, but he was sure of one thing; he didn't think he could find a better best friend.

CHAPTER FIVE

Across campus, Brooke and Sarah Polk retrieved their mail from the bustling corridor of mailboxes in the Middleton Hall student center, where hundreds of mail slots covered two long corridors. Brooke was standing over a trash receptacle, calmly sorting through the contents of her mailbox and disposing certain items without opening them. Sarah had put her pile into her bag to be opened at a later time. She had noticed two letters postmarked Chapel Hill, NC. One would be from her grandmother, who still preferred the postal system over the internet and, therefore, was the only person Sarah could count on to write weekly letters. They conveyed almost identical information about the weather and what her dog experienced that week, but were appreciated nonetheless. The other envelope came from her mother. Every week she sent a few brief sentences on a notecard along with articles cut out from the local paper chronicling the results of Sarah's brothers' high school football team in the fall, and their lacrosse team in the spring.

She looked around at students fumbling through their bags for their mailbox keys. The girl next to her retrieved a yellow card, which indicated there was a package waiting that did not fit in her box.

Sarah watched students walking up to the second floor of the student center. The second floor contained a food court and an adjacent lounge area where people relaxed in leather club chairs to chat with friends, read, or do whatever else they felt like doing to pass the time. The mail area and the campus bookstore were on the ground floor.

Brooke looked up with her usual poise and smiled at Sarah as she tucked her remaining mail into her backpack. Brooke felt a sort of kindred spirit with Sarah, as much as she probably ever would with anyone. Brooke respected the way Sarah managed a busy schedule of studies, soccer team commitments, and working to earn her spending money. They had become friends because Sarah was always up for a run on the weekends, provided she didn't have a soccer game. It was rare for Brooke to find another woman who could match her pace and endurance.

"Take a book out of your backpack so it looks like you came in carrying books," Brooke instructed in a quiet voice as she moved closer to Sarah. Brooke removed her genetics text book from her bag and casually held it with one arm. Sarah did the same. Brooke proceeded to walk into the bookstore and Sarah followed, her heart beating so rapidly she needed to take deep controlled breaths to try to slow it down. She felt warm; she was close to perspiring, as if they were a few miles into a run. She contemplated taking off her sweatshirt but she was too worried about messing up Brooke's plan, whatever it was. Her face felt flushed and her senses were hyper-alert. The last time she experienced these sensations she was the final person to take a penalty kick in a tie game for her high school state championship soccer semi-finals.

"Can you believe that assignment we got for chemistry yesterday?" Brooke asked Sarah in a conversational tone as they walked by the cashier and the checkout counter. "It wasn't at all related to the lecture."

"Yea, um, it didn't make sense to me," Sarah responded nervously.

She glanced over at the man working the register. He was looking down to read a newspaper, both hands placed on the counter before him to support some of his weight. His balding head suggested he was in his forties at least. A pair of black-rimmed glasses was slipping down the slope of his nose as he leaned forward. He was immune to the constant sounds of the students talking and laughing in the hall a few yards away.

Brooke walked purposefully through the "Room and Home Essentials" section, past the Vera Bradley gift counter, and turned right at the wall of hanging Everett bumper stickers and decals. The school colors, a mix of forest green and navy blue, were present to some extent on the majority of items in the store. A few visitors were milling around the apparel section, trying to choose from the multitude of clothing bearing the Everett logo. There was no one in the textbook area at the back of the store. The books had been picked over, since the current semester started two months ago. Some of the typed course labels sat under empty shelves, not to be replenished until the start of the next semester. Brooke located the chemistry books and selected the book she needed, a very expensive heavy textbook titled Principles of Inorganic Chemistry. She nonchalantly placed it on top of the biology book she was already carrying and Sarah followed her lead.

Brooke and Sarah's chemistry class had initially required two textbooks; one was the main book, the other a reference, along with other materials. Because their funds were limited, Sarah and Brooke had each purchased everything except the reference text. Yet so far, all of their assignments had come from that book, and none had come from the book they bought. For Sarah, the cost of the unnecessary text book represented thirteen hours of working at the front desk. It was maddening when she thought of it that way. There were a bunch of things she needed and the only thing keeping them at bay was her lack of money. Because she grew up in North Carolina, her winter wardrobe was sparse. She had found out the hard way freshman year that "cold" in New Hampshire did not have the same meaning as "cold" in North Carolina when she experienced a mind-numbing frigidness beyond her imagination. By the time she purchased toiletries and other necessities with the money she earned working the front desk each week, there was never money left for the winter essentials she still lacked. If it weren't for the cold weather soccer gear Everett gave her team, she would be perpetually freezing half the year.

A copy of the chemistry book was available at the library, but relying on it being available when needed, not to mention having to go to the library for every assignment, was becoming tiresome. Last night Sarah had waited at the library's circulation desk for the library copy to be returned, saw Brooke return it, and they had a conversation about their situations.

"It's just not right. These books are crazy expensive, and then it turns out we don't even need them all. Ms. MacIntyre is so inconsiderate!" Sarah had said.

"She either made a mistake or she did it just to mess with everyone. Ms. MacIntyre is the worst professor I've ever had in terms of organization and professionalism. She's got some serious issues. In any case, I've decided that being dependent on the library's copy is ridiculous. We don't have time for that." Brooke was matter-of-fact.

They were in agreement. Sarah felt fired up when Brooke said they would remedy their problem. And now here they were, enacting Brooke's plan. While it had never been spoken, Sarah had a pretty good idea what it entailed and her stomach was reacting violently due to nerves and fear.

Brooke's demeanor was oddly no different than if she was taking a stroll through campus to admire the scenery.

Brooke marched back out of the store exactly the way she had come in, this time carrying two texts in her arms instead of one. She paused in front of a cooler of vitamin waters and protein drinks. Sarah stood beside her, and pretended to also read the drink labels. She felt ill and shaky, almost feverish; she could not have read a simple sentence with comprehension.

"I don't think I want a drink after all," Brooke announced, then turned and headed out of the store. For Sarah, the walk from the chilled drinks past the register seemed to stretch ahead like the last leg of a triathlon course. Her heart felt like it was beating at a rapid pace up into her throat, her hands were trembling; she felt like she was experiencing heat stroke. She wanted to just sit down and cry, but knew it wasn't a good option. She could see the man at the register by the door. He was still head down, engrossed in reading an analysis of last night's football game. It had been a close game, so fortunately for Sarah, it was a long article. A young man in an Everett cap was heading to the register carrying a stack of printer paper and gum. Sarah was worried the man at the register would look up just in time to see them walking out and somehow he would immediately be able to tell that they were carrying a book for which neither of them had paid.

"Have a nice day!" Brooke said to the balding man as she passed, causing him to look up so she could make eye contact, smile, and offer him a wave of her free hand before he proceeded to ring up the other guy's paper and gum. Sarah was shocked, she couldn't imagine what Brooke was thinking by calling attention to herself, but by then she had passed the register and both young women were out of the store and into the mail corridor. Brooke pushed open the double doors leading outside. Sarah felt an overwhelming sense of relief and had to consciously stop herself from turning to look over her shoulder.

"My heart was racing," Sarah whispered.

"That's good right? That's how you know you're alive."

"That was so scary. Weren't you nervous?" Sarah asked.

"No." Brooke shook her head. "I wasn't nervous. We deserve these books. Good thing they didn't have sensors."

"What?!" whispered Sarah, in a frantic tone. "How do you know? Are you sure they don't?"

"I think they would have gone off while we were leaving the store. I know they have sensors on the chemistry texts in the library, that's why no one can take those copies."

It had never occurred to Sarah to take the library copy, just as it had never occurred to her that a textbook would have a sensor. That oversight and its possible consequences made her feel ill all over again. But the deed was done and she was holding thirteen hours' worth of sitting at the front desk. She told herself that was a good thing, but it didn't feel good at all. With the experience still fresh in her mind, she knew she would never, ever be doing that again. Never. Ever.

How could Brooke be so unaffected by what they had just done? It was as if she was incapable of experiencing fear.

CHAPTER SIX

Robert drove a dark green BMW because he had spent last summer as a salesman at a BMW dealership. It was his first real job, and it wasn't so bad. He enjoyed participating in intellectual discussions with potential buyers about the vehicles' engineering, but he had little interest in forcing a deal. Despite a motivation that was generally necessary for sales, his name was engraved on a plaque hanging up in the showroom for being the salesman of the month in July. This was mostly due to the fact that his father had supported Robert's efforts by purchasing a new car for everyone in their family.

In Robert's mind, his substantial trust fund carried with it an enormous responsibility to make something of himself. He had no excuses. Yet he was still far from figuring out who he could or should become. He had entertained a few ideas: something with history or politics. Perhaps he could be the next Donovan Wright with his own political talk show. He wanted other men to respect him and he intended to try to earn that respect.

***

Jessica wasn't asking for an extension on her English paper when she reluctantly spoke to Dr. Menkin after class, at his request. She explained the importance of her charity drive and how the necessary and extensive time commitment had interfered with her ability to get her paper done. She was aiming for absolution and understanding with her response, nothing more. She didn't want to do the paper then and she didn't want to do the paper now. She could live with a zero. She had already convinced herself that if she did well enough on the rest of her assignments her grade might just average out to be almost okay. But Dr. Menkin thought he was doing her a big favor by granting an extension and now she still had to do the damn paper, along with a bunch of other work that was accumulating too quickly to ever get done.

The authors she had to analyze for the paper were Sylvia Plath, Virginia Woolf, and Ernest Hemingway. She hadn't finished the books she was supposed to read, but she was aware that all of them had committed suicide. The authors were supposed to be incredible talents and whether or not she enjoyed reading their work was apparently not relevant to that determination, it had already been decided. Apparently, she surmised, there was a correlation between being brilliant and mentally unstable.

Jessica decided to write about what the authors had in common because it was easier to Google their biographies on the internet and produce an essay about their mental illnesses and suicides than to try and speed read through their books and come up with something else. She opened her browser and began her search for details. Virginia Woolf had killed herself by filling her pockets with stones and wading into a river until she sunk and drowned. Her body was found three weeks later.

What woman in her right mind would want to kill herself like that? Maybe a quiet and painless overdose, but not something messy like drowning yourself. Didn't she think about how awful she would look when they found her?

Thinking about it sent shudders down Jessica's spine.

Maybe she didn't really kill herself. Did anyone see her do it? How hard would it be to put a gun to someone's head, load their pockets with stones and then force them to walk into the river? Didn't the mob do that all the time? They did in the movies. And detectives were terrible in the olden days. They didn't have the benefits of technology and there were no surveillance cameras on buildings. So no one knows what really happened!

Next she googled Sylvia Plath and discovered with horror that she had stuck her head in an oven until she expired. The article claimed that Sylvia had made several suicide attempts and was taking anti-depressants.

That doesn't prove anything. I'm taking anti-depressants. It doesn't mean I have any interest in killing myself, it just means I want to be thinner. Just because she tried to kill herself doesn't mean she wanted to die. The previous suicide attempts might have been just for attention. Maybe she had a crappy boyfriend who didn't make her feel special. Maybe he was the only one who didn't like her books. Or maybe he was a jerk who said he wouldn't even read her books, even though all of the rest of us have to. Someone could have totally killed her and then put her head in the oven.

And suddenly she came up with an excellent idea.

Maybe that's the real story here! Maybe all of these authors were murdered! And all this time the public was so quick to jump on the suicide bandwagon. It wasn't at all fair to these women. It made them look bad.

For a few fleeting moments Jessica was excited about the possibilities for her essay. She believed it was going to be revolutionary. In her excitement she unknowingly reached for a chocolate brownie weight loss bar and ate it as she thought.

Then she read further documentation regarding Sylvia's previous suicide attempts. Sylvia had admitted to taking an overdose of sleeping pills, spent months in a mental institution, and said she had definitely wanted to die. And years later when she stuck her head into the oven, she had gone to great lengths to protect her sleeping children from the carbon monoxide poisoning by stuffing wet towels under all the doors to the kitchen. Maybe she did want to end her life after all. Jessica switched back to Virginia Woolf and read that Virginia wrote a note to her husband that seemed very much to be a suicide letter and shortly before her death her house had been confiscated during the Blitz. Jessica didn't know anything about the Blitz but assumed it was something one wanted to avoid.

She grabbed another chocolate brownie weight loss bar and ate it in four bites. The excitement generated by her murder theory gradually waned as she did more research.

Now what? What am I going to write about now?

She was back to square one with her essay. If only there was a chance they had been murdered, it would have been a great paper. Murder was sensational, whereas suicide was just pathetic. It was for losers. Jessica was no loser.

Jessica's phone rang, interrupting her frustration. It was Megan O'Rourke.

"Hi. It's Megan."

"I know. I'm writing a paper. What are you calling about?"

"I'm going out for a Starbucks. Do you want to come with?"

Jessica looked around at the empty Red Bull and weight loss bar wrappers on her desk. She didn't remember consuming them. She had been so inspired by her ideas for a few moments. She wasn't sure if she had eaten anything else today, and if she was going to write this paper, she might as well go and get a Venti Latte to help her get through it.

"Sure...I'll go. Just give me a few minutes and I'll meet you downstairs."

***

Brooke had a dilemma. She was being politely pressured to go to Boston for the weekend with Ethan. Jessica's cousin, Bradley, a sophomore at Harvard, was having his fraternity's biggest party of the year and Ethan wanted Brooke to go with him, Robert and Jessica. They would stay at a condo that Robert's father's owned in Boston. Brooke didn't want to spend the weekend with any of them. She liked to be in control of her own schedule and she had better things to do than drive all the way to Boston for a party.

Aware that a fine line existed between acting encouraging and acting obsessed, Ethan had suppressed impatience and put well thought-out effort into convincing Brooke to come to Boston. It would be a cultural experience to stay in Craig Mending's condo because it had been featured in last year's Architectural Digest magazine. He pointed out that she hadn't left Everett since the semester started and that everyone needed to get away from campus and relax once in a while. He was persistent and patient while he dealt with the uncertainty of the situation.

"Do you know if you can come with us yet?" Ethan asked, because she had told him she might have to work, which wasn't true.

"I'm not sure yet, but I'll let you know as soon as I find out." She was lying, but she thought it would be nicer to let him believe there was a chance of her going. She felt like she owed him that at least. He was a really good guy and after all, she was using his car to get to Resolution Fitness several times a week. That was saving her a lot of time that she poured back into her studies. But the prospect of going to Boston held no appeal, until a few days before the party.

Brooke was flipping through a yoga magazine that someone had left on a step mill at Resolution Fitness. Under the title "Hot New Classes" she found an article about an instructor named Carlos Q. His new studio in Boston was getting rave reviews for its athletic mix of strength and revolutionary movement. He taught an advanced class every Sunday morning. Perfect! Before she could change her mind, she called Ethan from the gym.

"I decided to go to Boston with you this weekend, with one provision," she said hopefully.

"Anything." Ethan was grinning from ear to ear.

"There's a yoga class on Sunday in Boston that I want to attend. Can that work with everyone's schedule?"

"Absolutely. No problem. I'll make sure it works."

"Okay. Great. Thanks. I'm looking forward to it then."

She wasn't looking forward to the entire weekend, just the yoga. There was nothing Brooke loved more than taking an excellent exercise class. Any time she got a great workout it helped control the urges that might otherwise get her into trouble. She was also planning to take home new, cutting edge ideas to implement in her own class. And it might be good for her to escape Everett for a weekend. Maybe if she'd occasionally left Cedarhurst for some rest and recreation, she wouldn't have been forced to leave it forever.

CHAPTER SEVEN

It was a beautiful fall day when Jessica left for Boston with Robert. The sun coming through the windows warmed the car to a perfect temperature for napping. It would have been even better if Jessica had not been aware of who was sitting next to Ethan as he slept in the back seat. She had been exceptionally angry to learn that Ethan had invited Brooke along, but was pleased to notice that Brooke looked uncomfortable as she attempted to study with Ethan's head resting on her lap.

The passing suburbs and increasing traffic indicated they were getting closer to the designer outlet mall.

"We need to stop here," Jessica informed Robert. "I want to look for a few things."

"I might wait in the car," Brooke said as Robert maneuvered into a spot in front of J. Crew.

"Come on, it will be fun," Ethan told her.

Jessica couldn't understand why Brooke needed to be convinced. After all, Brooke needed new clothes far more than any of them. She should really try harder to fit in. A lot harder. It would be best if she could just become someone else entirely.

Jessica was a whirlwind of efficiency when it came to shopping. She cruised the store, and when she saw something she needed, she acted decisively. At the Brooks Brothers outlet she purchased a tight black sweater similar to one she already owned and a pink silk blouse, then moved swiftly on to the next store. In Ralph Lauren she saw Brooke pick up a plaid leather bag and search for the price tag. Brooke looked surprised and then quickly put the bag back down. Jessica understood then that Brooke didn't have the means to buy what she wanted. Coming up behind Brooke, Jessica scooped up the plaid bag, adding it to the shirt and scarves she had draped over her arm and then, with a smug smile on her face, purchased them with her father's credit card. Beside her, Robert bought some new socks.

Jessica waited inside while Robert rearranged the suitcases in the trunk to make room for the additional bags and Brooke stretched her legs using the side of the car for resistance. Three of the five new bags were Jessica's, one from each of the stores she entered. Once everything was in place, they climbed back inside the BMW to finish the trip.

In the front passenger seat Jessica sipped a Red Bull and talked to Robert, seemingly without needing to stop for a breath.

"Did I tell you that Bradley hooked up with Sofi, my tenth grade roommate at Miss White's? Her parents rented a house near his for the summer. She said she was so drunk that she doesn't remember, but he said she wasn't drunk at all and he was the one who was wasted. Do you remember Chip Talbot? He's in Bradley's fraternity. He was at the Hampton's with us last year. You remember him. He had those braces. He had to have braces put back on and he couldn't do the invisible ones for some reason. Can you imagine? I would die if I had to get braces again. And in college! I would just have all my teeth removed and get implants. His girlfriend was that anorexic model. She's not even remotely famous. She just thinks she is. Remember? Her skin was practically transparent and she was sort of blue because she was so thin. She was actually too thin." Jessica paused for a brief second. "Are you even listening to me? I can tell you're not listening. Nodding every so often doesn't count."

"I was just thinking about my father. I didn't ask about using the condo."

"I'm sure it's fine. Why didn't you ask?"

"My parents are in Switzerland. I didn't want to bother them."

"Is your mother out searching for new art to acquire? In her Bohemian attire? "

Jessica's tone was almost patronizing and Robert chose not to answer. Robert had enormous respect for his mother. His most useful advice had come from her. For instance—it's better to be remembered for having little to say than for expressing pointless thoughts. A few carefully chosen intelligent comments are all that is necessary to make one's mark. Robert took those words to heart. They defined his personality, and he found himself listening much more often than speaking during school and social situations. Jessica could have benefitted big-time from that advice.

"Honestly, I think it's admirable how she buys what she likes regardless of what other people think of it. That takes confidence," Jessica continued, her dig barely concealed.

Robert was silent.

"Well as long as you have a key and the security code I'm sure it will be fine. It's not like we're throwing a party or anything. You're always so worried about disappointing your father."

"Yea. Well—I don't want to disappoint him. He trusts me. And he's never disappointed me."

Jessica was tired of trying to engage Robert in an interesting conversation, so she turned toward the back seat. Ethan's eyes were closed again and Brooke was studying, which was all she seemed to know how to do, both of which irked Jessica. She had had enough of Brooke all focused and concentrating on her open notebook as if it was so important. She couldn't understand why Ethan couldn't have brought along someone more fun or interesting. Anyone would be a better choice than Brooke. She knew plenty of young women at Everett who would love to go away for the weekend with Ethan. Brittany and Megan would probably sleep with him in a heartbeat. Brooke didn't even seem to like him that much. Why was he with her?

"Oh my God, Ethan!" Jessica spoke loudly on purpose, successfully startling Ethan into opening his eyes. He was dazed at first and then wondering what was so important.

"I just remembered something!" she exclaimed in a volume that was unnecessary considering they were all in earshot.

Ethan lifted his head to stare at her. Now that she had his attention, she turned back toward the front of the car and continued speaking.

"Remember when all of us were in the Hamptons last year with Darien?"

"All of us" actually meant all of us with the exception of Brooke. "You two were down on the beach in the dark, doing who knows what for a long time!" She laughed as if it was hysterical. "Then you came up to the landing and you were carrying her because she lost her shoe. Then those people from Middlebury were helping us look for her shoe for like hours. Oh my God! That was the most fun night from the whole summer! We were so wasted!"

"Yes, you were," Ethan said, his voice deadpan. He sat up fully and squeezed Brooke's hand. He leaned sideways to whisper something in Brooke's ear. Jessica saw them in the rearview mirror and did her best to interrupt.

"Where do you summer?" she asked Brooke.

Jessica's question, though innocent enough and entirely appropriate for her friends from Miss Whites, was intentionally crafted to make Brooke uncomfortable.

"Um...like where have I been on vacation? Cape Cod I guess," Brooke answered.

"Where on the Cape?" Jessica asked. She was pleased when it took Brooke several seconds to respond.

"I can't remember. We actually only went there once or twice—it was a long time ago. I usually work all summer, as much as possible."

"Really?" Jessica asked, raising her eyebrows as if she couldn't possibly imagine such a thing. Before she could comment Ethan started talking, and Jessica was sure it was an attempt to save Brooke from embarrassment. He must have been worried that Brooke couldn't fend for herself. Brooke was pathetic.

"The last time my family went to Cape Cod my brother and I rolled around in sand dunes and ended up with poison ivy all over our butts. I'll never forget that trip. During the vacation, it spread from our backsides to our necks and faces. We looked diseased," Ethan said.

"It can't spread, it's not contagious," said Brooke, drawing knowledge from one of the plant based biology classes she had to take. "It was either still developing or you touched something that still had urushiol on it. That's the oil in the plant, that's what causes the allergic reaction. You have to wash everything you wear once you come in contact with it."

Jessica rolled her eyes. Brooke was a huge geek—not that Ethan wasn't. He was the biggest nerd in a jock's body that anyone could imagine, but at least he was rich and irresistibly handsome.

"I don't think I've ever had poison ivy, but my mother took a picture of me, years ago, when I had chicken pox. I had spots, giant spots, all over my face. She took the picture to a photographer who tinted all the spots green then she had it framed and it's still in our house. It's bizarre," Robert added.

"I've seen that." Ethan laughed.

"We've all seen it, Robert. It's hanging in your kitchen," Jessica added, again using "all" to mean "all except Brooke."

Feeling disappointed at the way the conversation had turned, Jessica took a book out of her bag and informed Robert they were going to get some of their homework done. They were in Theories of International Politics together. She began reading aloud to him from the text.

"What is the role of foreign assistance in international politics and foreign policy? How do the neorealist theories present in international realms effect decisions regarding foreign assistance and the establishment of foreign-policy?" Jessica sighed. "Whatever."

CHAPTER EIGHT

Craig Mending's condo in Boston's trendy Back Bay area was actually a loft. A bronze sculpture of an emaciated man greeted them from a chunky pedestal in the foyer, one of dozens of pieces of strange art.

"It's like a mini-contemporary art museum! Look at this sink!" Brooke exclaimed as she peered into the bathroom. A blue glass bowl sat atop a large horizontal section of polished and stained tree trunk. Everything was unexpected.

Ethan carried their bags into one of the downstairs bedrooms. Brooke followed him in and looked in that bathroom as well.

"Oh—the shower!" she called, her blue eyes widening with surprise.

There were no walls, just an open area with spectacular slate tile walls and floors.

"Apparently she's never seen professional decor before," Jessica said to Robert as she headed up the stairs to where a large master bedroom and bathroom took up the whole floor. "Let's use the master bedroom."

Robert was planning to use the other downstairs bedroom, but he supposed it didn't matter. They would have more privacy upstairs. It wasn't really his parents' bedroom. He wasn't sure if his mother had ever stayed here once she had finished the decorating. He surveyed his mother's work. Three framed charcoal drawings of something unexplainable hung above the bed, which was set unusually low on the ground. He grinned at the uncomfortable looking steel-framed chair in the corner, the most expensive object d'art in the condo. It was one of his mother's favorite finds and it always amused him.

Jessica immediately flung open the hidden closet doors. She pushed aside the clothes: pressed white dress shirts, a suit, khakis, a tuxedo and an assortment of ties and bow ties. She opened her suitcase and started hanging up her own clothes. When she was done arranging her clothes, she headed to the bathroom and set out her essentials: makeup, hairbrush, hairdryer, curling iron, hair products, toothbrush, toothpaste, electronic cleansing machine, face masque, lotion, serum, eye cream, foot cream, three bottles of pills, and a variety of other products. The initially empty countertop was now covered.

"Thank goodness for heated floors," she called from the bathroom, "that's one more thing I need if I can find a place to live off campus next year."

Robert switched places with Jessica in the bathroom as soon as she came out. Seeing that Jessica had made herself at home, he stuck his small bag inside the vanity underneath the sink. When he exited the bathroom she was lying across the bed, one eyebrow raised, holding a condom up between two fingers.

"Did you bring this?" she asked.

Robert looked at her, confused, trying to register the context of the question. He didn't know why she was asking, and with Jessica he always had to answer carefully or there might be trouble. Was he supposed to bring one? Had she told him to? He didn't think so. Jessica was taking birth control pills so Robert didn't use condoms.

"I found it in the drawer. On the side where you put your wallet and keys, so I just thought that maybe it was yours."

"Yea. It's mine, Jess. I had it with me, it's really old. I just wanted it out of my wallet. I put it in there."

The words just popped into his head, he was not sure why he chose them; it was unusual for him to lie without thinking first. He turned away from her, disturbed. Whose condom was that? It couldn't be his fathers. His mother had a hysterectomy shortly after his birth and couldn't get pregnant. Even if she could, wouldn't she be past the age that women need to worry about that? Had his parents even come here together? He couldn't recall his mother ever staying here once she finished with the décor, although how would he know? He thought his father was usually alone here for business. So if his father was here without his mother, why would he have a condom? The obvious reason was one he wanted to ignore, so he searched for another explanation. He was not shocked, just disillusioned and mostly disappointed because now he had this knowledge that he would rather not own. Didn't his parents have the best relationship, based on complete trust and respect? He and Ethan were the only people he knew whose parents were still on their first marriage. Maybe he was just jumping to conclusions. If only he and Jessica had just used the other downstairs bedroom. At least Jessica had put the condom back in the drawer and was not asking him, "Why? Why?" like she was accustomed to doing in most situations until she was satisfied.

Jessica already had plans for them. "Come here," she said, patting the bed and smiling.

Robert walked toward her.

"Wait, be a doll and make me a drink first," she said, using her seductive voice. "Then tell them we're going to take a nap."

Jessica woke up two hours later, just in time to make another round of drinks before they had to leave. While descending the stairs, she was caught off guard by the woman sitting at the table, her back toward Jessica. A gorgeous mane of silky blonde hair cascaded across her shoulders and a lovely blue sweater. Jessica didn't recognize Brooke because she had never seen her hair out of a ponytail. Then she noticed the laptop, books and notes spread across the table.

What a surprise, Brooke is studying. She has got to be the most anti-social person in the world, even if her hair can look nice once in a rare while.

Jessica headed into the kitchen where Ethan was standing behind the counter. He had found a cutting board and a knife and was creating perfectly equal slices out of an apple Brooke had brought from her dorm.

"What are you doing? You're like so anal," Jessica chided with an arrogant lift of her chin.

"I'm trying to impress Brooke with my culinary skills." He laughed.

"By cutting apples? Besides, I don't think she'd notice if you set the kitchen on fire. She's so busy studying."

Ethan shrugged his shoulders, but Jessica could tell that he was disappointed that his afternoon at the condo had been spent in an entirely different manner than her own. She would have been if she was in his shoes.

"Look, they're already rotting." Jessica pointed to the faint brownish color appearing on Ethan's apple slices as she passed him. From across the room she could see Brooke's textbook and ascertain from the illustrations that it was some sort of Science class. She remembered Brooke saying she was a Chemistry or Biology major. She thought for a second.

"It's too bad you don't learn anything in those classes that you can talk about with anyone." Jessica had heard someone say that science majors have nothing interesting to share at cocktail parties. She might have heard the line in a movie, she couldn't remember. She didn't know if it was true or not, perhaps it was a joke. Once she had said it out loud she realized it was a random comment but she didn't care. She felt compelled to keep Brooke in her place and the only way she knew to do it was by consistently putting her down. The trouble was that Brooke didn't seem to notice she was being insulted, or she didn't care. Either way it was infuriating.

Brooke looked up from her book upon realizing that Jessica was talking to her. Her response came quickly.

"Everything about science explains the world around us, so it just depends on what people think is interesting." She spoke in a calm and even tone, the one she used to explain exercises during her Pilates class. "Take that apple for instance, and the reference you made a minute ago." She gestured toward Ethan's slices on the cutting board. "When you cut into it, it starts to turn brown. It's a protective response at the cellular level. Enzymes inside the fruit combine with phenolic compounds and secrete an anti-microbial barrier. The brown we see is a defense line to protect its damaged cells. It's actually represents the opposite of rotting. We can stop it by inactivating the enzymes with an acid, causing a neutralization reaction. That's why lemon juice or vinegar is added to fruit salads and vegetable salads to preserve their freshly cut look. Any acid reacting with a base produces salt and water. Blanching and brining do the same thing to neutralize the reaction when cooking vegetables. I love understanding things like that. It's interesting to me." Brooke nodded and then went back to reading.

Jessica listened impatiently while Brooke was speaking. Ethan had moved into the other room to kiss Brooke affectionately on the forehead.

"You're as smart as you are pretty," he said with admiration, nuzzling his cheek against hers.

Seriously? Jessica scoffed to herself, continuing to stare at Brooke in disbelief. *She is so strange. Why can't they see it? And Ethan is clearly enamored by her. Whatever.*

"I'm going to make margaritas. So why don't you put your fancy culinary skills to work and cut a few limes for me," Jessica told Ethan as she noisily opened and closed the cabinet doors, searching for the items she needed.

"This is unbelievable." Jessica pressed her forehead against her fingers and shook her head in exasperation. "There are no margarita glasses. We're going to have to use wine glasses."

For the next few minutes Jessica was occupied with mixing and drinking, producing a batch of professional quality margaritas for all of them. Ethan took two of the salt rimmed wine glasses over to the dining table. He stood behind Brooke, drinking and rubbing her neck and shoulders with his free hand. Brooke thanked him for the drink and hesitantly took a sip. She grimaced as she put it back down on the table at the same time Robert joined Jessica in the kitchen.

"I'll have one of those." He poured the remaining mixture into a glass.

"I don't think Ethan's getting any sort of action with her," Jessica whispered to Robert. "They were both in the kitchen when I came down and she was completely studying. I feel so bad for him."

As Jessica waited for Robert's reaction, she noticed that he had to quickly suppress a smile. She figured he was laughing at Ethan's misfortune, but it was almost as if he welcomed the news and was happy to hear that Brooke wasn't doing anything to satisfy Ethan's masculine urges. As much as Jessica disliked Brooke, shouldn't Robert feel sorry for his deprived friend?

"I don't know. It's not our business. I know he really likes her a lot."

"Humph," Jessica snorted. If Brooke wasn't doing him any sexual favors, what good was she? Perhaps Brooke was playing hard to get and that was the appeal.

In a short amount of time Jessica had consumed three margaritas, and the pitcher was empty.

"Those were excellent if I do say so myself. Don't you think?" she called to Ethan and Brooke.

"Yes, excellent," Ethan said.

"What time is it, Robert?" Jessica asked.

"We need to leave in a few minutes."

"Let's go, everyone! We have dinner reservations," she announced next.

"I'll drive us tonight," Brooke offered. "I don't usually drink. That way everyone else can have a good time."

"You don't drink, as in, ever?" Jessica asked incredulously. A few minutes ago she didn't think she could possibly find Brooke any more irritating or any more of a complete social loser, but she had been wrong.

"Pretty much never. I don't like being dehydrated or hung-over. It ruins my workouts. And I especially want to feel great tomorrow. I'm looking forward to an excellent yoga class."

Jessica didn't know what Brooke was talking about, nor did she care.

"We're going to take a cab," Robert said. And Ethan nodded.

"Won't it cost a small fortune to take a cab from here to Cambridge?" Brooke asked.

"Don't worry about it," Ethan assured her. "Just relax. I really want you to have fun, more than anything."

The cab was waiting double-parked in front of the building when they got outside.

"Delaney's," Robert announced to the driver as he opened the front door and lowered himself into the front seat.

Brooke sat in the back sandwiched between Ethan and Jessica.

"It's very, very hard to get a reservation here," Jessica informed Brooke, adding a large hand gesture for emphasis. Jessica didn't think Brooke was capable of appreciating that fact, but she shared it with her anyway. "On a Saturday night it's almost unheard of."

"Oh, good," Brooke answered.

"I can't wait to see Bradley. His fraternity has the best parties. They turned the basement into a beach last year. They brought in dump trucks full of sand. And they don't just let anyone in the door. Although they'll let you in because you're with us tonight."

Thanks to the margaritas, Jessica was in a better mood than usual. Adjusting her red trench coat over her white silk blouse, she suddenly became preoccupied with picking invisible pieces of lint from her black pants. Everyone else was quiet, so she started singing out loud to a tune in her head.

"Can you sing, Brooke?"

"No. I can't sing at all. I have a terrible singing voice."

Jessica wasn't surprised to hear that, since musicality is a cultured talent. "I was in the honors choir at Miss White's and I'm in the church choir at Everett."

Jessica took off her silk scarf to readjust it, elbowing Brooke in the process. She didn't have enough room in the back seat to put it back on properly. When the cab stopped, she stepped out in a practiced way, twirling her scarf through the air and demonstrating the range of her excellent singing voice all the way to the front door of Delaney's.

"Mending, table for four," Robert said to the maître d' once they were inside. They did not have to wait.

"Right this way, Mr. Mending." A hostess whisked them away, leading them through the tightly packed candle lit room toward the front of the restaurant. The interior décor was elegant and simple. Sconces glowing with a faint flicker of light were the only adornments on the terra cotta Venetian plaster walls. Small tables with white linen tablecloths and cross backed chairs were arranged to accommodate as many people as possible.

"I'm really hungry." Brooke smiled at Ethan as he pulled her chair away from the table so she could sit.

"Bring us some bread when you have a chance please," Ethan said as soon as the waiter appeared with menus.

"No! No bread. I don't want it on the table," Jessica protested but then quickly conceded. "Oh, fine. Whatever. Bring the bread."

Brooke scanned the parchment paper menu up and down several times and Ethan noticed the concerned look on her face.

"I'm getting the NY sirloin. Please get whatever you want. It's on my Dad. Don't worry about it. Okay?" Ethan told her firmly. He put his hand on her knee under the table and gave it a gentle squeeze. Brooke nodded.

"I'll have the lemon grilled chicken," Brooke ordered.

"I'll have the shrimp cocktail," Jessica ordered next.

"Why aren't you eating?" Robert asked, although it was perfectly normal for Jessica to order only an appetizer or side salad for her meal.

"I don't want to ruin my buzz," she said, tilting her head to the side as she spoke in a manner she considered charming.

The waiter brought a carving board with a loaf of warm bread and butters. Everyone had some, including Jessica, and it quickly disappeared from the table.

"Are you a fan of fraternity parties, Brooke?" Robert asked.

"I've never been to one. This will be my first. What should I expect?"

"Really?" Robert and Jessica both asked at once.

"Didn't you have a Greek system at your old school, Brooke?" Jessica asked.

"No. It was too small."

"Oh. Cedarhill, that's what you said right Ethan? Is it a community college?" Jessica asked.

"Cedarhurst. It's a small private school," Brooke answered.

"Cedarhurst. Hmmm. I went to prep school in Connecticut, but I've never heard of it. I don't know anyone who went to Cedarhurst, so it must be very small."

Jessica noticed that both Ethan and Robert seemed peeved by her comment. Ethan had visibly cringed and Robert's face was set in that warning look he sometimes used. It was as if they both felt the need to protect poor little helpless Brooke.

"I've been to fraternity parties that were terrible and some that were brilliant," Robert said. "We'll find out soon enough which this is. The only sure thing is that there will be plenty of drinking," Robert said.

"She doesn't drink, remember?" Jessica stated, raising her eyebrows.

"It should be interesting, but we don't have to stay," Ethan offered, ignoring Jessica. "We can always walk around Cambridge or have coffee somewhere if you want out."

"Of course you're going to want to stay. It's going to be a blast," Jessica said to Brooke. "Well, maybe not for you. You might be the only one not drinking, unless there are some recovering alcoholics or something like that. There was this one girl at Miss White's who drank so much she had cirrhosis of the liver at like sixteen. She can't drink ever again or she'll die. God knows what she does at parties. Maybe there will be someone like her around for you to hang out with."

The meals arrived looking exquisitely artistic, the sauce and garnishes artfully arranged on triangular plates, but the actual portions were miniscule. Brooke's chicken medallions were balanced precariously in a small stack interspersed with fried onions.

"Glad we had the bread," Ethan said, as he cut into his steak and offered Brooke a piece from his fork.

"It's delicious," she said.

"Would you mind not sharing your food? It's a little gauche," Jessica told them, with a sneer.

They were almost finished eating when their waiter returned to see if they needed anything else.

"I'll have a long island iced tea," Jessica said.

"I just need to see your ID," the waiter responded.

"I'm sorry, but I don't have my purse with me. I didn't want to get robbed here in the city. I completely forgot I might get carded somewhere. I'm just not used to being carded," Jessica told him confidently.

"Sorry. I'll need to see your ID." The waiter had been through this before. He remained the consummate, cordial professional, playing along as if her story was remotely plausible.

"We're just going to have one drink, now that we've finished our dinner. Then we'll pay our bill, leave you a nice big tip, and be on our way," Jessica said in her imitation professional voice. She continued to look him in the eye as she turned her Cartier band around on her wrist.

"I'm so sorry, Miss. Unfortunately, I will need to see identification before I can bring your ice tea." His smile was unwavering.

"Seriously?" Jessica asked, much too loudly for the environment. "Do you know who his father is?" She tilted her head toward Robert, and the waiter followed her gaze.

Robert looked uncomfortable, then apologetic. He sent Jessica a warning look, delivered much too late, and shook his head. In a few seconds Jessica started laughing as if it was all a good joke.

"Just bring us the bill please then," she instructed, making another swirling hand gesture that knocked two pieces of silverware to the floor.

After dinner, Jessica and Brooke stood inside the waiting area of the restaurant while Robert and Ethan were outside flagging down a cab to take them to Cambridge.

"Did you enjoy your dinner?" Jessica asked while eyeing Brooke with disdain as if she was the most unattractive person Jessica could imagine and it was all she could do not to look away.

"Yes. It was excellent. Did you like your shrimp?"

"Yes, it was just a shrimp cocktail. Shrimp cocktail really can't be particularly good, although I suppose it can be particularly bad. I just wish we hadn't had that bread on the table. It's not good for you, you know. And now I need another drink." Her desire for another drink unfulfilled, she was in a hurry to get to the party before her current state of drunkenness waned.

***

Brooke believed she had made a mistake by coming to Boston, but it was too late now. The meal had been delicious; it would have been a good way to end the evening. She had endured more than enough socializing for one night.

Brooke didn't know what to think of Jessica, who seemed to think very highly of herself for no apparent reason. When Jessica's phone rang, Brooke hoped it was the cousin calling to say the party was cancelled.

"That was Robert. Come on. They have a cab," Jessica said without looking at her.

No such luck.

To get through the rest of the evening, Brooke reminded herself about the yoga class she couldn't wait to take. And maybe she could get in a long run in the morning and explore the city. The weather was supposed to be cool and pleasant all weekend. That helped take her mind off the looming party that was next on the agenda.

CHAPTER NINE

Robert sighed as the cab dropped them off in Cambridge outside the Harvard walls. They were on a street similar to Everett's downtown area, only with ten times the amount of activity. As he expected, Jessica began calling the shots immediately because she knew her way around Cambridge and the Harvard campus.

"Come on," Jessica called. She was weaving through the buildings on a mission, hurrying to get into the party and out of the cold. Ethan, Robert, and Brooke strolled along behind her, with Brooke looking this way and that, taking in the surroundings.

"I don't think they're going to run out of alcohol," Robert said. In his head he had been reliving Jessica's comment from dinner and finding it progressively more offensive. "Do you know who his father is?" He sure as hell hoped they didn't. After that he had pretended that he forgot his credit card, forcing Ethan to pay the entire bill because he didn't want the waiter to have his name, even though the reservation had been for Mending. That had slipped his mind until now. He imagined the waiter laughing about him back in the kitchen.

"Some little prick named Robert Mending thinks we should serve his underage friend a drink, risking our liquor license, because he has a big deal father. Does anyone know who he is?"

He didn't want there to be any possible way for Jessica's comment to come back to his parents or to be associated with him. They would be so embarrassed. Then he remembered his father might be an adulterer, so maybe he deserved a little embarrassment.

But he didn't know that for sure. He needed to stop thinking about that condom and what it might mean. Forget about it completely. In any case, his mother would have been horrified if she had seen Jessica's behavior and his mother was the last person he wanted to upset right now, particularly if his father was cheating on her.

"Here we are. Come on." Jessica stopped at a brick building with white columns on the front. A buzzing noise emanated from inside. She marched up the front steps and introduced herself to the guy screening the guests at the door. "I've already texted Bradley that we're here. He should be on his way down."

The fraternity house was similar to the formal areas of the dorms at Everett, with deep crown moldings and cross beams on the ceiling. But a leather chair was torn and the sofas were worn and visibly stained, as was the carpet. It had surely seen better days. As they waited inside the front door, one of the fraternity brothers eyed Ethan's Everett Lacrosse jacket critically. Ethan took it off and folded it over his arm. A young man, handsome had his face been visible through his carefully arranged mess of long hair, cruised around the house with a tray of purple drinks. Jessica spotted him and beckoned.

"Nice watch." She noticed his Bulgari as she took one of the plastic champagne glasses for herself and one for Robert. Robert graciously offered his purple concoction to Brooke.

"I know you said you didn't drink, but I don't think this qualifies as a real drink," Robert said with a smile. "It's more of a dessert, although it might be strong." Robert's hand inadvertently brushed against Brooke's as she accepted the drink. A pleasant tremor passed through his body with the touch.

"It reminds me of a grape Popsicle," Brooke said, sipping the sweet purple liquid before placing it, nearly full, on a side table where it joined other discarded drinks.

"I need a beer," Ethan said.

Robert was the first to spot Bradley Carroll. He was dressed much like Ethan, in green pants, a belt with nautical objects floating around it, and a plaid collared shirt. Bradley greeted Robert with a back slap, harder than what was called for.

"Hey Robert. Glad you could come. Well not really. Ha. Ha. I'm well on my way to being inebriated. I've spent the last two weeks making a select few young ladies feel very special and I'm certain at least one of them is going to end up in my bed...willingly this time." He laughed, speaking in a conspiratorial tone. "I need you to make sure that Jessica doesn't ruin it for me. You know more than anyone how bossy she can be."

"Jessica? Bossy? Are you sure you have the right person?" Robert joked.

"I'm just kidding with you. But I am glad you'll be in your condo tonight and not crashed in my room because that would ruin my well-laid plans. Ha. Ha. Get it?"

"I get it. You don't need to worry. I don't think you could get Jessica to crash in your room unless you've recently transformed it into a spa. A spa with a lifetime supply of Red Bull."

Robert stepped to one side and that was when Bradley's face lit up as he first spotted Brooke. Robert was not okay with the way Bradley's eyes moved up and down Brooke's body, or with the grin that came across his face.

"That's the hottest girl I've ever seen," he half-whispered, giving Robert a hard nudge in the shoulder for emphasis. "Where the hell did she come from?"

Robert could understand how Bradley was feeling. Her defined cheekbones, the dark lashes that framed serene blue eyes, her amazing dancer's body, all that blonde hair, and the complete innocence she seemed to have regarding her effect on men. But why did Bradley's comments bother him so much? Normally he would have just grinned and agreed, but instead he found himself feeling offended for the second time tonight.

Ethan had noticed the direction of Bradley's open-mouthed stare. He held Brooke's arm in a way that looked unabashedly possessive, but Bradley didn't seem to care.

"I'm going to take that girl for a ride in my new Mercedes and she's going to love it." Bradley was whispering so that only Robert could hear him. Robert had never even come close to starting a fight, but he felt the urge to punch Bradley in the face, although there was zero chance of him actually doing it.

"Shut up," Robert said, as if he was only mildly annoyed. "You're not driving anywhere tonight or your Mercedes will end up kissing a tree and it won't look too sexy in the morning."

"Bradley!" Jessica exclaimed when she noticed him talking to Robert. She gave him a dramatic hug.

"You've met Ethan, of course," Jessica said. She didn't bother to introduce Brooke, but it wasn't like Brooke didn't have Bradley's full attention already. It was obvious to Robert that Brooke was put off by Bradley's open admiration. She avoided his gaze but tentatively shook the hand he offered, pulling her own hand away when he clasped it between both of his.

"We need to put our coats and bags in your room. Make sure you lock it," Jessica said as they followed her to Bradley's room. Everyone took off their coats and Brooke also removed her sweater so it wouldn't get ruined by the sweat or smoke that was present around them. She pulled it gracefully over her head revealing a fitted black cotton camisole. She carefully folded the sweater and placed it inside her coat.

"Holy Moses!" Bradley muttered. He couldn't take his eyes off Brooke's body.

"What can I get you to drink?" Bradley clasped Brooke's elbow and leaned in closer, treating her as if it was just the two of them in the room. Ethan glared at him. Only Jessica was oblivious. She was arranging things on Bradley's dresser so that they were more suited to where she thought they needed to be.

One of the fraternity brothers appeared in the doorway carrying a tray of orange Jell-O shots shaped like pumpkins. Everyone except Brooke took one.

"We've got a problem," the guy with the Jell-O shots said to Bradley. He looked concerned. Ethan seized the opportunity to take Brooke's arm and bolt from the room, away from Bradley's lascivious gaze.

***

Ethan got out of there before succumbing to his urge to beat the crap out of Bradley. What a jerk the guy was for openly coveting his girlfriend while Ethan was standing right there.

"I need to find a beer," he said, supporting Brooke's arm at the elbow as he led her back down to the first floor, and then toward some basement stairs. He had to bend down and yell into her ear to be heard as they descended because of the rising noise level. The temperature in the basement felt like the sub-tropics and the smell of old beer had permeated the entire area. The floor was covered with it as if flood waters had recently receded there, leaving behind a permanent stench. They heard a collective holler as someone on top of the bar fell out of a full handstand; their beer funnel was knocked sideways and gold colored liquid poured out onto the ground.

Ethan located a keg and waited in a line to fill two cups. Brooke shook her head when he offered one to her. They headed to the next room where people were playing ping pong, beers in hand sloshing out of their cups, and found a place where they could stand without being knocked about. Ethan rested his hand on Brooke's shoulder as they looked around. He rarely saw her arms and shoulders bared. He wanted to cover them back up because he knew he wasn't the only one appreciating her. He smiled at her hopefully, he wanted her to have a good time, but he didn't know if he could enjoy himself, as he noticed that every guy who walked by looked admiringly at her. Drinking was liquid courage and guys who wouldn't normally have the guts to try and seduce her with their eyes were just going for it. That made him a little proud, a little apprehensive and a little angry. Brooke didn't seem to notice or care.

He was determined to stay close to her and be completely attentive. He second guessed his determination to have her join him in Boston at this party; maybe he should have taken her somewhere else for the weekend. They could have gone anywhere, his parents' place in Nantucket, a bed and breakfast somewhere, assuming he could have found one with a gym. And he was concerned about that yoga class, the one she was so excited about, the one he had promised she could attend. If anything or anyone prevented Brooke from going, she would probably never talk to him again. Ethan had been ready to throttle Jessica because she had been so awful to Brooke earlier, shooting snooty comments her way during the car ride and at the condo. Ethan was determined to tolerate Jessica, after all, she was his best friend's girlfriend, and no one was perfect, although in his opinion Brooke certainly seemed to be, but Jessica was making it really hard.

Catching the beat of the music, Brooke began to move her body to the high energy dance rhythms blasting through the darkness.

"I use some of these songs in my cardio classes," she said, although Ethan couldn't make out what she was saying because of the noise. "It's impossible to hear them and not dance."

Two girls moved into the open space to start dancing and Brooke immediately wanted to join them. She was about to ask Ethan when she saw Bradley pushing his way through the crowd. He was looking around in all directions. When he spotted Brooke, he made eye contact and a knowing smile spread over his face, leaving her no doubt he was coming straight for her. She quickly averted his gaze, turned, and pulled Ethan down toward her, kissing him long and deep.

Ethan was pleasantly surprised and wondered what he had done to deserve her uncharacteristic display of affection. Before he knew it, she had broken the kiss and was leading him toward the other dancers.

Ethan was a terrible dancer with abysmal timing, but he had already decided he would go along with whatever Brooke wanted to do. Fortunately for him, they were quickly surrounded by other people, mostly attractive women that had come to the party to dance with their friends. He felt more comfortable in the middle of the crowd and he kept up with Brooke, moving awkwardly and sometimes imitating her moves, dancing through song after song. Brooke was having a great time, he could tell, and he was relieved. Her moves were sexy and athletic and natural all at once. Ethan was aware that everyone else was noticing her, too, because she looked amazing. There were plenty of other beautiful young women dancing around them, occasionally knocking into each other. They stole glances of approval or envy at Brooke.

Eventually, Ethan's movements became less forced and more fun. He didn't expect to, but he was having a good time dancing too. He had only drunk one beer, emptied long ago, but the longer they danced the more he felt as if he had consumed additional drinks. He felt comfortable, forgot to be self-conscious and started to think that he might not be such a bad dancer after all. Maybe he was even pretty good. He was really enjoying being on the dance floor with Brooke. As more people crammed in to the basement, their space got smaller. They were so packed together now that everyone had to adjust their dance styles. Brooke was moving around closer to him, her body undulating around and against his. He had his hands all over her shoulders, her back, and her sides and she didn't seem to mind. Sweat was dripping down his forehead and down his back because the temperature was rising as it became more crowded and because he had never danced continuously for this long before. Brooke wasn't sweating, which seemed impossible, but she was glistening; a light sexy sheen across her forehead and shoulders.

Ethan noticed he was incredibly thirsty, but toughed it out through several more songs until he couldn't take it anymore. He thought they must have been dancing for over an hour when a guy behind him started getting too close for comfort. At one point the guy seemed to be intentionally touching his back so he jumped forward reflexively. Something about the incident felt strange and combined with his thirst, it was enough to bump him out of his feel good zone. He stopped Brooke from dancing, holding her still with his hands on her shoulders.

"Let's get drinks," he said, his lips touching her ear. He felt another hand graze his back and reflexively stepped forward.

Brooke looked questioningly at him.

"Drink!" he tried again, but he knew she couldn't hear him so he gently directed her off the dance floor. He heard two guys say "hey!" as he led her away. They were disappointed that Brooke was leaving.

They started weaving and pushing their way through the crowd, which had increased significantly while they were dancing. Brooke appreciated Ethan's imposing build parting the way like the Red Sea before her. She didn't want to stop dancing, but she could definitely use a drink of water.

Ethan stopped. He turned sideways and angled Brooke's body so that she could see around him. He shielded her from the people pushing around them as he pointed across the room. Brooke followed his gaze and saw Jessica dancing on top of the bar; she was singing while swiveling her hips and twirling her scarf around her arms. Without warning the lights went off completely and for a split second, the basement was immersed in blackness. High-pitched screams filled the air and drowned out the music. Before the shouts died out, black light filled the void and everyone could see again, just differently. The basement was enveloped in a purple glow. Jessica had resumed dancing on the bar, or else she never stopped. When she turned away from Ethan and Brooke, the black light revealed fluorescent ink across the back of her blouse. The words Snooty Drunk lit up clearly.

People were laughing at Jessica now that her back was visible, but she was not the only one wearing unexpected commentary. Anyone with a white shirt had been a target for the fraternity brothers who had been busy writing without being noticed. It was easy to do when your target had enough to drink. A sophisticated looking girl with jet black hair was craning her neck to catch a glimpse of her back and she looked furious, but most everyone else was laughing at themselves or others. Jessica seemed oblivious to what was happening around her. She wasn't looking for white shirts to read like everyone else was. The whole scene felt extremely surreal to Ethan. He was aware that Brooke was laughing and seemed to think it was very clever, which seemed good.

"Check the back of my shirt," Ethan said, angling his back toward her. He was wearing a white dress shirt and was worried about what it might say. He turned to face her again, bearing a questioning look.

"There's nothing!" Brooke assured him, mouthing the words and simultaneously moving her head slightly side to side in a way that Ethan found remarkably endearing.

They headed back upstairs where they could hear each other again.

"Did you see that guy in the dark blue shirt on the dance floor? He kept getting really close to me. I kept inching away because it was too weird. I didn't know what his problem was. He must have been trying to write on my back," Ethan told her.

"I saw that, too. I had no idea what he was doing, but it looks like he didn't succeed." Brooke laughed. "Good thing you kept moving. Don't you think it's funny?"

"Yes! Since it happened to other people and not us."

"I'm glad I removed my sweater. It wasn't white, but in any case, if someone had written on it I think I would have flipped. I was totally safe in this black top."

Ethan found bottled waters and they made their way slowly around the house, scanning and reading white shirts for entertainment. Some of the phrases were for mature audiences only, but most were witty or stupid.

"Dancing makes me feel so relaxed," Brooke said. "Maybe parties aren't so bad after all."

Ethan guided Brooke to a dark corner and tried to recapture the electricity she had ignited with her earlier kiss. He sensed that she was letting herself go and thought that perhaps they had reached a turning point in their relationship. As he kissed her, and felt her respond with more enthusiasm than he expected, he concentrated on remembering everything he had ever learned about how to make a girl feel good. It wasn't about him, although he was enjoying himself immensely, it was about pleasing her so much that there wouldn't be any question in her mind about continuing on later in the evening.

***

Robert was the first to get bored with the party, not long after encountering Bradley as he came out of a bathroom.

"Where's the girl you brought?" Bradley was officially wasted and it only made him more arrogant.

"She's with her boyfriend," Robert told him.

"Can you get him to leave for me? I'll owe you. How about if the three of you leave without her? If you make that happen, I will so owe you Robert. Anything you want. I can score some incredible X or Meth for you. What do you say?"

"Drop it Bradley. You're not Brooke's type."

"Charming? Positioned to master the universe? That's not her type?"

"*You're* not her type. I promise. Give it up before the rest of your prospects go home and you end up jerking off alone."

Later on, Robert watched Jessica dancing on the bar. He was glad she was happy for a change, but by then he had had enough. He went upstairs for some fresher air. Near an open window he could partly see a girl sitting on a guy's lap in a large armchair. Her arms and legs were wrapped behind him and they were making out as if there was no tomorrow.

Get a room. He almost said it before walking away when something compelled him to do a double take. It was the long blonde hair, even more gorgeous worn down than he had imagined it before today. It was Ethan and Brooke. He felt a twinge of something in his gut. Disappointment? Jealousy?

"Get a room", he said, out loud this time. He wanted them to stop.

Brooke released her arms from Ethan's neck and swiveled at the waist to stare at him, reminding him of the first time he had seen her in the library. Beside her, Ethan's smile was so genuine that Robert felt guilty.

"Are you ready to call it a night?" Robert asked.

Brooke hopped up in answer. She was ready.

"Let's get our coats and find Jessica," Robert said, turning away from them.

"Will you get my coat? I'll wait right here," Brooke asked Ethan. She didn't want to go back to Bradley's room.

"I'll get everyone's stuff. Wait here. I'll be right back," Ethan told her.

"Make sure you get my sweater too. Thank you," Brooke added as she let go of Ethan's hand and he walked away.

"Robert! There you are. There's someone else I need you to meet. Come with me." Jessica was walking haphazardly toward them. Robert was grateful that they wouldn't have to go searching for Jessica after all.

"No. We're going now," Robert said while Ethan bounded up the stairs two at a time to get their coats.

"It will only take a moment."

Much to Robert's dismay, Jessica managed to lead him out of the room. When he turned back, a new crowd of drunken coeds was blocking his view of Brooke.

"This is one of my old friends from Miss White's!" Jessica cooed. Though distracted, Robert managed to be polite and endure a bit of small talk.

Minutes later, Ethan came down the stairs carrying all of their coats.

"What took so long?" Robert asked.

"Where's Brooke?" Ethan asked, without answering. His body was tense, his brow furrowed.

"I don't know. Wait here with Jessica and don't let her leave. I'll look for Brooke."

"Okay," Ethan said, somewhat reluctantly. "Hurry up."

Robert said excuse me repeatedly as he pushed people aside to search for Brooke, scanning for a trace of her blonde hair and black top. Where could she have gone? He was nearing the end of a long hallway and was about to head back in the other direction when a door opened in front of him. Brooke emerged looking smug, which quickly changed to surprise.

"Robert."

She leaned to her right to yank the door closed beside her.

"Brooke." He wasn't sure what else to say. What was she doing down here? He felt nervous and excited being alone with her as they made eye contact and Brooke tucked her hair behind her ears and gave him a slight smile. She looked down at her hands and then seemed self-conscious as she rubbed them across the back of her dark jeans before clasping them behind her back. The moment felt significant.

"Ready?" she said. "Let's go." She briefly looked back toward the closed door before letting Robert lead the way to the front of the house.

"We're going now," Robert said to Jessica when they returned.

"But we don't even know where the after party is!" she exclaimed.

It was always the same with Jessica when Robert wanted to leave a party. It was rare that she was ever ready to call it a night. Jessica would have protested more, but she was too drunk to resist. She sighed with resignation and leaned heavily against Robert.

"Oh no. I didn't get a chance to say goodbye to Bradley. We haaaave to go back," Jessica was slurring some of her words.

"We can call him later," Robert told her, already glancing around for signs of a cab.

"But he was sooo sweet to invite us. They each only get so many invites and he gave us four."

"I'm sorry, but your cousin is sort of an ass," Ethan said with a snort.

Robert burst out laughing.

"Ethan! I can't believe you said that! Robert! Tell him!" Jessica perked up and looked shocked.

"He's a total ass. I can't stand him. He's going to get what he deserves some day," Robert said quietly.

Jessica was upset about their comments, but fortunately she was too drunk to be furious and by the time their cab arrived she had forgotten entirely.

"Wasn't that fun? Did you have fun, Ethan?" Jessica asked as she plopped ungracefully down in the back of the cab.

"Yes," he responded. "The party was good, but it was my date that made it great."

"Are you going to sleep in the same bed tonight?" Jessica asked, all of her tact having disappeared and been replaced by numerous alcoholic creations with food coloring.

"That's not our business," Robert said dryly, because he didn't want to hear about it or think about it.

"I hardly saw you," Jessica said, turning her attention to Robert.

Even after a few drinks Robert was as quiet and introspective as usual.

"I met someone…", he began to say, but before he could finish Jessica had settled into his arms and was snuggling into his neck and kissing him. In a few minutes she would be passed out, her head against his chest.

Brooke leaned forward, putting a little distance between her and Jessica, so she could talk to Ethan, who was seated in the front. "That was really fun."

"Yes it was," he answered.

"I didn't know we'd be dancing," Brooke said.

"Neither did I."

Ethan reached behind him, through the center of the seats, to take Brooke's hand, bumping the cab driver in the process.

"What's this?" he asked, squinting down at her skin. There were dark sticky splotches across the top of her hand.

"Some of that purple drink spilled on me."

"When did that happen?"

"While you were getting the coats. Someone knocked into me with their drink."

"I'm sorry. I should have taken better care of you. I didn't want to leave you alone there for a second."

"It's not a big deal. I'm just glad I wasn't wearing the sweater your mother gave me when it happened." Brooke released her hand and leaned back, a satisfied smile on her face. She was still happy, but farther away now, as if her thoughts were occupied elsewhere. Something had changed.

CHAPTER TEN

Jessica did her best to appear put together on the outside to compensate for how she felt inside. She expected Robert to appreciate her cute short-sleeved dress, adorable cardigan, and fantastic black shoes. Makeup expertly in place, hair perfectly smooth under a headband, but inside, her stomach felt menacingly unsettled and her head was positively aching. She had already consumed a slew of aspirin.

She walked cautiously down the stairs to find Ethan and Robert reading newspapers at the kitchen table. Ethan looked a bit slovenly. Although still attractive, there wasn't much he could do to change that, in an Everett t-shirt. Robert was dressed in his predictable L.L.Bean attire—duck boots, jeans, and a plaid collared shirt under a navy sweater. He had just returned to the condo with the newspapers, breakfast food, and coffees: three medium roast and a large skinny vanilla latte with a triple shot of espresso for Jessica. A tray with bagels and cream cheese was set out between Robert and Ethan.

"Oh...excellent. Perfect timing," Jessica said with gratitude, lifting her drink to her lips.

"There's an extra coffee if you want it," Robert said. "I didn't know that Brooke doesn't drink coffee, so you can have that one, too, if you need it."

"Brooke doesn't drink coffee. Now why doesn't that surprise me? Is it some health thing or will that mess up her workouts, too?"

99

"I don't know, but if you don't want it, I'll probably take it. I could use more than one this morning," Robert replied.

"Is she still sleeping?" she asked regarding Brooke's absence.

"No, she's running," Ethan answered.

"Whatever," Jessica responded.

Jessica sat down as carefully as she could so as not to move her head any more than necessary.

How could she be out running when I can barely stand up without having vertigo? It's because she's crazy. Only crazy people exercise that much and don't drink. Maybe if she drank, she wouldn't need to be exercising all the time.

"I'm wondering where she is though. I was sleeping when she left, but I think it was hours ago," Ethan commented.

No one responded. "Oh yea. This is important," Ethan said. "Brooke wants to go to a yoga class that's supposed to have a famous instructor. I promised I would get her there. It's why she agreed to come with me. It's at eleven," Ethan informed them.

"Are you serious?" Jessica asked, hearing more than enough to make her angry. "Is that all she does? Exercise and study? What is wrong with her?"

"Nothing. There's absolutely nothing wrong with her," Ethan responded emphatically, challenging Jessica with his gaze.

Robert had tuned back in to the conversation at the sound of raised voices. "Maybe you have to work out that much to look like that," he suggested with an innocent shrug of his shoulders.

"Oh, thanks," Jessica shot back. "Well, some of us have other things to do."

"It's also her job," Ethan responded defensively. "All that exercise is how she buys her clothes and food and all the other things that you just put on your dad's credit card."

"As if you don't?" Jessica shot back. "Whatever. Well, I want to go to church before we leave."

Jessica didn't actually want to go to church. Her head was killing her, and she had no desire to sit upright on a wooden bench for over an hour. She didn't know how she would possibly make it through a church service, but it was the first thing that came to mind that might keep Brooke from doing what Brooke wanted to do.

"Do you want to come?" she asked, gazing at Robert and altering her voice to sound as sweet as it possibly could in her condition. He gave a non-committal look. "I know you don't, Jew boy," she said, turning back to Ethan with a smirk. She knew Ethan was sensitive about his Jewish heritage, even though he had never been to synagogue and his family had a huge Christmas tree every year.

Before Ethan could respond, they heard the front door open and close, and then Brooke was standing before them, absolutely beaming. The first person she noticed was Robert. His gaze was one of open admiration before it quickly changed to concern. Ethan looked angry and Jessica looked irritated, as usual. It was clear the alcohol had worn off and Jessica was back to her usual self. It was also evident to Brooke that she had interrupted something. Her smile gradually faded. They were all looking at her and no one said anything right away.

"How was the run?" Robert asked her, breaking the silence.

"It was great!" Her smile and enthusiasm returned. She couldn't help it; she was still feeling high from her run and the fresh cold air.

"Boston is incredible. Sidewalks and cross walks everywhere. I passed Faneuil Hall and that golden dome state building."

"The Massachusetts State House," Ethan told her.

"It's so easy to get around. There was hardly any traffic."

"That's because everyone else is still in bed." Robert laughed.

Jessica could barely conceal her grimace and turned away from Brooke. *I can't stand her. She went to public school. And why doesn't she get that chipped tooth fixed? Ever heard of a dentist?* Then she had to close her eyes for a moment because the aspirin hadn't completely kicked in and there was a throbbing pressure tightening along both sides of her head.

"You ran far. Are you hungry? We've got bagels and sandwiches," Ethan offered.

"Later," she answered, offering a brief smile. "I'd better take a shower." She went to the bedroom to clean up, leaving the other three alone again.

"So, if she needs a ride to yoga at eleven that obviously makes getting to church a little difficult. Clearly, we should have taken two cars here," Jessica said as soon as Brooke was out of the room.

"I'm going with her and we'll take a cab," Ethan answered Jessica curtly. "It's not a big deal. We'll meet you somewhere for lunch if you want and then head back." He looked at Robert, then got up from his chair and followed Brooke into the bedroom.

Robert noticed Jessica move two pills from her hand into her mouth.

"What were those? I thought you only took those pills to help you study?"

"I'm starting a diet today," she announced. "It's a good day to start because I'm too sick to eat much." She took a sip of latte and broke off a piece of sesame bagel. Her insides convulsed uncomfortably after she swallowed. "I don't even know why he likes her."

"I can think of a few reasons," Robert said under his breath so that he wouldn't be heard.

"I think I'll feel better once I have some solid food in my stomach." Jessica cringed as she took another bite. "Her dad's like a teacher or something," she continued scornfully.

"I think he's a professor," Robert answered, pushing the tub of scallion cream cheese toward Jessica's plate. Probably not the most helpful thing for her diet, but she was already reaching to put it on her bagel.

"Do you see her fingernails? I don't think she's ever heard of a manicure, or a nail file. Her hands were so dry they were almost cracking."

Robert listened and his growing distaste for her words would have been evident if Jessica had been looking at him instead of at the cream cheese.

"I guess she doesn't even go to church," Jessica continued airing her thoughts out loud.

"Yes, and neither do I." Robert gazed at her incredulously with an eyebrow raised, but she didn't notice. She was now focused on spreading the cream cheese.

"Whatever," she answered. "I'll just have to skip church then. Where should we go to lunch?"

***

After Brooke showered, she ate her perfect post-workout meal—two pieces of whole grain toast with peanut butter and a banana. She had brought all of these things from the dining room at school in a Tupperware container in her bag, just in case. Now she was on her way to yoga, with Ethan, and she was incredibly excited.

"I'm glad we called the gym. I'll get on one of their treadmills while you do the class," Ethan said.

"Good," Brooke said as she studied his face. "You haven't worked out in a while have you?"

"I wouldn't be going at all if it weren't for you. I don't know if I should be thanking you or blaming you." Ethan laughed.

"Thanking me of course."

Their cab dropped them off in front of the studio. It didn't look like much from the street. Ethan insisted on paying both their guest fees, no matter how much Brooke protested. She was so appreciative to be there that she would have happily paid for the both of them. The studio wasn't much inside either. It was basically an empty room with a wood floor. The yoga room was adjacent to a corridor lined with cardio equipment. Brooke told Ethan she would see him after and then went to find the ideal spot to put her mat, which was always in the front row just right of the immediate center.

Carlos started the class in silence focusing on their breath. At some point, he started the music, but Brooke was so enthralled by then that she didn't notice. Only later did she become aware that an eclectic arrangement of inspirational spiritual chanting and contemporary rap music was playing. Brooke loved it and tried to remember some of the songs so she could purchase them to use for her own classes.

The class moved with a clever artistry, yet was completely unpredictable. They flowed from one asana to the next, through moves requiring strength and balance in a rhythm with their breath, almost as if they were dancing. The energy in the room was fantastic. Eventually Carlos began to cue deep stretches on the ground, a sign that the class was winding down. For most of the class, Brooke had completely focused on her own experience, but during the stretches she started to take notice of the people immediately around her. The man to her right had the muscles of a gymnast. He had been shirtless since the beginning of class, letting his sweat drip freely onto his mat. She observed how his arm muscles rippled under his shining skin, all three heads of his triceps clearly visible as corded bundles.

If only I could have a cadaver like him when I'm in medical school.

The class ended with the lights off for a full five minutes of Savasana or Corpse Pose as it was called. A piano piece played lightly in the background. A refreshing scent consisting of tea tree oil and mint wafted through the air, barely perceptible. This final resting pose was normally the most challenging pose for Brooke because it required complete relaxation of the body and mind. Her thoughts were generally racing on to whatever she needed to do next and her body was always anxious to get up and move on. Everyone thought Brooke was perpetually calm, being the yoga instructor and all, and because she did look that way on the outside, but they couldn't see what she felt. Sometimes it was like a flip switched inside her and she was filled with a relentless energy and fury. It was really hard to reverse, and it was awful to experience. Alleviation came only with the passage of time or long, intense, grueling workouts. But today, Brooke felt completely fulfilled. She let the weight of her body sink into the ground. Her mind was at peace. She didn't want to move a finger. She wished she could feel like that all the time.

After the class while Brooke was rolling up her mat, Carlos came up to her and introduced himself.

"You are new to my class?"

"Yes, I'm just visiting from New Hampshire. I read about your class in a magazine actually. That's how I knew about it."

He put his hand on her bare shoulder. "You have a very beautiful practice. I enjoyed watching you."

"I loved your class! It was so athletic. It was wonderful!"

"How long have you been studying yoga?"

"Just a few years. But I teach also. I did ballet and gymnastics when I was younger, a lot of it transfers to the mat."

"Yes," Carlos responded. Someone else was waiting to speak with him so he turned from her with a parting nod.

Ethan came up beside her. "I could see the class from the treadmills. That was really impressive. It was really different from the yoga I've done for lacrosse. You were amazing."

"It was a great class. Thank you so much for bringing me!" Brooke gave Ethan a giant hug, and they beamed at each other.

"I'm glad you're in such a good mood and that I'm mainly responsible for it, by getting you here," he said. "It's been a good weekend."

"Yes it has," Brooke agreed.

"Robert called. Jessica isn't feeling well, and…"

"I can't imagine why," Brooke said facetiously, interrupting him.

Ethan laughed. "She's sleeping. So you and I will grab lunch on our way to the condo and then we'll go back to school."

"Okay. Great." Brooke smiled at him again, a huge smile, and nodded. She was happy to be having lunch alone with Ethan. She was also starving and didn't think she could have waited to go all the way back to the condo and then out to lunch. It was turning into a perfect day.

After a relaxing lunch at a sandwich shop, and a shower at the condo, their time in Boston had almost come to an end. Brooke walked into the main room rolling her small suitcase behind her, carrying her coat over her arm. She was wearing a cotton button down shirt, one of the dressier shirts she owned. She felt so good from her long run, the incredible yoga class and then a healthy lunch. She was definitely glad she came, but now her relaxed state of mind was wearing off and she was anxious to get back to her dorm to prepare for tomorrow. She planned to use the ride home to write down everything she remembered from the yoga class so that she wouldn't forget, and then she would get back to studying.

"Oh...we're wearing the same shirt," she commented to Jessica. Jessica had changed since breakfast because her dress was constricting her waist. Now both young women were wearing similar white shirts.

"I don't think so," Jessica responded, then hurried away to find Robert, who was still upstairs.

"Seriously? Seriously? Can you believe she said that?" She shook her head at Robert. "I can't wait to tell Brittany. Her shirt is like from the Gap. Mine was custom from my father's tailor. It looks nothing like hers, anyone can see that!"

Jessica continued her tirade while Robert ignored her. He had already made the beds and meticulously spread his father's clothes out evenly in his closet.

"I have to admit that she did have a beautiful cashmere sweater on at the restaurant last night. I don't know where that came from. If only she had the sense to add some decent jewelry, like the bracelet and earrings I wore when we saw Phantom last semester. Remember those? They would have made the difference. She's hopeless!"

Jessica followed Robert back downstairs. She felt like crap, and having Brooke around, positively bursting with her sporty energy, was incredibly irritating.

"What are you doing?" she said to Robert when she realized he was sweeping the floor. He had already paced around the condo picking things up and emptying all of the trash cans. It was making her feel queasy. She certainly didn't recall him rushing around and cleaning the place the last time they were here. They had just walked out the door leaving almost every room in disarray.

"What are you doing, Robert? Why don't we just leave everything for the cleaning lady?" Jessica suggested, sitting down at the table.

"Can you wipe down the sink with some paper towels?" He used his elbow to point toward the kitchen because his hands were full. "And the master bathroom, too."

Seriously? Do you know how awful I feel? My head is killing me. I'm not moving. Jessica thought, as a scowl took permanent residence on her face and she pretended she hadn't heard him.

"I'll get it." Ethan dropped his bag next to Brooke's suitcase and they both grabbed some paper towels to wipe the sinks and counter tops together. Brooke crouched down, sitting on the back of her heels and reaching under the cabinets to wipe crumbs into a pile and scoop them up with her wet towel. Robert bent down beside Brooke and wiped the floor under the cabinets on the other side.

"Thank you," he said, just inches away from her. "I think we're good to go."

They finished by dropping their used paper towels into the trash bag Robert was carrying.

"Thanks guys." He nodded in gratitude to Ethan and Brooke. "Okay, Jess, ready to go?"

They left with a large trash bag containing all evidence of their time at the condo. Robert put it in the trunk with their luggage and shopping bags and he drove them back to New Hampshire. He had virtually erased every trace of their stay.

***

They were thirty minutes away from Boston when Jessica's shriek pierced through the car.

"Oh my God! Oh my God!"

"What is it? Did you forget something?" Robert asked.

"No! This is terrible! I just got a text from my mother. It's Bradley. He's in the hospital."

"What happened? Did he get alcohol poisoning?" Robert asked. "Or did he crash his Mercedes? I told him not to drive."

"No. It's worse. Someone literally bashed his head in with a rowing trophy at the party last night, or after the party. They're not sure. Oh my God. They don't know what happened to him. They don't know how or why this happened."

"He was fine when I saw him last," Robert said.

"Me too. That's unreal," said Ethan.

"What else did they say?" Brooke asked, for the first time expressing an interest in something Jessica had to say.

"He's in a coma. And he may never come out of it. He might be in a coma forever." Her voice shook as she repeated the information she had been given.

"What else?" Brooke asked again.

"There's nothing else. They don't know anything else." Jessica sounded horrified.

"They must have told you something more?" Brooke prompted.

"No," Jessica said harshly, tears streaming down her face. "I don't know. I don't want to know." She clenched her jaw and began texting furiously, not wanting to discuss the terrible incident that had befallen her cousin, and particularly not with Brooke. It was none of Brooke's business.

CHAPTER ƐLEVEN

Riding a particularly strong wave of academic frustration and apathy, Jessica attempted to construct a paper for her psych class. She had done the research; she just needed to assemble the pieces together in a way that didn't amount to crap. Her professors had told her several times that it wasn't enough to just regurgitate the facts when writing a college paper. She heard them, and she got it, she just wasn't sure what she was supposed to do instead. It should have been an easy assignment, but the news about her cousin had devastated her. She was emotionally drained, not to mention tired and hung over from the weekend.

She struggled to get started, hoping an opening sentence would magically write itself and guide her thoughts. The topic for the assignment was the psychological disorder of each student's choice. Jessica had chosen psychopathy. She used the word "psycho" liberally when speaking about anyone she thought was strange, so she figured it would be a good opportunity to truly understand the term. The research was mildly interesting. Psychopaths exhibited anti-social behavior, diminished ability to feel remorse or empathy. They were incapable of forming significant and deep emotional attachments. Jessica had figured that much from watching films. But who knew that a psychopath generally had above average intelligence and considerable charm? And that psychopaths were often highly motivated toward goals of achievement and success? That last characteristic could set them up to be quite successful, provided they didn't get eventually get caught doing whatever it was that psychopaths do. And if they did, according to her research, they were confident that anything they had done was completely justified and their victim deserved whatever they got. The combination of viewing their victims as objects and having no remorse or guilt allowed them to pretty much do whatever they wanted, robbery, assault, fraud, even murder. And they could feel good about all of it. In some respects Jessica felt a psychopath had some of the qualities necessary to be a ruthless tycoon on Wall St. But she couldn't write that because it was silly and she certainly wasn't referring to her father and didn't want to even remotely suggest that she was. Whoever violently assaulted Bradley and left him for dead in his fraternity house was certainly a full-blown psychopath, that was for sure. It made her ill to think about it, although too much caffeine on an empty stomach sometimes made her feel that way, too.

She continued to stare at the information running down and across her laptop.

How? How? How to string the facts together so it makes an essay with a point? What is my point?

It was almost 11:30 at night and what little steam she had was evaporating exponentially. If she had another Red Bull she might be alert for longer than required, so instead she settled for a regular cup of Hazelnut roast coffee. She had taken another ephedrine an hour earlier. Her stash was almost gone. She needed to ask Brittany for more immediately in case it took a few days for it to arrive. Brittany had to get it from her mother, who got it from her father, who was some kind of physician. Perhaps Brittany would like Jessica's gray fur stole in exchange. It would be a nice gesture. She hadn't given it to charity after all. It was too expensive, but Brittany might appreciate it. She paused to send Brittany a text about the ephedrine, which they referred to as "tic-tacs." She put milk and sugar in her coffee, took her first few sips, and then tried to refocus.

The problem with these assignments is that they don't pertain to my life, so why should I be expected to care? I'm not the type of person who would ever associate with a psychopath.

110

She gazed with admiration at her beautiful new red leather shoes, lying where they had been tossed in the center of her floor.

I wouldn't have minded writing about shoes, new lines of fall shoes. I could have done that without doing any research. It would have been relevant and informative and interesting. Something people would want to read. But unfortunately shoes don't have anything to do with psychological disorders. Ohh!

A light bulb went off in her head as a result of her brief brainstorming session.

I could have written about shopping for shoes, compulsive shopping for shoes! Compulsive shopping is a psychological disorder. But I've already done this research! Damn! Okay, how can I start this paper? What do I have to say about psychopathy? I'm tired.

What did it matter to her if psychopaths had a hyperactive dopamine reward system driving their behaviors? What did that even mean? She thought dopamine was the substance produced in the brain when people exercised. And exercise made her think of Brooke. She couldn't stand thinking about Brooke. She couldn't stand that girl.

Oh My God! Whatever! I just have to write the paper. I'm going to pick an opening sentence and go with it. It doesn't have to be perfect.

She sighed, resigning to her fate of turning in another paper that would be less than stellar. She began her essay with the following:

Understanding the characteristics of someone suffering from psychopathy is important so that you will know one when you see one. Otherwise you might be sorry.

Good enough.

CHAPTER TWELVE

When Robert heard his new ring tone and saw it was his mother calling, he still hadn't decided how to get to the bottom of the condom issue, or if he should just forget about it. One of his plans had been to ask his mother if any of her friends had used the condo recently, particularly the master bedroom. Then, if she said yes, he would know that someone else was responsible for leaving it there. Although, who would stay at someone else's condo and leave their birth control behind? That was rude. And if she said no, then he would know for sure that it was his father's. He didn't want his father to know he had found it. It would be awkward enough to know his father was an adulterer; he didn't need the added stress of his father knowing that he knew. That's why he had cleaned the entire condo before leaving Boston, so the housekeeper wouldn't report that someone had been there. If only he and Jessica had slept in the other guest room.

By the time he said hello, he had vowed to forget about the whole issue.

"Robert. It's your mother. How are you?"

"Hi. Good. When did you get home?"

"Last night. I'm exhausted. I couldn't sleep on the flight. That's the last time we fly commercial on such a long flight, even though I'm the one that insisted this time. What have you been up to? Did you come home at all while we were away?"

"Not home, but I stayed in the Back Bay condo with friends for a weekend. We went to a party at Harvard. It seemed easier to stay

113

there." He wasn't in the mood to mention Bradley and how he had somehow ended up in the ICU with a massive skull fracture.

"Oh. I haven't been to that condo since I finished decorating it. How is it holding up?"

"Fine. It looks great. Everyone loved the way it was decorated." Jessica had not, but it didn't matter, he was just talking in order to avoid what was really on his mind. Robert felt torn. He didn't want to keep anything from his mother, but what would be accomplished by telling her about the condom and his father's probable affair, which he hoped was a singular incident. The only possible outcomes all resulted in his mother being hurt.

"I'm asking because your cousin Kevin was staying there for a few weeks. He's trying to figure out his next steps, according to Sofia. He's made one terrible decision after another. Sofia worries herself sick over him, but she's his main enabler and unfortunately for Kevin, she's spoiled him since he was a child. He's never had to work hard and he's never stopped partying long enough to develop any serious interests."

"I didn't know Kevin had been staying there."

"Yes, and he wasn't alone. I got to know the woman who lives next door when I was doing the remodel. Lovely couple, no children. She called me just to be sure I knew that there was someone staying there. She told me that he had different women coming in and out every night. So I asked Claudia, the woman who does the cleaning. She's a dear and she would never tell me this if I didn't pry it out of her, but the poor woman had to pick used condoms and empty beer cans off the floor. I gave her something extra because I felt so sorry for her. She didn't sign on for that. But we don't need to be talking about Kevin when I haven't spoken with you in weeks. So who did you come up with? Did you say?"

Robert felt like a child again. His ideal world could remain intact. He had been wrong. He had jumped to conclusions about his father after Jessica found that condom in the nightstand. He should have known there was a more reasonable explanation. He was never so relieved to find out he had been incorrect. That would teach him to worry about something before he had the facts.

"I went up with Jessica and Ethan and Brooke."

"Is Brooke Ethan's girlfriend?"

"I guess."

"Well that's wonderful. I know you said that all the girls chase Ethan. She must be something special."

"She is. She's different too. She's super-smart, probably one of the best and brightest of the best and brightest. She spent every extra second studying when we were there. I don't know that she's all that into him though. It's interesting. You would like her. She's very independent. Oh, and she teaches yoga and a bunch of other exercise classes. She went to a yoga class when she was there. She was really excited about this class. There was a special instructor, Carlos something, I think. I wondered if it was one of the classes you took when you there."

"I'm still doing yoga almost every day, but I haven't been to a studio in ages. I have two different people that come to the house. It gives me more time to work on my other projects."

"Well apparently Brooke is really good, even though she's young. She teaches around ten classes a week and tons of people go."

"Brooke does sound interesting. I'd love to meet her." Yvette had never heard her son speak about a girl with so much open admiration. Did he even realize how he felt? It made her a little bit wary, since this girl was supposed to be Ethan's girlfriend, and Robert was with Jessica. But Yvette did not consider Jessica to be the type of girl she wanted her son to end up with. Jessica was too superficial, too high-maintenance. Each time Yvette spoke with her son, she was hopeful he would tell her that Jessica was no longer in the picture.

Robert wasn't sure if Brooke and Ethan had slept together and he was sort of clinging to a hope that they had not. In his mind he had relived the semi-awkward moment he and Brooke had shared in the hallway before leaving the fraternity party. It felt special to him, and he believed it had somehow been special for her because of how she had looked into his eyes as if wondering what he was thinking.

She had also appeared uncharacteristically nervous. That had to mean something.

"I don't know how long she's going to be with Ethan. Like I said, she doesn't seem to be too interested," Robert said, as much to himself as to his mother.

But you definitely are. That was clear to Robert's mother.

"And how is Jessica?"

"Good."

The contrast in his response was telling.

"Glad to hear it." She felt happy for her son and nervous for him all at once. Having a serious crush could open up the doors for heartbreak.

CHAPTER THIRTEEN

Everett had a century-old bell in the center of campus that rang on special occasions. One day out of each semester it would ring six times at six A.M. in accordance with a tradition established in 1885. It was the signal that Mountain Day had arrived. All classes and sports practices were cancelled. Members of the crew team were the only students who got a heads up from their coach the night before. They normally rose for practice before the sun and would have been half way through drills by the time the bell rang. They were sworn to silence, and held accountable by the honor code, so that they, too, could enjoy the luxury of sleeping in that day. Students properly following tradition packed a picnic lunch and hiked up one of the surrounding mountains.

The ceremonious bell ringing went unnoticed by Brooke, even though she was dressed and doing a quick review of her chemistry notes to pass time until the dining hall opened and breakfast was served. When her phone buzzed, she was curious as to who was sending a text before breakfast. It was the official message from Everett declaring it was Mountain Day. Brooke recalled hearing or reading about this surprise day off, though she had since forgotten about it.

"Great," she lamented. "What exactly does that mean for my day?"

Brooke was disappointed that her entire schedule would be messed up. She wondered if all scheduled tests and quizzes would be pushed back. She heard hoots and hollers from the hall as her

117

dorm mates received the same text and celebrated what they considered great news.

Breakfast in the dining hall was unusually quiet. Most of the students had decided to go back to sleep and "seize the day" a little closer to lunch time. Brook was alone as she took a tray and started down the buffet line.

She selected three whole-wheat blueberry pancakes. She bypassed the syrup, topping the pancakes with a scoop of trail-mix and two ladles of fat free Greek yogurt. At the end of the buffet line she filled the rest of the space on her tray with a banana, an orange and an apple. She would put the fruit in her backpack and take it up to her room later. She did this at every meal. Her room was stockpiled with any and all portable foods that were served in the dining hall. She was perpetually hungry, thanks to a high metabolism and several hours of exercise every day, she couldn't afford to buy snacks, and she needed extra food for all the days when she had to miss lunch to teach her noon time sculpt class.

Dozens of round mahogany tables filled the South Vernon dining room; most of them were empty. Brooke sat down, deposited the fruit into her backpack and removed her chemistry book again. She always read or studied while she ate. Five minutes of studying here, ten minutes there, that's what made the difference. Chemistry was proving to be her most difficult course, even though she was allocating more study time to that class than any other. It was ridiculous. The lectures were only remotely related to the quizzes and tests. She felt like she was self-teaching the material. Everyone in the class was struggling. That generally meant it was the teacher, not the students, but there wasn't much they could do about it. By the time Brooke finished her food there were more women starting to sit down around her. She said hello to a few people she recognized and then left the dining area.

Sarah had just positioned herself behind the front desk for her shift when Brooke walked past from the dining hall. Mountain Day did not apply to the people working the front desk either. Brooke crossed the large foyer to talk to her. As she approached she could hear Kate Newman-Shultz's shrieking voice from behind her apartment door yelling "Eli!" then a giant bang. Then nothing. Brooke looked at Sarah, who rolled her eyes before they both resigned to laughing.

"They're starting early today," Sarah commented shaking her head from side to side. "What are your plans for Mountain Day?"

"I'm not sure," Brooke answered honestly. Less than an hour ago every minute of her day had been planned. Now she was disconcerted to have a wide open day with no structure. Her entire schedule had been dumped overboard and she felt lost.

Sarah pointed and flexed her foot, then massaged her calf muscles while she and Brooke talked. Sarah had been playing sports since she was five years old, focusing solely on soccer once she started middle school. She was lucky that her body had, so far, avoided any major injuries. Her legs, powerful and strong, were perpetually sore and on the verge of cramping, regardless of how many bananas or potassium pills she consumed. Her calf and hamstring muscles were particularly tight. Sarah and her teammates never spent as much time stretching after practices and games as they should—a couple of minutes at best. It was no wonder she was tight.

"I'm going to tell you again," Brooke said, teasing yet sincere, as she watched Sarah make a fist and massage it into her lower leg. "You need to come to one of my classes. If you come, I'll do an extra stretching session just for you. Or you should do a Yin yoga class. It's where you hold stretches for two to five minutes, getting deep into the muscles. When it's over, you'll feel like you have a new pair of legs."

"I know. It sounds great. I would love to. I just need to find the time. I promise I will get there before the semester ends," she assured Brooke sincerely.

"And the club doesn't charge for the first class, so no excuses."

Suddenly the Newman-Shultz's apartment door burst open and Kate came rushing out with her coat in hand as if there was a fire inside. Sarah and Brooke turned instinctively toward the noise. When she saw them looking at her, Kate immediately changed her entire demeanor and composed herself. There was a few seconds of awkward silence as Kate walked coolly past the front desk, head held high, and out the front door of the dorm.

Brooke's phone chimed as it received a text from Ethan.

"Be ready at noon. Picnic. Bring appetite."

"Who is going?" Brooke typed. She needed to know if Jessica was part of the plan before she agreed.

"You and me. Can't wait," Ethan replied.

"It looks like I have plans," Brooke told Sarah and then read the texts aloud to her. "Would you like to come with us?"

"First of all, no thank you, because I have plans for later. Part of which involves taking a nap first." Sarah laughed. "And even if I didn't, did you not get the part about 'you and me'? I don't think it means you and me and also one of your friends. He seems to really like you. And it's like too good to be true that someone as hot as Ethan can be so sweet."

Brooke had to think about Sarah's comment. "Is he hot? Really? You think?"

"Of course he is. Are you kidding? How come you sound surprised? He looks like a God."

"Hmm. Well, he definitely is sweet. He's very considerate. I'm going to go for a long run. I wish you could go with me, but it's probably good for you to have a day of rest. I'll see you later."

She was pleased that there would be time enough for a long run, core exercises, and a few solid hours of school work before twelve. In her mind she compartmentalized activities into the next five hours. She felt better about the unexpected turn of events now that she had a new schedule developed. The only kink in her agenda was that she didn't know what Ethan had planned or how long it would take.

During her run she thought about her relationship with Ethan. He frequently and consistently asked her to go places and do things with him. Unlike other guys, he didn't seem discouraged that she didn't reciprocate. And he had never pressured her to do anything that she didn't want to do. Apparently he really cared for her. She thought he was a great guy and she almost wished she could feel the same way about him, or anyone for that matter. It might be nice, as long as it didn't get in the way of her goals. When they were at the Harvard fraternity party, she had tried to pretend like she was really into him, just to see what happened. She was actually having fun, probably because of all the dancing, and who knows what might have happened later, if not for Bradley Carroll. Her mood had completely changed when Bradley managed to corner her at the end of the hallway. The way Bradley had assumed she would want to be with him and the way he had tried to touch her had made her really angry. As if she would be impressed with his pretentious car. He was as awful as Jessica.

But maybe if she gave it another try with Ethan, and acted as if she truly cared, she might start to feel that way for real.

Ethan was sitting on the stone steps outside Brooke's dorm waiting for her when she came outside. She took a few seconds to study him before he noticed her. He was wearing jeans with a collegiate looking sweater and a forest green cap with a large capital E on the front. His shoulders were hunched forward, his long legs stretched before him.

"Hi, Ethan."

He stood up when he saw her and gave her a hug, which she returned.

"Hi. How are you?"

"I'm fine." She smiled at up at him. "I heard you were hot."

"No, it's actually very cool. It's good you brought a jacket."

"Never mind." She laughed. "What do you have planned?"

"Since this is your first Mountain Day we're going to follow tradition. First stop is the New Farms Deli for our picnic food." He picked a stray blonde hair off her shoulder and let it float away with the wind.

Brooke immediately felt conflicted about buying food at the gourmet deli in town when the dining halls were open for lunch, a lunch she had already paid for, with substantial student loans, through the meal plan.

"We can eat here first," she suggested. She had already planned the salad she was going to make at the salad bar.

"No, this has to be special. Let's go." Ethan put his arm around Brooke and started leading her toward the student parking lot. He unlocked his car when they were a few yards away. Brooke was happy to get in and shut the door. It was a beautiful fall day, but the intermittent gusts of wind made her wish she had worn another layer of clothing. She hadn't minded or even felt the chill earlier when she was running outside.

Ethan had to move the driver's seat back a ways in order to accommodate his height because Brooke was the last person who had driven his car. When they arrived in town, they discovered how many other people had the same idea. They had to circle the parking lot several times before waiting for a car to pull out so that they could take its place.

"It's so crowded we could have walked here by now," Brooke said.

"Yes, but after we pick up the food we have to drive to our picnic location a few miles away. I know you wouldn't think anything about walking that distance, but I'm not going to." He laughed.

"Okay. I can't wait to find out where we're going," she said, but she was thinking, *I don't like this type of surprise. It better not be too far away. I can't be gone all afternoon. I have work to do. I should have said I couldn't come.*

"It's not too far. You'll see soon enough. It's not a big deal though," he added. "I don't want you to expect something great and then be disappointed."

Ethan opened the door for Brooke to enter the New Farms Deli. She had only been there twice before, both times with Ethan. She enjoyed browsing inside. The store was decorated to look like the inside of a barn, with weathered, paneled walls and numerous shades of red and black. Large open barrels lined the walls, filled with shiny bags of unusually flavored chips. Toward the back, tables were made from salvaged wood and cut to resemble barn doors. The aisles were crowded with Everett students who were intent on purchasing picnic fare in their tell-tale forest green attire.

Ethan grabbed a basket and started to cruise the store. The line for making custom sandwiches was long so he asked Brooke if she could try to find something from the pre-made area. He selected a large sandwich after only a quick scan of the refrigerated shelves, and then left Brooke to make her choice. She was completely overwhelmed by the number of gourmet choices. She quickly examined the ingredient list on each sandwich before turning them over to see the price tag.

Ethan was back at her side, his shopping basket full. Brooke had finally narrowed her selection down to two sandwiches, one she really wanted and one she didn't want as much that cost less. She had never been out with Ethan when he didn't insist on paying for her, but still she didn't want to assume that would always be the case. She couldn't help but wonder what would happen to all of the food waiting at the dorm if everyone bought their lunch and had a picnic. What a terrible waste.

"Is there anything you like?" Ethan asked her.

"Just one minute," Brooke said, without looking at him. She was starting to get stressed. The psychiatrist she had seen a few years ago had labeled her "impulsive" and said she took "excessive risks." How was that possible, she thought, when it was absurdly difficult for her to make little decisions like this? With a deep breath and a forced exhale, she picked up the less expensive sandwich and headed toward the checkout counter where Ethan was waiting, credit card in hand. He took her sandwich and quickly paid for everything. Once they were in the car, he transferred all of the new purchases into his picnic basket, the one his mother had brought him.

They left the Ash Street shops behind them and drove back through the main gates of campus. There were as many students as ever outside, but instead of walking purposefully toward classrooms, they were collected in groups, talking, throwing footballs, and sitting on the lawn. Brooke wondered why they didn't have more important things to do. A day off was meant for getting ahead, not for wasting time. Again she hoped that the picnic would be quick.

As they meandered along through campus, Brooke admired the Everett buildings that had become familiar to her over the past few months; the dormitories with their lushly landscaped quadrangle areas and the academic buildings, one for each field of study. The Jeep slowly drove past the pond, then the athletic complex, and headed to the more remote areas of the campus, which housed the physical plant facilities and garages. Ethan made a turn onto a smaller road that curved behind a maintenance building. He traveled around another bend, which brought a narrow gravel road into view. They traveled slowly over the bumpy ground as it led slightly uphill and culminated at an opening in a giant sloping stone wall. The large round stones, massive in height and width, dramatically marked the rear property line of Everett College.

"We are officially off campus," Ethan stated as he made a left turn onto a single lane unpaved road.

It was as if they had traveled back one hundred years in time, maybe more. Endless empty fields stretched out to meet the horizon.

"I've never been back here before," Brooke said.

"Most people haven't. It's like a well-kept secret. Except there's nothing out here, so really there is no secret to keep."

"It's different," she mused, wondering where the road would take them.

"It's called Stonewall Road. I thought it would be a nice place to picnic. I wanted to take you somewhere you've never been before."

"When have you been out here before?" Brooke asked. *I hope we're not going too far away. I can't spend all afternoon out here. I have to study. There's no telling what we're expected to know for chemistry, thanks to Ms. MacIntyre.*

"Once, last year during Parents Weekend. My mother wanted to see the countryside so we followed the navigation system map through the campus to where the GPS showed nothing. Nothing map worthy."

Brooke glanced down at the navigation screen. The map was covered with many symbols representing aspects of Everett College, but blank just beyond it.

A low stone wall, positioned parallel to the road, meandered across the dips and slopes of the land and continued farther than her eyes could see. Enormous trees were visible in the distance blazing with the colors of fall foliage. The mountain peaks stuck out behind them, miles and miles away. A little further along a second stone wall started up alongside the road on the opposite side as the first. Brooke studied the undulating line of stacked gray stones, decomposing in some places. Up ahead a grouping of long abandoned dead apple trees sat just inside the wall. Ethan maintained a slow speed because there were plenty of deep holes along the route. He was relaxed, his left arm draped over the top of the steering wheel so that his body was slightly angled toward Brooke.

"I see how it got its name," Brooke commented.

"These walls were built in the 1820s. The farmers that settled here had to move them in order to work the soil. They used oxen and draft horses and probably moved a lot of them by hand. I bet that's what their children did in their free time, when they weren't washing their one other pair of pants in the stream."

Brooke liked that Ethan was a bit like her and had interesting facts to share.

And apparently other people think he's hot.

She watched him as he drove, trying to see him as if for the first time.

"That would get old pretty quickly," Brooke said.

Dragging her dirty clothes down to the washers and dryers in the basement every week was one of the only things Brooke hated about college. It was an inefficient process that took up a huge chunk of her time and caused her to worry that someone would take her clothes while they were unattended. She put it off as long as possible, essentially until she was down to her last clean sports bra.

"They moved the stones to the edges of their land to mark the boundaries. Now the walls are considered historical landmarks. There's a fine for getting caught stealing the stones."

"Why someone would steal a stone?" Brooke mused.

"Landscaping projects mostly."

"And probably for fraternity pranks when Everett had fraternities, like seeing how many stones a pledge could carry before they collapsed," Brooke suggested, causing Ethan to laugh.

"Doesn't it seem like these fields should be dotted with cows? Like the cows are missing?" she asked.

"Most of the farmers left by the 1880s, just before Everett was being built. They sold their land to the state."

"Wow, they missed out, I think. Surely they would have benefitted somehow by being here while Everett was being built. At the least they could have sold some of their stones. In fact," she said as she pointed out the window at the crumbling stone wall still running parallel to their route, "see that wall over there with all the missing stones? I think there are some exact matches to those around the front side of my dorm. I think the South Vernon builders would be up to their necks in fines if they were alive today," she joked. "How do you know all of this, about the history and the stones, I mean?"

"A history book about the area. I think I read it here at school. I know so much about everything I can't keep track of where I learned it. And my brain could explode."

It was the first time Ethan had ever heard Brooke joking. Joking and laughing…that was a good sign that she was comfortable.

I wonder how long we'll be out here. After this, I'll go to the library until dinner. I'll start with the new chemistry chapter first.

Then Brooke remembered her earlier intention to pretend to feel what she imagined other girls felt about their "boyfriends." She reached over for Ethan's hand and brought it back to hold against her thigh. He smiled at her, and she smiled back.

They traveled for another mile and then made a left turn onto a tree-lined road. An old iron bridge loomed ahead. It was impossible to tell if it was originally red or black or brown. Steel-framing arched from one side to the other. Brooke peered out her window to see the dark water flowing underneath. As they crossed the bridge she let go of Ethan's hand so that she could instead put her own hand on Ethan's leg. Intrigued when she sensed his surprise, she circled her fingers lightly across his thigh, thinking it was something she should do to act like she cared.

"I'm looking for a spot to have lunch," Ethan said.

Now that they were trying to find a place for their picnic, the landscape was not as smooth and empty as it had looked from afar. The ground was a hodge-podge of tough grass, weeds, thicket, wild flowers, and shrubs. After another mile, Ethan finally pulled the car over to the side of the road.

"I don't think we're going to find a better clearing," he admitted, frustrated that the perfect spot was nowhere to be seen. "This might have to do."

All of the land was uneven, since it was farmed before the days of backhoes and levelers, but the chosen area was relatively flat and clear enough that they could sit down. Ethan turned off the car, climbed out and opened the back door.

"Are you hungry?" he asked.

"Yes. Definitely."

Ethan walked a few yards from the car before shaking out a striped green stadium blanket and spreading it across the ground. He went back for the picnic basket, then opened the passenger-side door, where Brooke was still sitting. Immediately a gust of wind swept in.

"It's a lot colder here without buildings to block the wind," she said.

"I'll help you stay warm. Come on." He took her hand and helped her step out of the car, first pulling her against him for a kiss. Brooke curled her body into his chest to evade the wind, but pulled away after a few seconds and sat down on the stadium blanket.

"I have a special treat. Russian caviar. Do you like it?" He held up a small jar for her to see.

"I don't know. I've never had it."

Ethan opened the jar, used a small spoon to transfer the translucent eggs on to a cracker and handed it to Brooke on a napkin. She took a small bite while Ethan had made one for himself and popped the entire cracker into his mouth.

"I'm sorry. I don't really like it. It's the texture."

"Don't worry about it. Someone gave a whole crate to my father. He gets all sorts of random appreciation gifts from patients. He doesn't like it either, so my mother sent some to me."

"He gets presents from patients?"

"Someone from Saudi Arabia gave him a Porsche once after he operated on the guy's son."

"Wow."

Brooke enjoyed her sandwich, matching Ethan bite for bite. They dipped pita chips into hummus until they were gone, then started in on dark chocolates. When they were satisfied, they lay back on the blanket and watched clouds moving rapidly across the blue sky. Brooke snuggled into Ethan's side, her head on his shoulder, their fingers entwined, her mind racing. In the distance a flock of crows lifted out of the trees, and fanned out into the sky, making distinctive *caw!* sounds that quickly died off as they flew. Even under her sweatshirt Brooke's skin was covered with goose bumps and she was starting to shiver. She pressed even closer against Ethan. He had a feeling that her behavior, which might have appeared affectionate, was probably a result of her attempts to keep warm. He was grateful it was cold.

"So why do you want to be a doctor?" Ethan asked.

Brooke could almost feel her body light up inside.

"A surgeon. Like your father. I've known since I was nine years old."

"How?"

Brooke's eyes sparkled as she spoke. "I was in third grade. At my elementary school there was a pretty large section of woods between two fields, with a creek running through it, that doesn't matter actually, about the creek. Anyway, one day during recess a friend and I discovered a dead cat in the woods, next to the creek. It was a gray, short-haired cat just lying on its side as if it was sleeping, but on closer inspection it was obviously dead. We moved it around with a stick. Rigor mortis had set. I remember being amazed that its body maintained the exact same position no matter what we did. We concluded that it had been strangled because its brain was literally coming out of its ear. It looked like a tiny bouquet of light grey cauliflower bulging out of the ear canal. So we called it the cauliflower cat." Brooke spoke enthusiastically as she remembered the intense curiosity the carcass had sparked.

"I'm not sure I want to hear this," Ethan announced with a grimace. Thinking about misplaced brain material made him uncomfortable. He had to look the other way when he had blood drawn at the doctor's office. However, Brooke was more animated telling this story than he had ever seen her. Normally so focused and serious, for once she sounded dreamy and for that reason he wanted her to continue.

"Listen. This is really interesting." Brooke poked him gently in the shoulder. The scene was vividly returning to her as she spoke. "I went to visit that cat every day before school, during recess and as soon as school got out. At first I was just curious because it was dead, maybe it was the first time I'd seen a dead animal, and because part of its insides were visible. But then it started to decompose and change. It was fascinating. It became bloated, its stomach distended, that was the body breaking down from bacteria and its own enzymes. I didn't know any of that at the time though. It was covered with blowflies and flesh flies. They laid their eggs all over it. Its fur disappeared, its skin thinned, fluids came out of all the orifices. Eventually you could see the putrefied internal organs, and the skeletal structure. The whole body was swarming with larvae. I remember it smelled terrible, the decomp gases. I just pulled my sweater up over my nose while I studied it and poked it every day…"

"Enough!" Ethan laughed, but he was dead serious that he didn't need to hear anymore. "This is a disgusting story."

Brooke continued with a far off look in her eyes and her voice much louder than usual. "One day, after a few weeks had passed, I went to visit the cauliflower cat at recess. I remember I was excited that day because I had found a face mask that my father used for sanding. I was going to wear it to block out the smell, even though I was pretty used to it and the smell was diminished by then. When I got there with my little mask, the cat was gone. Someone from the school finally disposed of it. I was devastated. Hard to believe it was out there for so long, now that I think of it."

Brooke hadn't thought about that cat in maybe ten years, and she had never before said it was the catalyst for her fascination with death and disease, but it seemed apparent to her now. She still remembered it perfectly. Her sole reason for jumping out of bed for those two weeks had been to monitor the cat's decomposing carcass. She had thought about it continuously at the time, imagining how it had died and why. It had fascinated her.

"That's an awful story. I assure you I wouldn't have asked if I thought that was the explanation you were going to share," Ethan commented, half-serious.

"What about your brother? Michael, right?"

"You want to know about my brother?"

"What kind of physician does he want to be?"

"Probably a surgeon, like my father."

"How did he know?" she asked with interest.

"Got me. Actually, now that you mention it, I can think of one thing. When I was younger, years ago, I accidentally slid the top of my feet across the dock at the Yacht Club, don't ask me how, but I remember top of my feet were filled with splinters. And it hurt like hell!"

Brooke listened patiently. "And?"

"And Michael used tweezers to slide out each piece of wood. It took at least an hour, and it felt like forever. Anyway, my Dad was so impressed because Michael had the patience and his hands were so steady. He said Michael would make a great surgeon." Ethan didn't mention how he had been overcome with tears because of the splinters and how his clumsy misfortune had allowed Michael yet another opportunity to earn his father's praise. That was one of those times when Ethan needed to remind himself that Michael had never been All-American, or All-State for that matter, at anything. Most likely why Ethan had stuck with lacrosse as long as he had.

Ethan studied Brooke's small hands. He was thrilled that one had finally made its way over to his thigh earlier, and wondered if they were adept for surgery. It bothered him that after weeks of what he assumed was "dating" he still didn't know firsthand if her hands were skilled in any other way either. He was becoming a prime candidate for a celibacy award. Yet for Brooke, he was willing to wait an eternity, or at least a few more months.

"How about you? What do you want to do, Ethan? Who, apparently, is hot."

Ethan raised an eyebrow, not certain he had heard her correctly or understood what she was saying.

"I'd like to work for a few years and then go to business school, or law school. Not sure exactly what I want to do though."

"Well what do you love doing? Don't you have a passion?"

"I really don't know. It remains to be determined. I don't have a story like yours, that's for sure. I would have thought you would want to do something with exercise. Make exercise DVDs maybe; be famous."

"No. I love fitness, there's no question about it, and I always will, but teaching classes is just a good job for right now, it's not my dream. Shhh. Listen," whispered Brooke.

There was nothing to hear. It was almost eerily quiet, except for the whistling of the wind.

"It's so quiet!"

Then a crinkling noise stirred the silence as an empty pita chip bag blew out from under a bottle and off the blanket, first moving in spurts of just a few inches, then much faster. Brooke jumped up and ran after it but it was lifted into the sky and out of reach. She laughed and ran back to the blanket and into Ethan's arms.

"It's too windy!" she yelled, laughing. *See, "fun Brooke" can make an appearance every once in a while,* she thought, pleased with herself for managing a lighthearted attitude.

Back in the car, Ethan placed the basket on the rear seat and threw the blanket in after it. He started the engine and they warmed up instantly, protected from the wind.

"Ready?" Brooke asked.

Ethan started driving, but he didn't want to go back to school yet. He wanted to do something memorable for Brooke, but he couldn't think of anything.

Brooke had placed her hand on the back of his neck and was gently kneading his muscles.

This is where the brain stem is most easily severed, she thought as she felt around the cervical vertebrae, identifying the bones and joints with her fingers.

When they reached the bridge, he decided to pull off to the side of the road.

He grabbed two quarters out of the spot where he placed his spare change in the car.

"Let's walk out there. Come on."

They ran to the center of the bridge and stopped to lean over the rusty iron railing. The large creek moved powerfully around large boulders underneath them.

Ethan put his arm around Brooke's shoulders and they stood silently for a few moments watching the water cascade mesmerizingly around the rocks.

Brooke was trying to savor the moment, trying to convince herself that what they were doing was beneficial because it was relaxing. The only time she felt completely at peace was during a workout or immediately after, although it was short-lived. She was very aware that they were wasting valuable time and she had things to do. She stared down at the water while she tried to patiently wait for their date to end. The water made her think about molecules, which made her think about chemistry, which made her feel angry and tense. The class could potentially ruin her perfect grade point average. It was the teacher's fault. Perhaps it was time to do something about Mrs. MacIntyre.

"Here, make a wish." Ethan handed her a quarter, looking at her expectantly.

Brooke tried hard to suppress her impatience and envision whimsical, fun thoughts, but nothing came to mind except for the obvious: a transcript with straight As, graduating first in the class, top medical school, top surgical fellowship. And she knew that wishful thinking had nothing to do with accomplishing any of those things. Only hard work mattered, which is why she needed to get back to the library and study.

"Close your eyes," Ethan said, his voice soft. He straddled her from behind, his strong arms circling her torso, his chin resting on top of her head.

She closed her eyes and tossed the quarter out into the air.

I wish that nothing will ever get in the way of my goals.

Ethan began to gently kiss her neck and Brooke hesitated before breaking free of his embrace. Thoughts of chemistry ruining her perfect GPA had ruined all chances of returning Ethan's affectionate.

"Okay, we have to go back now," Brooke insisted, heading toward the car.

She knew how to make her wish come true.

CHAPTER FOURTEEN

It was the beginning of December. At that moment, there was no place Brooke would rather be than in the Bisaillon Library with Ethan. She had exercised for a combined total of four hours, waking up extra early in order to get in a really long run followed by an hour of her own yoga practice, then later teaching a sculpt class. She felt relaxed. She was wearing comfortable stretch jeans, her Everett sweatshirt, and her softest, thickest socks. Ethan's coat lay across her like a blanket. They had just eaten dinner together in her dorm, and she didn't have to teach at Resolution Fitness tonight. She sighed with contentment. Her club chair was facing Ethan's, and her legs were extended from her seat to his. He was rubbing her feet with one hand in his lap as he read from an online textbook on his iPad. He had massaged her feet for the first time a few days ago, and Brooke thought she had died and gone to heaven. Incredibly, he seemed able and willing to do it for what seemed like hours while he read.

She was still worried about a big chemistry test she had to take tomorrow, but she had enough time ahead of her to study. She allowed herself to close her eyes for a few minutes. It was raining outside, but not storming, causing a soothing pattern of sounds to echo down from the roof.

"That feels so good," she practically purred. It was so rare to feel this relaxed, to just be still and let her thoughts float away. She wanted to enjoy every second of it.

Ethan didn't raise his eyes from his reading, but his lips formed a smile for her.

Suddenly, she was aware of other voices and her feet being moved aside. She had fallen asleep. When she opened her eyes, Mac Maraska was standing above Ethan. He and Ethan had gone to high school together. He looked shaken up and...was he actually crying? Ethan's face looked serious, confused.

"No way." Ethan shook his head from side to side. "When was this?"

Brooke searched their faces, struggling to figure out what was going on.

"I guess this morning...this morning. I just heard." He glanced at Brooke for the first time, then back to Ethan. "Your phone was off, and I just wanted to come tell you. I guess I needed to tell someone, see someone who knew him." He paused. "I can't believe it."

"Holy shit," Ethan said softly, looking down at the gold bit crossing his leather shoes, temporarily leaning his head into his hands.

"What happened?" Brooke asked quietly, tentatively, and then she waited. Mac looked at her apologetically. Ethan didn't answer right away.

Mac turned back to Ethan. "I'm going back to my room to call a few people, see if we can figure out what was going on. Let me know if you want to talk or something." Both Mac and Ethan were silent for a few seconds, and then Mac continued. "I'm going to go to the funeral. If you want, we can go together, whenever it is." He looked at Brooke again, feeling self-conscious that his eyes probably showed signs of recent tears. "Sorry to ruin your night." Then he turned back to Ethan again. "I'll talk to you later man." He put his hand on Ethan's shoulder as he said this.

"Okay, thanks Mac–for finding me." Mac turned and walked away, shaking his head.

"What happened?" Brooke asked again, gently. She leaned forward so her hands were on Ethan's knees and she was looking up into his face.

"Shit," Ethan said. Then he looked up at Brooke. She was kneeling on the floor, looking up at him earnestly. Even right now he couldn't help but think how incredibly beautiful she was.

"Who died?" Brooke asked more insistently.

"A guy named Dan Hattenski. He was at Bucknell. He was like my best friend when we were little. We were still friends in high school, sort of, just not as much." Ethan needed to collect his thoughts.

"How did he die?" prompted Brooke.

"He blew his head off with a gun, according to Mac."

"Oh no. I'm so sorry." Brooke wasn't sure what else to say. She started to imagine the scene.

Did he put the gun to his forehead or in his mouth? It would make a big difference in terms of impact.

She stood and put her arms around Ethan, who was still sitting. She wondered how long she had been sleeping and hoped she hadn't lost too much time. She checked the giant wall clock and was relieved to find that she had only been asleep for twenty minutes.

At Ethan's request, Ethan and Brooke wordlessly packed up their belongings and left the library together. They headed toward his dorm, Ethan carrying both of their backpacks over his left shoulder, his right arm tightly wrapped around Brooke.

"After what happened to Bradley Carroll, it seems like a lot of bad stuff is happening to people I know," Ethan said.

"Well one thing has nothing to do with the other," Brooke said confidently.

Ethan wasn't sure what to think. He and Dan were best buddies when they were young, their friendship facilitated by the fact that their mothers were very close. He remembered his earliest play dates being with Dan. It took them both years to realize that "Santa" bringing them the same gifts every year was not a coincidence. Their mothers made these decisions before Christmas so that they would have more fun together. If Dan got an Airsoft gun, Ethan would get an Airsoft gun. Then they would spend weeks together wearing their goggles and vests, running and ducking from each other, scattering the Airsoft pellets that so annoyed their mothers all around their yards. When Ethan found new skis under the Christmas tree, so did Dan. Then they had semi-private ski lessons together and ski outings until their mothers grew tired of driving to the ski slopes. As they got older, they progressed from playing with action figures to playing video games, paint ball, and exploring the woods. How many times had he looked up at his mother, employing his sweetest most earnest expression to ask, "Can Dan sleep over?" It was more times than he could ever recall. And at Dan's house he remembered them struggling to keep each other awake until Dan's parents were asleep so that they could sneak back downstairs and silently watch horror movies or anything rated R. Their mothers had made sure they were on the same community basketball team every year. Dan was always a point guard and Ethan was the big man, expected to get the rebounds. The best part of basketball was going out to lunch with Dan after the games.

Then toward middle school, for no particular reason, they started growing apart, even though they attended the same schools. Now Ethan felt guilty that they hadn't been close friends.

"Why would Dan do this?"

Outside the dorm, Ethan removed his arm from Brooke's shoulder, took out his phone and dialed his mother.

"Hi. Mom?"

"Ethan," she said, her voice full of concern. She cried as soon as she spoke his name, indicating that she had already heard. She was still close to Mrs. Hattenski and had been consumed with the tragic news which gave her many reasons to worry as well as grieve.

"Mac just found me in the library and told me about Dan."

"So terrible," she cried. "Unnecessarily terrible. I can drive up to Everett tonight so you won't be alone."

"No, but thanks. It's not necessary. I'm fine. I've got a few things to finish up, and then I'll come home for the funeral with Mac."

"Please, please tell me if there is ever anything bothering you. Nothing should be so important...that poor child. His poor mother..."

"I'm happy here. Nothing is bothering me. Everything is good. I would tell you. You don't have to worry…Do you know why he, um, why he did this?"

"I don't know. I can't imagine. He was your best friend when you were little. Do you remember that?"

"Of course I do."

Ethan finished the conversation with his mother when they reached his room. Brooke placed her backpack on his bed and went to use the restroom. As soon as she got back, he immediately reached for her, forcefully pulling her close as if she was in danger of being yanked away. He wrapped his arms around her upper back and held her tight. He didn't want to let her go. Ever. Brooke held still for what felt like a long time before slowly backing out of his embrace.

"Hey. I've got to go back to my dorm. I'll see you tomorrow?"

Ethan's phone rang; it was his mother again.

"Just one moment," he told Brooke, while he took the phone call.

"I'm okay, Mom. Don't worry…I'll see you in two days…okay, let me know…I love you too…I'm fine…Brooke is here."

Ethan ended the conversation with his mother and put his phone down on his dresser. He hugged Brooke again in a way that was both strong and gentle.

"I really want you to stay. Do you mind?"

"Okay," she said, "but I need to study for chemistry. I have a big test tomorrow."

An hour passed. Everyone who knew Dan felt compelled to reach out to someone else who also knew him.

"They haven't found a note," Ethan informed her. She nodded without looking up.

"He had a girlfriend at Smith," Ethan said a few minutes later. He continued to scan social media for updates and respond to tweets.

"Someone thinks he got caught cheating at school."

"Sounds like no one knows why he did it yet," Brooke said, unable to mask her irritation.

***

Brooke returned to studying and another thirty minutes passed. She had heard Ethan share the little information he had to several different callers from high school, the same story each time. His occasional comments to her had not stopped, even though she had done her best to ignore him. He was becoming louder and more emotional as the night wore on, and he drank from a bottle of Scotch. Was it really necessary that she stay in his room? He seemed to have plenty of other people to talk to.

She tried to keep her head down and block out Ethan, but it was getting harder to focus while bracing for the next interruption. She wondered how long Ethan and his friends would continue to speculate. Didn't they have work to do? It was all too distracting. But whoever had found Dan was incredibly lucky. If only she could have been in that person's shoes when he or she found him. It was the only aspect of the whole incident that she found acutely interesting, yet she still hadn't heard Ethan mention anything about it. In fact, it seemed to be the one particular fact about the suicide that Ethan had yet to discuss with someone. She couldn't understand why. It must have been a fascinating mess. Finally she had to ask.

"Did you hear anything from the person who found his body?" she asked hopefully. She was dying to hear the details of the gruesome scene.

"No."

Then there was a tap on the door.

"Come in," Ethan called.

"Hey. Did you finish the theory paper yet? I have a question." Robert stood in the now open doorway holding an array of papers in his hand. A quick scan of the room told him something was out of the ordinary. He saw Brooke on the floor studying, her legs bent in unusual angles.

"What's going on?"

Ethan filled Robert in on the whole drama, starting from the beginning. Brooke watched Robert sitting motionless on Ethan's bed, patiently listening. He gave Ethan his full attention.

140

This is how it's done, Brooke thought. *Not interrupting, not multi-tasking. I'm glad Ethan has such a good friend. Ethan needs him, and I can't help that I need quiet in order to concentrate, and I suck at being supportive. I have to completely master this entire chemistry section tonight. I can't count on anything Ms. MacIntyre taught us in class.*

Robert turned his head and nodded to her while he continued to listen to Ethan. Brooke smiled at him, a smile that was appropriate enough for the mood in the room.

She knew she didn't have much time left before she would be too tired to focus. She started packing up her stuff. Now that Robert was here to take her place, it was a good time to leave. Yet before her last book was in her backpack, Robert was lifting his hand from Ethan's shoulder and leaving the room, nodding at her again before exiting. Before Robert was out the door, Ethan crossed the room, enveloping her in a hug.

"I know you have a big chemistry test tomorrow. I know you're worried about your chemistry class. Thank you for staying. I really appreciate it." He wrapped his arms around her, holding her shoulder and the back of her head gently against his chest. Brooke noticed the smoky scent of scotch on his breath mixed with a fresh smelling aftershave or maybe it was his deodorant. It wasn't unpleasant. She decided to wait a few more seconds before she raised her head to tell him she had to leave now. Ethan bent down, his lips grazing her ear.

"I love you," he whispered, and hoped beyond hope that she would say it back so that something good would have come out of this sad evening.

"I love you, too," she said, unable to come up with any other appropriate response. She didn't feel like she loved him, but maybe she did and she just didn't know it. Maybe love was nothing more than not minding having someone around most of the time and being able to put up with their inconvenient distractions. But she knew that other people could feel more. She lightly rubbed Ethan's back and let him hold her. Her shoulders dropped with a sigh. She knew it wouldn't kill her to stay over, if it really mattered to Ethan. She definitely deserved an A for supportiveness.

CHAPTER FIFTEEN

Jane MacIntyre was unhappy, aware of deepening wrinkles around her mouth and sagging skin under her triceps. Just recently she discovered that if she sat for too long, her hips started to ache. Her life was more than half over and seemed to have reached its climax. Being surrounded by young coeds didn't help. Some were brilliant, and she did respect their intellect, but she was no longer pleased with the intelligent ideas they posed in the classroom. Unfortunately for her, the principles of chemistry had not changed in the years she had been teaching. The good questions had all been asked, over and over. She could not remember the last time a student had been able to surprise her with any original questions or novel insightful comments.

Jane had always been shy, directing her lectures to the whiteboard or her notes as if they were the audience rather than speaking directly to the students seated before her. But now she had pretty much stopped caring whether the students understood molecular orbital theory or not. She didn't have any desire to interact with them at all. Recently she had left out entire sections from her lectures because she just lacked the motivation to deliver them properly.

Let them try and figure it out on their own if they're supposed to be so brilliant.

At the last minute, she switched the textbook she had been using for all scheduled assignments, just to vary things for her own sake, but she continued administering the same tests that she had used for the past several years. As a result, the students found many of the test questions had little connection to the lectures or the current textbook and required an almost impossible leap of understanding. The changes failed to make Jane's life any more interesting. In fact, it only made for more tedious work on her end.

Outside of the classroom, the students made her feel more like the Grinch than anything else. She was bothered by their noise, noise, noise, their laughing, their ability to easily move on to the next new endeavor while she was stuck doing the same old thing month after month, semester after semester.

She was also bored with her partner, who seemed content to get old in their quaint, as in "outdated," faculty-appointed house and accept that it's all a slow decline from here. Jane needed something more. She could not go on like this; it was becoming unbearable. She felt it was now or never if she wanted to make a change, but she didn't know what changes to make.

At the beginning of the semester, she saw a sign on campus advertising an exercise class for faculty. She thought it would be something different, maybe just what she needed to get out of her rut, to transform her body and improve her bone density. But she knew it was unlikely she would follow through and actually attend the class. A day later she saw the same sign outside the auditorium. Then the day after that, the same sign on the inside of the stall door in the ladies' room.

On the designated start date, with a sudden burst of determination to change her life, she packed a change of clothes in her large purse and marched straight from her Polymer Chemistry class to the gym. She recognized the young woman teaching the class as one of her students, Brooke Walton. She was familiar with her name because she was the girl who had transferred to Everett after finding her academic advisor unexpectedly dead of a heart attack or something like that. Jane had overheard the story but couldn't remember the details exactly. Jane immediately felt she had made a mistake by coming to the class, although she had no idea why. She looked to the door, planning to escape as if she hadn't meant to be there in the first place, but there were people streaming in, looking for places to stand and filling up the doorway. Jane was surprised by the number of her colleagues who were there to participate. Before Jane knew it, Brooke had started welcoming them, saying she was so glad they came. Jane got caught up listening as Brooke explained the concepts behind the class, and then they had begun to move and it really was too late to leave.

To her surprise, she enjoyed it. She really, really enjoyed it. She left the class feeling awake and alive in a manner she wasn't sure she had ever felt before. Brooke segmented the workout into sections for upper body, thighs, gluteals, and abdominals, working each area of the body through a series of precisely controlled movements. Then they lengthened their fatigued muscles with stretches and yoga poses to change their shape. There was a certain comfort to the regimented nature of the work, the focus required to complete the sets, and the detailed physiological explanations that Brooke provided for each exercise. The scientist in Jane could really appreciate Brooke's impressive understanding of anatomy and physiology. After just a few classes, Jane was getting stronger and tighter without that bone-jarring jumping around that she previously attributed to group exercise. Each week she arrived as early as she could so she could take her spot in a back corner of the room. She was partly protected there with one wall to her left and one wall behind her, leaving only two possible places, instead of four, where someone might stand near her. At first, she wished there weren't so many people, although at least there was no one else from her department. Then, over time, as the class size grew, she realized there was more anonymity in the larger group. She recognized the depth of her commitment when she made a trip into town to buy a pair of yoga pants, and then again just one week later to buy a second pair and some fitted tops. She began attending all of Brooke's classes, on campus and at Resolution Fitness and would have gone twice a day if it was an option.

Jane sighed with relief as she completed her last lecture of the day. The only thing she still had to do before her students would leave was to hand back their recently graded tests, which had been a disaster. Then she would have two hours to herself until her exercise class, the only thing she really looked forward to lately.

"I have to say, ladies and gentlemen, in general the results of this test were not very good. There were a lot of very low scores. Many of you will need to work harder to understand this material for the final exam." Ms. MacIntyre was facing the students but gazing up and over their heads, past the elevated rows of stadium-like seats so that she didn't have to make eye contact with anyone. It was her fault that almost everyone failed, but she didn't need to tell that to them. She managed to push aside the guilt. She could always adjust the grades on a curve.

Just hours before the test was administered, she was rummaging through her office, which was, quite simply, a mess. She couldn't find the test that she used every year for this section. It wasn't filed where it should have been. Her office became a wrecking zone as she quickly scanned through papers, dropping them wherever they fell.

The logical solution was to postpone the test until she found the misplaced copy or made a new one. She didn't want to do that. In all her years of teaching, she had never postponed a test for any reason. Instead she began searching for a different exam she could give the class. She was dealing with huge personal issues, she was exasperated, depressed, and she was too emotionally exhausted to care about a minor issue like administering the correct chemistry test. She found a test from a similar Inorganic class she used to teach and called for an assistant to quickly make her copies.

***

Brooke, seated in her usual spot in the center of the front row, generally loved to get her tests back. There was almost always an A written on the top affirming her hard work. Today was different. She would prefer to hold off on seeing the grade for this particular test. Thanks to the situation with Ethan's friend's suicide, she lost a lot of her preparation time. Added to that unforeseen obstacle, the test was far more challenging than expected. At this level of academia the students were expected to extrapolate from the course material, and she would never expect to see test questions that were identical to what they had studied, but in this case, there were several things on the test that she wasn't even familiar with from class or from the chemistry book. It seemed ridiculous. She knew she had not done well and it was very hard for her to accept. She had never experienced a class like this before. Other students had already complained to the administration, but Brooke wasn't inclined to do that because it would make her look weak. But, as far as she was concerned, the course was a complete disaster and Miss MacIntyre should be fired.

There were anguished sounds as her classmates turned over their exams. Every student in the room had scored a five on their high school AP science exams; none of them were okay with the grades they were currently receiving. Brooke waited quietly as Ms. MacIntyre flapped Brooke's exam face down in front of her.

"This was the highest grade," she whispered to Brooke, without actually looking at her.

Brooke was hopeful that she didn't do as poorly as she thought. She took a calming, hopeful pranayama, a yoga breathing technique, and exhaled slowly before she turned her test over.

Christ! She screamed inside her head. She couldn't believe it. She was so upset she could feel her body tightening all at once from the outside in. She got a seventy-five! That was a D. She had never received a D before. She had never received a C before. She could even count the number of Bs she had scored on tests throughout her life because there were so few.

No way. No way. This is not happening. I did not just get a D on a major test.

Brooke remained seated for a moment, her back ramrod straight, the top of her head stretching up toward the ceiling, appearing calm and poised from the outside. Inside, she was seething, her jaw clenching, and the vessels in her forehead straining.

She never, ever expected to see a test or paper with her name and a D on it. This had to be a bad dream. She squeezed her hands into fists on her lap. All of her thoughts had converged into a tornado like channel of anger swirling with crazy clumps of desperation and urgency. She needed to go for a pounding run or get on a bike and pump her legs for two hours; something brutal to dispel the intense energy flooding every cell of her body, or someone would be sorry.

Instead she rose from her seat and traveled through the rain to the biology building where her genetics class was held, her thoughts racing in multiple directions. She had no recollection of moving from one class to another, she noticed nothing on the way, not the cold rain falling around her, not the other students, oblivious to her fury. She was completely consumed with her anger. The minutes passed by quickly in her genetics class, and the macroeconomics class that followed as her mindset channeled between desperation and intense determination fueled by anger.

Brooke caught a glimpse of Ms. MacIntyre as soon as she entered the studio. That was no surprise, since her chemistry professor had not missed a single class in months. She was standing in her usual spot in the back. Brooke couldn't bear to look at her; the woman was singlehandedly ruining her entire life.

"We're starting with inner thighs. Place your block between your legs. Rise up on your toes, as high as you can. Back is straight as if you have a wall behind it. Neutral pelvis. Keep that form, contracting your lower abs against your spine and we're going to lower down for two counts, up for two, half way, tiny movements. Drop your tailbone, think of allowing space to grow between your vertebrae. Squeeze that block like you want to pulverize it."

She was barely through the second set of counting to twelve; she never did an odd numbered amount of repetitions, when her thoughts were hijacked by chemistry worries. She pushed the thoughts out of her mind, but they returned almost immediately. She had been revisiting the current state of her chemistry grade repeatedly for the past two hours and she couldn't seem to stop. It was like the fever dreams she had as a child when her mind would trace the outline of a shape over and over again, around and around, finer and finer until it had the effect of finger nails on a blackboard.

Two tests, three quizzes, four lab grades, and a homework grade. The lowest so far has been an 88, most are high nineties. Two tests, three quizzes, four lab grades, and a homework grade...

Her brain accounted for each number, going from lowest to highest, determining the average for each category: test, quiz, lab, homework, then calculating the relative percentage of each sub group. Again and again her mind returned to determining the exact exam grade she would need in order to finish the course with an A. She had already figured it out several times, but she couldn't stop, as if keeping it in the forefront of her thoughts would make a difference.

"Lower your body all the way down to the floor, as low as you can go. Heels stay lifted. Pull your abs in as hard as you can. Shoulders back and down. You should feel your thighs working now. You should feel your heart rate increasing. Let me know if you don't and I'll come over and make adjustments. No one is going to waste their time in my class and it's not working if you can't feel it."

Luckily, she could teach the class in her sleep, because her thoughts were elsewhere. '

***

Jane MacIntyre was secretly excited when she saw Brooke. After she returned the tests, she felt guilty about giving Brooke a low grade. Brooke was a brilliant student and to say that Jane appreciated her exercise classes was an understatement. She was completely addicted and couldn't imagine how she would cope with her miserable life if Brooke stopped teaching.

Jane's guilt, however, was short-lived because she had come up with a fantastic and redeeming idea that would surely rectify the situation and give Brooke the honor she deserved. She couldn't wait to do what she needed to do so her idea could come to fruition. Just a few more weeks until the next faculty meeting.

CHAPTER SIXTEEN

It was five o'clock. The dark gray sky added to Brooke's sense of despair. The rain had been steadily falling all day while the storm brewing silently inside Brooke surpassed the intensity of any of the outside elements. She had spent the last three hours in a genetics lab meticulously separating and counting the white- and red-eyed offspring of her third generation drosophila flies. It required intense concentration and all the while she felt like she was teetering on the edge of her sanity and her life was close to spiraling beyond her control.

As soon as she exited the biology building, it began to pour with the kind of rain that caused flash floods and washed small children away. Brooke became soaked as she jumped over puddles, trying to protect her backpack and its contents as best she could. She ran into the library for a few moments of shelter. Umbrellas of varying sizes and colors were scattered all around the perimeter of the entryway, dripping water across the marble floor while their owners used the facility. Brooke looked them over, considered her options, and then selected a plain red one.

She opened it up on her way out the door. She was shielded from the rain for the rest of the walk to South Vernon, but she was drenched already so the new umbrella did little to alleviate her anger.

Back in her room for the first time since before breakfast, she couldn't tear her clammy clothes from her body fast enough. She had been damp all day. She deposited the clothes in her dirty laundry bag, noting with resentment that it was near full. After putting dry exercise clothes on, she hurriedly began to straighten everything in her room—lining up her few pairs of shoes, tucking a pile of papers into as neat a stack as possible, using a damp towel to wipe down every surface until everything was spotless and dust free. Everything needed to be in perfect order right now or she didn't think she could handle it. With nothing left to straighten, she perched on the edge of her bed, trying to be still for just a few seconds in an attempt to calm down. She needed to scream out loud at the top of her lungs, but she didn't. After an anxious moment, she remembered that she hadn't checked email or texts all day. She had a message from Ethan. It was sent at the same time she had received the chemistry test that was threatening to ruin her life. She read the text.

"Just leaving campus, driving home to RI with Mac for funeral. Back on Sunday. Will miss you. Call me after classes. Love you."

All sorts of uncalled for responses filled her head, but she managed to push them aside. Since she wasn't in the mood to be nice to anyone, she didn't respond. A gear in her brain had shifted into anger mode and it was stuck. She may have still looked the same on the outside, but that meant nothing. She had time to get some of her written homework completed before grabbing a quick dinner, which was normally exactly what she would have done, but instead she lay back on her bed and stared at the ceiling for a full ten minutes, trying to get a grip.

Downstairs, after eating a meal she couldn't even remember, she opened the front door and gazed outside. Giant ugly puddles had formed all over the quad. The precipitation hadn't let up but the cold wet drops had changed to sharp stinging sleet. She expected no less. In fact if it started thundering the weather would be even more in tune with her mood. And of all nights, she realized with disgust, this would be the first time in months that Ethan's car was not available for her to drive to the gym.

She was not going to ride the bus to Resolution Fitness. She didn't have the patience to wait for it in the rain tonight. It was too cold and wet to run there, and she was so done with being cold and wet. She was upset that she considered not showing up to teach, or calling in sick, but even in this mood she couldn't fathom acting that irresponsibly. She knew there were probably several people leaving campus in their cars to take her class in town, but she didn't want to text people and wait for their responses. She needed an immediate action plan.

Then she remembered something that provided a flicker of hope. Without wasting any more time, she ran upstairs to her room. She deposited what she needed into her small lightweight backpack, the one she used when she didn't plan to shower at the gym. She left the dorm and ran across campus to the student parking lot to see if she might actually have one bit of good luck tonight. Even with her new red umbrella she was pelted by the freezing rain and the wind stung her wet cheeks. She didn't know what she would do if her idea didn't pan out.

Her first sense of relief came when she reached the parking lot. Sitting in its usual spot in the far corner of the west lot, next to the hedge border, was Jessica's pretty blue Volvo. Brooke had seen it many times on her way to get Ethan's car. She headed straight for it, remembering what Ethan had told her about Jessica when he gave her the key to his Jeep. She crouched down close to the front right tire, removed her glove and felt around the inside of the fender. Cold raindrops slid down her wrists and under her sleeves. The parking lot was lit with strategically placed lampposts, but there was no one to see her. Now that it was sleeting, most everyone was staying inside. The one other person heading to his car was running with his head down, his visibility hampered by his umbrella and the onslaught of rain horizontally assaulting him. Brooke might as well have been invisible.

She was successful on her first try. In less than five seconds, she was holding a magnetic box, larger than she expected. An entire remote key fob was inside the box.

Who does that?

She remembered Ethan saying those same words and smiled for the first time in what seemed like days. She pressed the button with the unlock symbol, and the Volvo emitted a confident beep as its interior was illuminated.

She got in and closed the door beside her. She leaned back against the soft, dry seat and sighed with relief at the sheer pleasure of temporarily escaping the rain. Inside the Volvo the steady drone of the sleet was reduced to comforting white noise. Brooke started the engine. Music instantly erupted from the radio and flooded the car until she located the button that turned it off. Music with a steady beat was essential for her cardio classes, running and dancing, but under any other circumstances she found it irritating.

The Volvo's heater was immediately responsive and her body began to warm. She took her time accustoming herself to the knobs and levers on the dashboard, finding the switch for heating the driver seat, and then calmly reversed the car out of its spot and headed away from campus. She cruised through downtown on Ash Street, driving the nicest car she'd ever driven, and took the turn toward Black Gum Road.

Black Gum was industrial and unattractive, unlike Ash Street with its specialty shops, charming cafes and boutiques. Black Gum Road was where people came to have their cars serviced, their television problems diagnosed, and to work out at Resolution Fitness. There were a few vacant buildings and the stores that were in business were spaced far apart. Brooke parked the car to the rear of a printing business next to the gym. It was closed at night; the parking lot was dark and deserted. She opened the driver-side door quickly, hopped out with her backpack, and took off through the rain, not bothering with her umbrella or to lock the car.

Everyone at the gym seemed happy to be inside rather than out. Brooke found their enthusiasm provocative, in a bad way. Her body was surging with a seemingly unlimited supply of restless energy and she wanted to smack their smiling faces. Wearing herself out physically was the fastest way to quell her anger. But her body was insatiable. She crammed in as many repetitions, power moves and cardio sets as she possibly could until she had to end the class. She aimed for exhaustion so that it would displace her anger, but when the hour was up she wasn't even close to feeling okay.

One of her regular attendees approached Brooke as she was unplugging her iPod from the stereo system.

"Tonight's class was much harder than usual." Her comment was just short of a complaint and she searched Brooke's face for an explanation.

"It's good to work harder once in a while," Brooke told her. She usually appreciated any feedback, but not tonight. She didn't want to talk to anyone. She skipped her usual shower, put on her coat, hat, and gloves and headed back out to the car as soon as the class was over. A foggy mist had enveloped the parking lot. It was colder than when she arrived, but the rain had finally stopped.

The excitement of driving the Volvo had diminished. Teaching the class had provided a temporary distraction, but now that she was done, her chemistry-related anxiety returned with a vengeance. It was driving her crazy. She knew her incessant concerns were not accomplishing anything, but they kept sneaking back in to dominate her thoughts as they had mercilessly throughout the day. Her mind was an anguished mix of racing thoughts and numbers and so much anger that even she was surprised by it. She tried to make sense of the restlessness inside her, the surging intensity to do something. What could she do? There was no way she would be able to go back to her dorm and study in her current mood.

She drove back to Everett without consciously paying attention. She was about to return the Volvo when she saw a large group of students walking toward the parking lot together. She didn't want anyone to see her driving Jessica's car. She made a split second decision to keep driving. She steered the car around and through the darkened campus using the high beams, past the fitness center and the sprawling athletic complex, vaguely recalling the way to the sloping stone wall behind the campus as she saw relevant markers. She took a wrong turn twice and ended up on the far side of the baseball stadium before she backtracked and recognized the maintenance garage and finally found the gravel road she had traveled on with Ethan. She exited the campus, turned onto Stonewall Road, and continued heading away from Everett.

The road seemed longer and more desolate now that she was alone with nothing to see except darkness. She felt the car bouncing through ruts and water filled ditches. Her eyes were peeled for the next turn.

She took a left and kept going, her gloved fingers tapping impatiently against the leather steering wheel. She felt her mind clearing into focus along with a stir of excitement.

She was about to accelerate so she wouldn't be driving all night, when she saw a familiar landmark, the old iron bridge. She impulsively decided she didn't want to be this far away from campus. She slowed the car to a stop and made a hasty three point turn before the bridge, marveling at the car's maneuverability. The sodden ground was easily disturbed by the turning tires and fresh mud erupted from the parted grass. She drove one mile back the way she came and pulled off the road next to a dense grouping of trees. She let the car idle slowly until it stopped with the front half sloped down into a natural depression in the earth.

She grabbed her new umbrella, shook it vigorously to remove the remaining raindrops, and then put it into her bag. She turned off the engine and leaned forward to put the backpack on, wiggling into it while still sitting. She didn't hang it over one shoulder as she was usually inclined to do, but slipped each arm through its proper strap so that it was secure on her back. She opened the door, letting the cold air whoosh in. For a split second a clean pine scent prevailed until it was quickly replaced with the damp, earthy smell that had permeated the area. She got out, leaving the door open so that the interior lights were on, and headed toward the back end of the car. The saturated ground yielded to her weight and she sunk slightly with each step. She popped the trunk with the key fob and waited as the trunk rose on its own accord. She was completely startled by something that looked like a sleeping gray dog. She quickly jumped away from the car, almost tripping over an obtrusive shrub.

It didn't move, so she stepped forward again. On closer inspection it turned out to be a balled up grey fur coat. Brooke pushed it aside along with the rest of the trunk's contents: an ice scraper, a camera, and a case of bottled water. There was a zippered pouch with the words VOLVO attached to the inside of the trunk. She unzipped it and found a flashlight. She turned it on to see if it worked, and it did, so she tucked it into the side pocket of her coat. Pulling up on the floor mat revealed a sparkling clean spare tire neatly harbored into a recessed area. Resting on the center of the tire was a lug wrench with a socket on one end and a pry bar on the other. Brooke could not imagine them getting used, as if Jessica would ever change a tire.

Brooke removed the tool and clenched it tightly while she stood still for a few seconds, looking around her. Beyond the area illuminated by the car there was complete blackness in every direction. She sensed no other movement. The silence and stillness seemed an absurd contrast to the disquiet she felt inside.

She approached the front of the car. Her gloved hand raised the wrench high into the air then sent it sailing down full force into the front windshield. As it made contact she listened intently, expecting a satisfying shatter, but there was only a dull cracking noise. The Volvo's safety glass cracked to resemble a giant spider web, but every piece stayed in place. Brook smashed it repeatedly, her frustration growing. The glass was destroyed but still intact within the windshield frame. She bit the edge of her lower lip in anger, lifted, and contracted her arm and took a swing at the headlights. The red and orange tinted glass shattered on contact with a crack and a spray of plastic shards erupted. She continued to swing and smash, increasing her pace as she moved along.

She circled the vehicle, pounding into it without pause, breathing faster, until there was nothing left of the outer lights. Wires spilled out from destroyed compartments on all four corners of the car.

Brooke surveyed her work, catching her breath as she stared at the mess. Moments ago the Volvo had appeared smug and stately. Now it looked completely violated. She turned away from the road and heaved the wrench and then the keys upward and outward toward the treetops. She watched as they were swallowed by the night. She closed her eyes, breathing in the darkness and the solitude, her arms extended by her sides in Mountain Pose. She remained that way for a full minute, aware of her heart beating quietly inside her chest. She enjoyed the sense of serenity washing through her. Finally. When she was ready, she sat sideways in the driver's seat to put her running shoes on and place her boots in her backpack. She circled the car twice in her running shoes to have a last look before she used the light emanating from inside the car to guide her to the road. It was extremely dark; the moon and stars covered by clouds. She remembered the flashlight tucked into her coat and paused to take it out and turn it on. She started walking toward campus again, her strides growing longer and faster until she broke into a jog back. Then her jog turned into a run, her fit body responding with a peaceful sense of purpose. She no longer needed to run herself into the ground; instead she enjoyed how very perfect it felt to calmly move at a steady pace all the way back to her dorm.

CHAPTER SEVENTEEN

Wearing tightly-fitting stretch jeans, a black cashmere sweater, and a pink wool pea coat, Jessica headed toward the west student parking lot. She was running late for an appointment in town: a lip, eyebrow, and bikini wax. Her journey was slow going because everywhere on the ground were dark puddles, seeping from the grass, making the sidewalks impassable without getting her feet drenched. She wished she hadn't worn her soft black leather boots. They were perfect for her outfit, but perfectly inappropriate for the weather. It was a concentrated effort to keep them from being ruined.

There were lots of disgusting things on the ground. Numerous worms, dead or dying, lay spread across the cement. Piles of sodden, decaying leaves were visible at curbside and under bushes, accumulating despite the constant efforts of the grounds crews. Jessica detested the cloudy damp days that had recently settled over Everett. The sky was a dull shade of gray, the air dank and cold. The most annoying part of it was the wind. Its fitful gusts whipped her hair around her face, into her mouth and eyes and made the temperature seem twenty degrees colder than it actually was. Each gust delivered a chill to her bones, cutting right through her cute wool coat as if it was non-existent. She wrapped her arms around her chest, her purse slipping down to her elbow in the process.

She was thinking about enjoying a cold weather cocktail later. Something warm with whiskey or rum, like a hot toddy or something creamy, like a Sneaky Pete. The combination of whiskey, coffee liquor and crème seemed perfect to dispel the chill she was experiencing. She would need to get some crème from the dining hall. She planned to send herself a memo so that she wouldn't forget, once she was inside her car with the heat running.

Jessica looked around in confusion, certain she had parked in her preferred spot, the last spot in the first aisle. A silver Toyota Prius now occupied that exact spot. After scanning the general area where she always tried to park, she still didn't see her car. So she stood still, for lack of something better to do, as if the car would appear if she waited long enough. The wind continued to gust in sharp biting waves.

"Where the f— is my car?"

She started to walk down the aisles of the parking lot, huddling into herself to brace against the wind, glancing left and then right, looking for her shiny blue Volvo. She passed aisles of cars, none of them her own. She felt self-conscious and irritated and hoped no one was noticing her. So many dark colored cars, all of them with a coating of grayish mud and in need of a good wash. She noticed the license plates, New Jersey, Connecticut, Pennsylvania, North Carolina, Massachusetts, Ohio, and Nevada. She couldn't believe that someone had driven all the way from Nevada in that piece of crap.

She reached the end of the west lot and crossed the street dividing the two student parking areas. She stood on the perimeter of the east lot, scanning the cars even though she had never parked there before. She turned and walked back to the place where she was certain she last parked her car. Her nose was running. She reached into her coat pocket for a tissue and found she had none. She recalled with annoyance that she recently put a box of new tissues in her Volvo. She continued walking and passed Explorers, Tahoes, Hondas and even a station wagon with wood paneling that had to be decades old. She saw one other Volvo sedan, but it was silver and she knew immediately it was not hers because the back was plastered with bumper stickers. Her car had two decals, "Everett—the peak of Education" with its simple depiction of a snow-topped mountain peak on the right corner, present on almost every vehicle in the parking lot, and then a pink monogram of her initials, JBC, on the left corner of the back window.

Jessica was startled by movement inside a Ford next to the silver Volvo. She wasn't aware anyone was in there until he had leaned sideways. It was a man with dark skin and a shaved head. He must have been there since before she arrived. What was he doing sitting alone in a car in the parking lot?

She returned to the place where she thought her car should be, as if it was the logical thing to do. She took out her phone and called Robert. While she listened impatiently to the ring tone, she glared at the Prius as if it was to blame for her situation.

"What a pathetic excuse for a car," she said aloud.

"Hi. This is Robert's phone. You can leave a message."

His voicemail message responded immediately because his phone was turned off. She remembered he had a class at one on Fridays. That damn class had prevented them from leaving campus early on several weekends, and now it was keeping him from coming to her aid. She was about to leave a message but then hung up quickly. If it turned out she was going to find her car before he got her message, she would rather he not know about her current dilemma. She dialed Brittany. No answer.

"Great! Thanks, everyone, for being there for me!" she muttered out loud. The wind was pressing against her, blowing the sides of her coat apart. She hung up and dialed her mother, Shari. Again no answer, but this time she did leave a message.

"Mom. It's Jessica. I'm having trouble finding my car. I think it was stolen. Call me when you get this. I'm not sure what to do." The urgency was rising in her voice as she spoke.

The fact that no one was available to answer her call increased her panic. She walked briskly around the perimeter of the parking lot, the preservation of her black boots forgotten. Feeling ridiculous, she retraced her steps down each aisle just in case. In frustration she dialed her mother's number again, the wind whipping her hair around her phone. Still no answer.

I can't believe this is happening! And I'm freezing!

She just wanted to go back to her dorm, warm up and then come back out to find her car and pretend none of this confusion had ever occurred.

She decided she had to call her father.

"Hello, Jessica. How is everything at Everett?" his assistant asked when she answered the call.

"Rebeka," Jessica said very matter-of-factly. "I need to talk to my father right now."

"Your father is busy at the moment; can I help you or take a message?"

"Tell him it's an emergency." Jessica thought she was sounding business-like, imitating her father, but she was simply sounding rude.

"Okay, just one moment, Jessica." To say that Rebeka did not adore speaking with Jessica was an understatement.

***

Foster Carroll sat at his imposing desk in his generously appointed office on the fifty-third floor of the Ignite building. He was supposed to be in a meeting for which he was currently late. Everyone in the adjacent conference room would be waiting on him to start. As he listened to Rebeka relay Jessica's message, he squinted critically out his window and across the city. As Jessica's call was transferred to his line, he hoped her idea of an emergency agreed with his. Not that he wanted her to be in danger, but he wanted to avoid feeling frustrated with her, which is what he would be if she had labeled a trivial issue an emergency.

"Hello, Jessica. I'm about to go into a meeting. Can this wait?"

"I can't find my car. And Mom isn't answering her phone. No one else is around right now to help me."

"What do you mean you can't find your car? Where did you leave it?" he asked with irritation.

"Someone must have stolen it."

"Have you looked everywhere it could be? Did you let someone else drive it?"

"Yes! I looked! No one else drove it! It's not in the parking lot! It's not anywhere in the parking lot! I've walked around it like fifty times and it's freezing here!"

Beneath Jessica's anger and confusion there was a speck of uncertainty. During the summer after her senior year at Miss White's School she misplaced her car after a party and called the police. Prior to the police arriving to take her statement, a classmate informed her that she had driven the car because Jessica was way too drunk to drive. Jessica didn't remember any of that happening. But she knew this time that she was not out drinking and she didn't leave campus last night or the night before. She last drove the car to the pharmacy three days ago and she was certain that upon her return she parked in the front row, the last space next to the hedges, in the exact spot presently occupied by the stupid Prius.

"Call the police then, or wait and I'll do it after the meeting. No, on second thought, you need to call the police. They'll have questions for you I won't be able to answer."

"Does my car have a tracking chip sort of device?"

"No, it does not."

"Okay." Jessica sniffed bravely. "I'll call the police."

"Call your mother and let her know when you find it. Good luck." Foster sighed as he pushed a button to hang up the call. He had already risen from his seat and straightened his custom suit jacket in preparation for the meeting. When Jessica was accepted at Everett, which was no easy feat on his part, he did not intend for her to take a car. He told her she wouldn't need one there, the campus was self-contained. He didn't have a car when he was a student there. He recalled that it didn't take her a second to formulate a response.

"Well, Dad, you didn't need to get facials and manicures. You could wear one tuxedo to every formal dance and get away with it. Girls are expected to wear a different dress for every occasion, with shoes and accessories. I don't think I can get all of those things at the campus bookstore. Do you?"

Foster acquiesced. It wasn't an important battle to pick. The car cost less than one year of Jessica's room, board, and other expenses

163

at Everett, and far less than it had cost him over the past decade to secure her a spot at the school in the first place. His daughter had no idea how hard he had worked to have her admitted. She might never realize that her intellect and passions weren't quite on par with the average Everett student.

***

"911. Is this an emergency?"

"Yes, my car has been stolen."

"Is anyone inside the vehicle?"

"No."

"Hold on please."

A moment later the dispatcher returned and asked several questions.

"Did you leave anything inside the vehicle that we could use to track it with—an iPad, a smartphone?"

Jessica was hopeful for a second as she thought about the question. Unfortunately the answer was no.

"Where are you calling from?"

"Everett College. I'm a student here."

"Hold on please."

Jessica waited another minute; looking around her the whole time, half expecting to suddenly see her car sitting in the next aisle. She hopped up and down to try and keep warm. An emergency services recording began its third loop while she was on hold. Then the operator returned.

"Call campus security first. They can help you look for it and then call us back if you still can't find it."

"Okay." Jessica called the main number for campus, got connected to campus security and told them her situation. They said they would be sending someone over to the student lot right away.

"Are you really coming right now?" she demanded, "Because I'm freezing and I don't want to be waiting out here another ten minutes while you take your time!"

Once she was certain her car was definitely gone, she wanted to call Robert again. But before she called him her phone rang.

164

"Hello. Miss Jessica. You had an appointment today at 1:30. Are you coming?" It was the spa.

"My car was just stolen, so…no, I guess I'm not coming!"

She hung up and then instantly regretted it because where else could she get her brows waxed within twenty-five miles of campus? And without a car, how was she going to get it done at all?

Jessica's most urgent issue was getting out of the cold. She hadn't dressed warmly enough to get to her car never mind standing outside for half an hour. She tried to focus on what she needed to do, deciding to call Robert and leave a message.

"Call me as soon as you get this!" she screamed into the phone, as if Robert was the perpetrator. "Someone stole my car. I can't believe this!" The reality of the situation had hit home and her drama began to unfold.

***

Bob Finnegan, retired police officer, and Jim Johnson, young enough to be Bob's son, were patrolling the campus, doing their best to keep it safe and secure, when they got the call about a missing car in the west student parking lot. Along with the official message, they got a heads up from the security dispatcher that the young woman sounded like a handful.

"Potential seven two."

Seven two was their "unofficial" code for "spoiled brat." They had dealt with enough of these that the security office had developed an inside way to communicate with each other without ever actually using those words. There was also a signal for very drunk, the most often used "unofficial" code.

They headed over in their golf cart. It had thick plastic sheeting on the sides to offer them protection from the wind and rain, but it was still unbearably cold riding across campus. Muddy water splashed up out of puddles and onto the plastic creating dripping brown splotches as they made their way along the campus roads. As soon as they took care of this business, Bob planned to stop in at the security office for another cup of coffee. This one he would make extra-hot in the microwave before pouring it into his mug, the one that fit into the cup holders of the golf cart. He hoped there was still

165

French Vanilla creamer left. That stuff was fantastic. He needed to remember to tell his wife about it so she could pick some up to have at their house. Maybe even try the other flavors.

While Bob drove the cart, Jim noticed, not for the first time, Bob's sagging physique and protruding stomach. That stomach scared the hell out of Jim and he didn't know how Bob could live with it. He wondered if Bob's stomach had always been headed for disaster and it happened gradually, or if one day, BAM, he hit a certain age and his stomach came popping out. Each day he spent with Bob provided him incentive to do an increasing number of sit-ups and push-ups. He would be happy to grow old on this job, as long as his body didn't change into Bob's. Just saying he worked at Everett College made him proud. He was a local. None of his immediate family had ever attended college and even though he was not an actual student here, somehow it felt similar enough to him. He got to hang out on the campus all day without having to do any of the homework and studying. And instead of paying Everett to be there, they were paying him. He had a full healthcare plan, benefits, even paid vacation time. It was truly amazing. Sometimes he thought it was too good to be true.

As they got closer to the west lot, they saw a young woman waving them over. Jim noticed she was dressed up in a fancy belted coat and tight leather dress boots, as opposed to the sweatshirt and jeans that were popular around campus. Most of the female students were piled under layers of sweaters and coats these days. This girl was attractive and like all of the students on campus, just a few years younger than him. Jim imagined that they were about help a damsel in distress. He contracted his abs, puffed out his chest and sat up straighter. As they got closer, his attraction for her was muted when he noticed her bright red nose and angry features.

Bob stopped the cart, lifted the plastic up on his side and climbed out first, hoisting his waist band to support his stomach as he stood. Jim came to stand beside him, hands clasped behind his back, offering a helpful smile. She glanced at him and then Bob, but did not smile back.

"You called about a missing car?" Bob asked.

166

"Yes. Someone stole my car. It was parked right here." Her teeth were chattering as she spoke, but her voice was irritated, edgy.

"When did you drive it last?"

"Three days ago. I went to the pharmacy in town. I came back and I parked it right here." She pointed to the Prius accusingly, as if it had somehow magically displaced her car on its own. "And I was not drinking and I did not leave it anywhere else. I'm sure I parked it here." She spoke more forcefully than necessary.

Bob walked slowly around the Prius scanning the ground, leaning forward with his hands clasped behind his back, noting that there were no signs of broken glass. He did his best to ignore the sound of Jessica's teeth chattering. Nearby, Jim was more focused on Jessica. He was standing close enough to smell her perfume, and he thought it smelled nice.

"What type of car are we looking for then?" asked Jim, standing up to his full height in front of Jessica, who was more appealing now that she looked about to cry rather than yell. His damsel was back and he hoped to be her hero.

"Volvo S80," she said.

"Is it a sedan?"

"Yes, a two-door sedan. A bluish silver color."

"Let's have you climb in here with us if you don't mind and we'll take a tour of the parking lot again, just to make sure someone didn't move it. That's happened before," Bob spoke with kindness.

"Okay," Jessica agreed, and climbed in the back. She wrapped her arms around her body and shivered on the plastic seat.

Bob recounted stories about all of the misplaced cars he had found over the years. He didn't mention the part about how alcohol was always a factor. While Bob drove, Jim used his phone to Google "what to do if your vehicle is stolen" to make sure they handled the situation properly and he sounded experienced.

"Most stolen vehicles are used for temporary transportation. About eighty-six percent are recovered, within a few weeks, with little damage," he said aloud, facing straight forward so it was not apparent he was reading directly from the internet.

"Good, I guess," she responded with a snort, desperately needing a tissue for her nose.

"We don't know it's been stolen yet. I don't recall a car being stolen from Everett since I've been here. I've been here six years. This would be a first," Bob added.

"Well, if it's not where I left it and it's not stolen, then what exactly do you suggest happened to it? Or do you still think I might have been drunk and don't remember lending it out?" Jessica's words and tone reminded Bob that they were dealing with a seven two. It was wisest not to answer.

They continued to drive across the campus, searching the other lots.

"I've never parked over here, ever," Jessica insisted as they drove slowly through the east lot.

There wasn't much they could do other than drive around campus searching. Jim was out of ideas for engaging Jessica in conversation, plus it was hard to flirt with Bob sitting next to him and the cold making his feet feel like two blocks of ice. Bob's stomach was used to being fed at regular, short intervals, and he was anxious to get back to the office for a bite to eat. Eventually Bob conceded that Jessica's car was indeed missing. He took her back to the security office for hot coffee, a croissant, and unlimited tissues. Bob spoke with Rebeka and then Mr. Carroll and then helped Jessica file a police report.

***

"It's about time," Kurt Washington thought to himself as he pulled his AAA card out of his wallet.

A truck had just arrived to tow his Ford, almost an hour after he found it wouldn't start and had called for help. It wasn't the battery either, that was still working fine, but the engine simply wasn't cooperating. They had told him it shouldn't be more than fifteen minutes, so he had chosen to sit and wait in the parking lot inside his car. Fortunately there was a basketball game he could watch on his phone so it wasn't as bad as it could have been, although it wasn't exactly warm outside. It was a great game, he had missed it live because he had to cram for his advanced physics test, and he was quickly caught up in it, even though he knew exactly how it would end. He had no idea that he had not been the only person in the parking lot with car troubles.

CHAPTER EIGHTEEN

Jessica was exhausted from her long and stressful ordeal, and mostly from being bone-chillingly cold. Instead of having her feet massaged while she read magazines, she had spent the remainder of her Friday afternoon in the security office, which she found to be ugly and depressing. It was tedious work to fill out security forms while listening to Rebeka ask all sorts of questions that she said were necessary for insurance purposes. She was in desperate need of a huge caramel latte with a triple shot of espresso and she was so cold and hungry that she ended up eating an entire croissant, which she knew to be the evilest of all the fat-inducing breads.

When they were finally finished, Jim Johnson drove her back to South Vernon in the golf cart. She ignored his attempts at small talk and watched the students going about their business on campus. They didn't have a clue what she had been through today. She didn't want their sympathy, but some acknowledgement of the tragedy that had befallen her seemed appropriate.

"What do you usually do on Friday nights?" Jim asked her.

He had been particularly nice to her as they worked out the necessary formalities, but she was just too drained to be polite.

"I don't know," she answered curtly.

The golf cart stopped at the steps of the dorm. As she stepped out and saw her feet hit the ground she was devastated to notice thick white stains, undoubtedly permanent, creeping up the sides of her boots.

She stomped up the stairs and suddenly started to feel fired up. She was going to seize the opportunity to be a leader, not a victim.

"Put up a note on the door that says we're having an all-dorm meeting at seven," she announced as she cruised by the front desk and made a split-second decision.

"Not in my job description," muttered the young woman at the front desk, although she did it anyway.

In her room, after removing her ruined boots and starting her espresso machine, Jessica sent a group text to the distribution list for the dorm, alerting everyone about the meeting. As always, the group text ended with the words, "Signed by Jessica Carroll, South Vernon President." She took a long hot shower, dried her hair, reapplied her makeup and heated up a diet frozen meal in her microwave. While she was waiting for her dinner, she drank an extra hot espresso. She purposefully avoided talking to anyone in order to create anticipation and suspense for the meeting. Twice there was a knock on her door followed by Brittany's voice, but she ignored it so she could rehearse what she was going to say.

She carefully dressed in black twill pants, a loose dark floral printed blouse with a black camisole underneath, and a different pair of black boots. She added a thickly coiled black and red necklace that she had purchased specifically to go with the shirt. Just before the meeting, she popped an ephedrine. She always took an extra one before dorm meetings and class presentations because it helped her to focus while she spoke. She waited until five minutes after seven so that everyone was assembled and waiting when she entered the formal living room.

"I need to move this chair," Jessica said, pointing to a blue velvet wing back chair, essentially instructing someone to move it for her. While she waited for the chair to be positioned in the focal point of the room, she stepped aside and proceeded to whisper to a senior from her floor, an important part of the build up to her presentation. When the chair was ready in front of the fireplace, Jessica sat down, hesitantly, as if she had been injured during her ordeal. She placed her bottle of Fiji water on the hearth of the fireplace behind her. She fixed her mouth into what she visualized as a brave smile and looked around at the fifty or so women who had gathered before her. They were sitting on the couches, the chairs and the arms of the chairs, on the steps leading down to the formal room, and even on the floor in front of the fireplace. Some were standing and leaning on the furniture. She was disappointed that not all of the dorm's residents were there. She waited a moment in her chair while phones and tablets were put away. She scanned faces looking for Brooke Walton, who she remembered had yet to attend one of her dorm meetings. She did not see her, which irritated her to no end.

"Thank you, everyone, for coming to this impromptu meeting. There's something I want you all to be informed about. This afternoon, around one o'clock, I left the dorm for a very important appointment. When I got to the west parking lot, I had quite a shock." She inserted a long pause for effect. "I discovered that my car was stolen." Another pause. "I spent almost two hours with campus security trying to locate the car, and then the rest of the afternoon filling out police reports, then insurance forms." Technically, Rebeka had filled out the insurance forms, but that detracted from the tale of trial and tribulation that Jessica was aiming to share.

"It was emotionally exhausting. Before today I had no idea how much is truly stolen when someone else decides to take what does not belong to them." She paused again and let her audience whisper amongst themselves for four full seconds.

"Obviously, my car was misappropriated, along with everything inside it. I had to give a description of all of the valuables in my car. Unfortunately, I keep all of my gift cards in there so that I'll have them when I need them. They are all gone. I lost a music collection and a beautiful gray fur coat that I had yet to even wear. And I also lost my afternoon, something I can never replace. Spending hours in the freezing cold and then filling out paperwork was not what I had planned for this afternoon. Throughout the ordeal, I asked myself what I did to deserve this. My car was locked, my windows were closed. It was parked in the front row, the most visible spot in the lot, near a lamppost." She intentionally did not mention the extra key under her car, because she didn't know that it had anything to do with the theft. How would anyone know to look for that anyway?

"Yet someone felt confident enough to walk on to this campus and leave with my car. Just like that. It's truly baffling to me that someone had the nerve. More than anything, I feel violated. I feel like I have to watch my back, like I can't go outside without wondering who I can trust. I feel like I'm not safe here anymore. The thief has taken more than my car, more than the items inside it. He's taken my sense of security." Jessica sighed. "More than anything, I want to make sure that this is an isolated incident. I don't want this to happen to anyone else on campus."

Most of the students in the room didn't have cars anyway and were wondering how all of this applied to them.

"I'm going to speak to campus administration to see that our parking lots have attendants from now on. Perhaps that can be another job for people on financial aid, so it would help them as well."

"That sounds fantastic—standing in the parking lot all night in below freezing temperatures like human popsicles to make sure Jessica's car doesn't get stolen again," Jennifer Hayes murmured sarcastically to her friend. Jessica noticed that someone wasn't listening. She stared at Jennifer in a way that made Jennifer freeze, although there was no way Jessica could have heard her.

"Until then, I urge you to watch out for each other, and to take extra care in the parking lots, or anywhere outside of the dormitories and academic buildings. If you see any strangers or suspicious activity, particularly in the parking lots, report it to campus security immediately. I want to catch whoever did this to me."

When Jessica finished speaking, she saw Robert standing in the entrance to the formal room. She glanced over at him, smiled, and nodded to acknowledge his presence. She assumed he had received her messages by now. A slight frown crossed her face as she remembered how he wasn't available earlier when she needed his support. But being the center of attention had lifted her spirits.

Several young women, mostly freshmen, came forward to surround Jessica and tell her how sorry they were.

Megan and Brittany, their very thin bodies sharing a wingback chair with room to spare, were talking while waiting for Jessica to be finished. Brittany tried to catch Jessica's attention with her eyes.

"At first I thought she was going to say she was raped," Megan told Brittany, her voice hushed.

"Me too."

"So having your car stolen is better than getting raped," Megan said.

"Definitely," Brittany agreed.

"I have something important to tell her," Megan said intently.

"I have something important to ask her," Brittany added.

They both stood up as Jessica approached. Robert moved to join them.

"Jessica, I don't know if this is helpful," Megan began in a conspiratorial whisper, twirling a piece of her long straight hair around her finger, "but Madison said there was a dark skinned man hanging around the parking lot a few days ago. She watched him, he was just looking around, and then he walked away, the opposite direction of the dorms. She thought he was up to something."

"It's like anyone can just come on campus and steal a car now. What's next?" Brittany asked, as she struck a somewhat sexy pose by extending her arm with an upturned palm.

Jessica remembered the man she had seen sitting alone inside a car in the parking lot. He had a shaved head and dark skin. She realized she hadn't seen him leave in the car or on foot. Not during the time she was being driven around in the golf cart, but perhaps she hadn't noticed. It was strange, but she thought it was unlikely it had anything to do with her car being stolen. She mentioned it anyway, for lack of something else to say.

"I did see someone sitting in a car in the parking lot. I think it was a Ford. He had dark skin and a shaved head. It was unusual because he must have been sitting there for a long time, the whole time I was looking for my car, and I don't remember him leaving on foot or in the car. It's like he was homeless in the parking lot."

"Someone waiting inside a car? So? Nothing about that sounds suspicious. Maybe his roommate was getting lucky and he had to wait somewhere." Robert frowned, looking from Megan to Jessica. It wasn't the first time he had heard them say something stupid. "I wouldn't be speculating out loud like that, Jess."

"What? What did I say? I didn't say anything. It was just strange."

"You implied a few things; just don't be thinking out loud, okay?" Robert cautioned.

"Well," continued Megan, tilting her head and raising a knowing eyebrow, "If I had a roommate and she was entertaining someone else in our room, I would go to the student center, or someone else's room, or even the library, so your explanation doesn't make sense, Robert. I think Jessica should definitely talk to Madison and see if she remembers what he looked like and compare notes. It's probably the same person and I know he freaked her out."

"Okay. Thanks." Jessica took a long look at Megan in her super skinny jeans. She usually didn't take anything Megan said seriously. Megan was generally clueless. It was hard to believe that she was some sort of math genius. Her wardrobe was fantastic though. If Megan wasn't so tiny, Jessica would absolutely consider borrowing a few of her outfits.

"Jessica. I need to talk to you." Finally Brittany had her chance to speak. "Can I....Oh, I'm sorry about you losing your car. That's really a shame for you. Can I borrow your brown dress boots for tonight? The Cole Haans. I have a date with a new guy. I know exactly what I'm going to wear." She explained slyly, striking another suggestive pose and practicing her sexiest smile.

"Sure," Jessica answered. "But treat them like they were your grandmother. I ruined a pair of boots today because my car was stolen. I don't need to lose another."

"I'll take care of them like they were my own Nana," Brittany declared gratefully.

"I have to take a shower," Megan announced to the group and walked off. She was at the bottom of the staircase when Gretchen Kim and Maya Rao entered the dorm. They were finishing up a conversation from their Cultural Anthropology class. They noticed the sign about the meeting. Gretchen glanced at her watch and then caught Megan's attention since she had been coming from the direction of the formal room.

"Do you know what the meeting was about?"

Megan paused at the base of the stairs to explain, twirling her hair again, a jutting hip bone leaning against the main balustrade.

"Someone stole Jessica's car today."

"Jessica Carroll?"

"Yes. It was stolen out of the student parking lot."

"Do they have any idea who took it?"

"I don't think so, but Jessica said she might have seen the person, a black guy with a shaved head who was there yesterday and today, maybe, looking suspicious. He ran away when someone approached him. So at least they have a lead, if Jessica tells the police."

"How does she know it was him?" Gretchen asked.

"She doesn't *know* it was him. She just thinks it was him because he looked suspicious."

"What sort of suspicious?" Gretchen asked.

"I don't know. I guess he just looked like he didn't belong here. You'll have to ask Jessica." Megan gave a look like Gretchen was the clueless one and then continued walking up the stairs.

The front door opened again and Kate and Eli came in, holding hands and laughing. They also saw Jessica's sign. And Jessica was coming toward them, intending to walk right by.

"We didn't know anything about a meeting," Kate said defensively. She felt that she and Eli should be informed before an all-dorm meeting was held.

Jessica looked them both over disapprovingly before speaking.

It's too bad they weren't around in the sixties; they would have fit right in with the hippies.

"I sent a text using the distribution list for the South Vernon students."

"What was the meeting about?"

"Someone stole my car today. I needed everyone to know so they could be more vigilant in protecting themselves and their property."

Jessica continued walking, away from Kate and Eli. She didn't have time for them; she had other things to do. She needed to find someone with the school newspaper to write an article about her ordeal and include a picture. She would definitely wear the crème cashmere turtleneck with the new Burberry coat.

CHAPTER NINETEEN

On Tuesday afternoon, Evelyn Rossiter, Ph.D. was alone in the rural valley a few miles behind the Everett campus. She was fifty-eight years old, an ornithologist and expert on acoustic networks within sparrow communities. She had just arrived and was perched silently in her usual spot tucked between a crumbling stone wall and some bushes, staring into the copse of trees. Snow had fallen lightly a few times in the past couple of weeks, but there was yet to be any accumulation. A light frost was melting, leaving behind drops of glistening moisture. Her older model Subaru station wagon was parked to the side of the road. In it was her lunch, water bottles and recording devices.

This place was her preferred element. She had spent many hours, even complete days in this spot. She wore her typical field clothes: a fisherman's sweater she had received as a gift twenty-five years ago, a turtleneck, and brown corduroy pants. She loved the quiet she encountered outdoors, especially here in the New Hampshire valley. Just a few miles from the far end of campus and she could count on being completely secluded amidst the sounds of wildlife. Acres of undisturbed foliage attracted a wide variety of bird species. She was grateful that her research took her out of the classroom. It was the reason she had become an ornithologist, but in order to make a living at it, unfortunately, she also needed to spend time inside teaching. Today she was particularly content to be alone. She had a lot on her mind. Her partner of twelve years, Jane MacIntyre, was not happy with their relationship; had not been happy for some time. Evelyn's strategy for dealing with the situation had so far been to ignore it and hope it went away. If not for their tenured positions at Everett, Jane probably would have left her by now, or so she had said. It was hard to walk away from tenure and as long as they both worked at Everett, they would be forced to see each other on a regular basis anyway.

Based on Jane's increasing complaints, Evelyn categorized the nature of Jane's unhappiness into two major areas—boredom with teaching and dissatisfaction with aging. Whenever Evelyn had a problem, she approached it systematically, gathering as much information as possible. This situation was no different. She had extensively researched "mid-life crisis," which she had always believed to be a cultural phenomenon. Everything about Jane's behavior seemed to fit.

Reading through the characteristics of a mid-life crisis, she made a list and checked off one manifestation after another because Jane exhibited all of them: sudden concern with appearance, chagrin over unrealized goals and dreams, dissatisfaction with relationships, depression. Above all else, it was the depression and how it was affecting Jane's career that had Evelyn most concerned. Evelyn knew Jane had been neglecting her students and delivering haphazard lectures. Just the other day she was ranting that her office was a mess. She had behaved as if someone else was responsible for its condition. She had lost a test, used another one in its place, and subsequently caused almost all of her students to receive a failing grade. She seemed upset at first, but then she was laughing. It was very strange behavior. Evelyn believed Jane was testing the limits of how little she could care and how much she could get away with. She hoped Jane wasn't having a break down.

Evelyn hadn't had a mid-life crisis of her own, but she was astute enough to realize that she had never cared about her appearance: not when she was a teenager, not when she was in college, and certainly not now. Also, unlike Jane, she didn't have siblings who were newly able to talk incessantly about their grandchildren at every opportunity. Jane had never been upset about not having children, so it was a surprise to Evelyn that the lack of grandchildren had suddenly become such an issue. Anyone could have children and grandchildren. Anyone at all. On the other hand, how many people could produce breakthrough research on supramolecular chemistry? Jane had. Well, it had been a few years now, but that was once-in-a-lifetime work for anyone and certainly something to be proud of forever.

Instead of focusing on expanding her impressive base of chemical research, Jane suddenly developed a deep interest in critically examining her skin and muscle tone. She quickly morphed from a woman who used only a simple cleanser and moisturizer to one who purchased expensive wrinkle refiners, skin tone enhancers and cellulite cream. Cellulite cream! What self-respecting chemist in her right mind believed that was effective? This mid-life crisis had clearly messed with her ability to reason on several fronts.

There was some hope. The exercise classes that Jane now religiously attended seemed to be having a positive effect on her outlook. She looked forward to them like nothing else.

Maybe, thought Evelyn wistfully, I could start going to the class, too. Exercise is good. And I don't have any eleven o'clock lectures this semester so I can get over there no problem. Oh....who am I kidding? That's not going to happen. Dancing around inside wearing tight clothes isn't my thing. Maybe we could start skiing again? That was something we used to enjoy together.

Right now she just wanted to block out thoughts of Jane's unhappiness and forget about imposing changes on herself. She would ride this out, since it was likely a phase. She would be as supportive as possible and not take it personally. Evelyn needed to focus her own attention on starting a new research project that would lead to a publication. Everett expected its professors to be prolific publishers and this facet of her career alone generated enough stress for her without worrying about Jane. Writing a book, she knew from experience, required too much time inside writing and editing to suit her. She strongly preferred to be outside doing field research, so she had resigned herself to producing a constant flow of papers. For the past twenty years, she had published research on white-throated sparrows and tree sparrows, all plentiful in this landscape. Today's research involved recording their songs to determine the number of different notes per second and their frequency. Her analysis would produce enough insight for at least one new paper regarding their survival and evolution.

Surveying the trees through her binoculars, she ever so slowly scanned across the branches of an Eastern White Pine. She stopped moving and locked her gaze as she caught sight of a small splash of bright red. A common enough bird, the male house finch, and just that morning she had used him as an example to illustrate reproductive strategies during a lecture for her Behavioral Ecology course.

The house finch alighted from the pine. Evelyn smoothly followed his path with the practiced ease that came from years of looking fixedly through binoculars. He headed downward in a quick and graceful arch passing Silver Maples and landed again, about fifty yards to the right on the back of a car before taking flight again.

What?

This time Evelyn reluctantly ignored the sparrow and focused on its last point of departure. A portion of the back end of a car was visible from her vantage point. She could see an Everett sticker applied to the rear window.

Her first thought was disappointment that someone else was there. She had rarely encountered anyone else in the area. She lowered her binoculars and sighed. She thought it was probably a lost cause to collect any meaningful data now. She raised the binoculars to her eyes again as she realized that she had seen only a car, but no people. There was no movement and no sound associated with the discovery. She got up as quickly as her stiff joints allowed as it occurred to her that there might have been an accident and someone might be hurt. Evelyn's tall duck boots squelched with each step while she trudged across the mushy thick grass toward the car. She slowed to a cautious pace as she got closer. The car was on a slope, the front of it angled downward. When she was a few yards from the car, she saw that it was clearly abandoned and had been for at least a few days. The driver-side door was wide open. Water had collected in small pools on the leather seats. The car was filled with an array of natural elements, scattered leaves and small debris, blown in through the open doors. More unusual still, the body of the car was intact, but all of the windows were cracked and the exterior lights were destroyed. Shattered orange and red glass pieces were scattered about on the muddy ground. She scanned the vicinity, discovering it did not seem to be the scene of an accident. It was odd.

"Hello. Is anyone out here?"

She waited. All was quiet except for the birds' songs that she had been conditioned to hear.

"Hello! Is there anyone here?"

Evelyn knew she should call the police, particularly because of that Everett sticker on the back, but there didn't appear to be any sort of emergency, and they would arrive making all sorts of racket and that would be the end of her research for the day. She could call them when she finished. Or better yet, she could call them when she got back to her house.

CHAPTER TWENTY

Brooke was striding across campus, the sun streaming through the bare branches of oak trees lining the route, and her only immediate concern was chemistry. She currently had a B and that was not acceptable. She needed to ace the final. She wasn't sure what she was going to do, but she would secure that A if it killed her. *Or someone else*. Just thinking about the class released a surge of adrenaline that made her clench her jaw and feel the need for a long, hard run. But there wasn't time. She had to get to the lab. And first she had to call Ethan.

"Hi, Ethan. How are you?"

"Glad to hear your voice. What are you up to?"

"I'm calling to ask you for a favor."

"Sure. What do you need?" he asked, realizing this was the first time Brooke had called and asked him to do anything of any sort. It felt like a milestone moment.

"My sister, Amanda, is visiting me for the weekend. I need to pick her up at the bus station tonight night at five-thirty. Can I use your car?"

"Sure. Of course. But how about if I come with you to get her?"

"Okay. If you want to."

"I'd love to meet Amanda. Thank you for inviting me." He was joking, but Brooke didn't catch the humor. "How come she's visiting this weekend? What's the occasion?"

"It's her birthday present. She turns twelve this week and she wanted to stay with me for the weekend."

"I've always felt sorry for kids with December birthdays. It's too close to the Christmas holidays. They get everything they would have gotten for Christmas anyway, just split up over two events. Not fair. Let's do something fantastic with her."

With her sister's transportation arranged, she could shift her focus on the mammalian anatomy lab. She particularly enjoyed this course and its experiments, all of which involved animal dissections. She was incredibly proficient with the dissections. The purpose of this lab was to study the contractile properties of skeletal muscles, something near and dear to Brooke. The current experiment utilized a frog, but all muscle properties were similar and any insight gained could relate to muscle stimulation in humans. The lab was related to a hypothesis she had been developing privately, for the past year, outside the classroom. She hoped it might allow her to obtain some of the data necessary for the next steps.

She sighed with relief upon finding the lab empty. That was critical for what she hoped to do. With a flick of a few switches, the overhead lights brightly illuminated the large room. Rows of long lab tables laid in wait, all equipped with the latest technology, thanks to a recent large endowment to the biology department. Brooke busied herself setting up all of the supplies she needed at a table next to a window. Sitting on a backless stool, abs pulled tightly against her spine, back and shoulder muscles engaged, she prepared a small syringe with a milliliter of a diluted anesthetizing solution. She crossed the room to remove a brown frog from its enclosure, entering a password to unlock the cage. Before reaching in, she spent a moment watching one of the frogs, memorizing the pace of its breathing. Satisfied, she encircled it with her hand and lifted its passive body up and out. On the way back to the table, she held the amphibian just inches from her face. Although it remained docile, she could sense its fear through the change in its breathing pattern and the rapid heartbeat.

Brooke held the frog firmly while she injected the contents of the syringe into its leg. She waited a few seconds and then poked at its head to ensure its blink reflex was no longer available. It would now be motionless for the duration of the experiment. With practiced hands she stretched the frog's leg between two small clamps and wrapped coils around its body to secure it on top of a tube. Her hands found the dissecting tool and expertly cut through the thin brown skin on the dorsal side. She pulled the skin back with tweezers, revealing the white underside and the thick gleaming pink muscle tissue beneath. The next step was to identify all of the leg muscles. She checked them off her list one by one, separating the biceps femoris and semimembranosus to expose the larger adductor magnus. She used a needle to thread wire deep between the muscle's fibers. With everything in place she applied the electrical stimulus and observed the muscles contract. She did this repeatedly, varying the voltage and frequency. Marveling at the steadiness of her own hand, she proceeded through the experiment, moving the needle around, noting and recording the obvious, that the larger the group of muscle fibers, the stronger the contraction. She repeated the stimulation with a higher voltage. Periodically, she dampened the frog's skin with water to keep it moist, per the lab's instructions.

For the purposes of her assignment, she was supposed to record the rate of contractions versus frequency and voltage. Using her favorite pen, a smooth Mont Blanc that had been carelessly left behind by someone in the library, she painstakingly recorded her detailed observations. Her notes would later be expanded and encompassed into a final report worthy of an A plus.

After the experiment, she was supposed to inject a lethal four milliliter dose of anesthetizing agent to kill the frog. Instead, she administered a second small dose just like the first. She released the clamps and coils.

Brooke glanced up at the door to make sure she was still alone, then paused to savor her anticipation. A small surge of adrenaline coursed through her blood, making her more acutely aware of the moment. Life coursed silently through the frog's body in a rhythm of breath and heartbeat that Brooke could feel through her thin gloves. The frog remained motionless, unable to comprehend its unfathomable situation. Brooke pivoted her wrist, turned the frog over, and placed it on its back on the counter. Her fingers palpated the smooth light brown chest. With careful movements, she made a small and precise incision with the dissecting blade, exposing the small beating heart. Brooke watched it intently as it bulged and contracted. The cut was barely big enough to see through, but nonetheless the frog's insides began to leak out. She must have cut a vessel. Now she would have to rush before the frog expired on its own. Without taking the time to record the information, she counted the palpitations for five seconds. Then with two fingers of one hand holding the skin apart, she touched the electrode wire as gently as possible to the pericardium and delivered a low voltage of electricity through the membrane to the heart. It was messy inside the thoracic cavity, but she definitely saw the heart's rhythm change immediately, faster and erratic. She increased the voltage slightly, the response was magnified, and then it stopped.

Damn.

She would never know if the frog had died as a result of her rushed surgical procedure or the electrical disturbance to its heart. She sighed, feeling incredibly disappointed with her sloppy effort.

She looked toward the door again. There was no one there.

Strands of long blond hair had come loose from Brooke's ponytail. She pushed them away from her face using her forearm, because her gloves were covered with frog secretions. She then lengthened the opening down the frog's belly, rapidly identifying and removing the organs with the scissors and tweezers, for the sake of cementing her own knowledge. When its body was nothing more than an empty, sagging shell, she disposed of it, along with the pile of organs, and wiped down the counter area. The last rays of sun shone through the windows and across the counter tops.

She still had time to get another frog. She needed to determine how much voltage and frequency it took to hijack the frog's nervous system and stop its heart. Then she would do some size and weight calculations to extrapolate the amount required to stop a human heart. She needed this information for an extra-curricular project she had in mind.

En route to get another frog, the lab door opened and an attractive young man paused just inside the room. He stared at

Brooke and looked incredulous. Brooke was startled at first, instantly turning back to look at her lab area, confirming it was now clean of all but the instruments. It was just out of habit, she had nothing to hide yet, other than her intentions.

"Hello," he said, not having moved from the doorway yet, "this is a pleasant surprise. I didn't expect to find anyone else in here on a Friday afternoon."

"Hi," Brooke answered, without really looking at him.

"Are you alone in here?"

"Yes. Just finishing up though. It's all yours." She was disappointed that she was no longer alone. Continuing with her own experiment was no longer an option.

"I've seen you around campus. You teach the exercise classes don't you?"

Brooke didn't answer. The way he was intently trying to engage her in conversation reminded her of Bradley Carroll.

"I'm Jack. Are you sure you're finished? I hate the idea of working alone. Something about it seems Frankensteinish, if that's a word."

"Yes. I'm done. Enjoy." She attempted a lightness with her tone to belie what she was feeling. "You'll get more accomplished having the place to yourself." She purposefully did not offer her name.

"What were you working on?" he asked.

It was really upsetting when people pried into her business. Why was he so interested in asking her questions? She didn't like it.

"Nothing. Just a muscle stimulation lab." With her back to the newcomer she vigorously washed her hands, helpless to prevent the tension increasing across her shoulders, the tightness pulling at her forehead. She told herself she hadn't done anything wrong. There was no reason for her to be concerned. She hadn't done anything and he hadn't seen anything. She just wanted to be left alone. The last time someone had walked in on her unexpectedly, it had turned her life upside down. As she continued to scrub at her hands, she unwillingly began to relive that horrible scenario when the head of the Cedarhurst science department caught her in the lab alone.

***

It was also a Friday evening when it all started. Cedarhurst's lab was always empty then because everyone else was preening or partying. The door was supposed to be locked, so she was shocked to see Mr. Wilhelm approaching. She had been so engrossed in what she was doing that she hadn't seen him enter or cross the large room, and then there he was, much too close. Alarm bells went off throughout her body, she was caught off guard. She hadn't planned for this. Should have, but she had not; it was a terrible oversight on her part.

Mr. Wilhelm innocently acknowledged her with a friendly greeting. "Brooke. Good evening. Why am I not surprised to see you in here?"

Brooke was his favorite academic advisee and the daughter of one of his closest colleagues. She was working late in the biology lab alone, further evidence of her dedication to excellence in science and learning. She stared up at him, praying he would hold her gaze and that he wouldn't look down. Then, as he moved even closer to see what she was doing, he froze, his expression registering shock and confusion. It seemed like minutes that he just stood there, unable to avert his eyes from the experiment Brooke had set out on the counter. Brooke watched his face change to indicate full comprehension and then horror.

"What are you doing?"

It wasn't really a question. It seemed like a bellow, but maybe it was more of a hiss, she couldn't remember some of it properly anymore. She had tried so hard to forget. Droplets of spittle had flown from his mouth. The skin of his face had been alarmingly pinkish against his gray and white facial hair. He had been standing very close, but he quickly backed away.

Brooke's response, a slight smile, the result of nervous energy, only made the situation worse, although there may not have been any appropriate reaction for this situation.

"Don't ever do anything like this again."

That was all he could manage to come up with, begging her, his voice full of disappointment and fear, his eyes darting around the room, trying to explain away what he had witnessed.

"Okay. I'm sorry. I–"

"I don't want to know," he interrupted her. "Just don't ever let this happen again." He continued to stare at her in silence, searching her face. He didn't know what to do. He was having trouble processing his own thoughts, controlling his reaction. Brooke wasn't sure either. Should she finish it off immediately and start disposing of everything? Wait for him to leave? She kept watching him, not wanting to look back down at her experiment; it had been inexplicably ruined for her.

After what seemed like forever, Mr. Wilhelm said, "We'll talk about this tomorrow morning at our usual time."

And then he left.

Brooke and Mr. Wilhelm met every Saturday morning in the lab to discuss her studies. Their "usual time" was comfortable and informal, starting with him brewing coffee into his "Science!" mug and her stretching while they discussed and sometimes debated. Clearly it would never be the same again.

It was only a cat! Thousands of them are euthanized every day. No. They're used in labs all the time. And it was anesthetized for God's sake. It couldn't feel a thing. Why was he so upset? Was it his? Did it belong to his neighbor?

Brooke guiltily disposed of everything, unaccustomed to feeling dejected. She had never seen anyone so angry or disappointed because of her, especially not a teacher. She had always been the most perfect student.

Brooke left the lab and headed across Cedarhurst's concrete walkways to her dormitory. She had just experienced the most frantic, most uncertain moment of her life. Her thoughts raced around her mind. Was it really a big deal what she had done? Who would Mr. Wilhelm tell? Would she be expelled? What should she do? She absolutely needed his recommendation for medical school and how could she possibly get one from him now? She needed to pound out a long, hard run in order to calm down. She was angry, and getting angrier by the second.

By the time she returned to her room, she had refocused and had a new plan. She would transfer, and she had no time to waste. She chose two colleges, the top ranked schools in the country, Everett and Rothaker. She felt manic as she sat down at her desk and downloaded their transfer applications and financial aid forms. It was while filling out the applications that she decided that transferring wouldn't be enough to guarantee her an unblemished record. Mr. Wilhelm was too much of a risk to her future.

Everett's application asked why she wanted to transfer. Over the next few hours she produced a heartbreaking essay about her academic advisor, Mr. Wilhelm, a man she highly respected and with whom she had a close professional relationship. With poetic detail, she described the horror of finding him dead in his office and the subsequent distress she experienced as a result of his unexpected death. She carefully chose words to convey how she couldn't think straight. She couldn't eat for days, and it felt like her insides were hollow. Everything on the Cedarhurst campus reminded her of what an incredible mentor he had been, blah, blah, blah. She re-read her brilliant essay and felt pleased.

The remaining task was to turn her essay into reality. Exhibiting the utmost patience, she waited until late in the evening when the sky was at its darkest, then headed out into the night to take care of the rest.

***

"Are you usually in here on Friday afternoons?" Jack asked.

Brooke shook her head and managed to regain her composure. Her hands were scrubbed beyond clean. She gathered her belongings, readjusted her ponytail, and then deposited all of her things into her backpack. All the while she was uncomfortably aware that Jack was watching her, expecting her to say something. Trying not to look culpable, she avoided eye contact as she went out the door. She had done nothing wrong and even though he didn't know it, Jack was surely lucky for that.

CHAPTER TWENTY-ONE

The very distinguished professor of classic literature, Fred Herbert, addressed the lecture hall full of professors with the seriousness of a court room judge.

"Last order of business, we need to nominate the 'Peak of Everett' student for the semester. Does anyone have a candidate they feel strongly about? Someone who exemplifies excellent conduct, both social and academic? Someone who has made outstanding contributions to the community through service or leadership?"

"I do." Jane MacIntyre stood up, to the surprise of her colleagues and her partner, Evelyn. It was unusual that she had anything to share during the monthly faculty meetings.

"I have a student named Brooke Walton in an advanced chemistry section. She transferred to Everett this semester from a small college in Connecticut. Academically, she is one of strongest students I've ever had. She's motivated, disciplined, and intellectually gifted. She also teaches an exercise class for faculty and staff three days a week. I take her class. The level of professionalism and the depth of her knowledge as an instructor are quite brilliant. These classes are based on a very deep understanding of muscle fiber stimulation and response. I feel she's making a wonderful difference in her contributions to campus on several fronts. She also works at a gym downtown, out of necessity, just about every night, which I would say again sets her apart from her peers. She's a remarkable young woman and I would like to see her recognized."

Jane sat back down, feeling exhilarated and flushed after speaking her mind. She felt vindicated for her recent haphazard teaching as far as it concerned Brooke. The fact that Jane had never recommended another student for the award lent more weight to her nomination than anything she could have said about that student. It was the first time she had even stood up and had an opinion in this forum. Evelyn was the most surprised of all.

"I'd like to second that nomination." It was Robin Smith, beaming from ear to ear and feeling luxuriously svelte. "I met Brooke the very first day she arrived at Everett. I knew immediately she was something special."

Robin hadn't thought to nominate Brooke, but she agreed with everything Jane had said and frankly, she thought that anyone who could inspire Jane MacIntyre to stand up and say something positive without being manually coerced definitely deserved the award. She had heard from another faculty member that Brooke was an impressive student, which was saying a lot at Everett. And Robin didn't know what she would do once Brooke graduated; she had become so addicted to her exercise classes, attending Resolution Fitness in the evenings whenever Brooke taught. Brooke's classes were so informative; they were like receiving a crash course in exercise physiology at the same time you got a kick-ass effective workout. And Robin's ass was a good two inches higher as a result. She would never underestimate the power of feeling good about yourself.

Scott Talbot stood up and nodded his head strongly in agreement regarding the nomination.

"Excellent choice, she's one of my students. I agree she's exceptional, extremely focused. Her work is more insightful and theoretically advanced than my graduate students. I've been trying to convince her she should be an Econ major. She's the whole package and just the type of student we should have representing the spirit of Everett College."

Other nominees were suggested by professors who did not have the pleasure of knowing Brooke. In the end a list was compiled with Brooke's name on the top. A vote would be taken at the next meeting.

CHAPTER TWENTY-TWO

"I can't stand this closet!" Jessica yelled to no one in particular.

She was alone in her room. She had been feeling somewhat shaky all day, and she was still recovering from a bad cold. For three days her nose was red and raw and her eyes were so irritated that she couldn't wear her contacts. She missed the last two days of classes to stay in bed and recuperate, downing ibuprofen, antihistamines, and herbal teas while she watched television and tried to sleep. Today, feeling considerably less congested but not too great, she multi-tasked by drinking a double espresso while attempting to rearrange her clothes. The stress of the last week had taken its toll. Even though her car was found, it was practically ruined and she had to wait for the glass to be replaced and the interior to be professionally cleaned. She was behind with all of her schoolwork and would need to get the notes from the classes she missed from someone before the final exams. She had started doubling up on energy drinks in order to stay awake during the day, but then she suffered sleepless nights. She had not had her lip and eyebrows waxed in weeks. Her nails were a disaster, they reminded her of Brooke Walton, although not that bad. Brittany had agreed to drive her to the salon later today so they could both get a manicure and pedicure.

Jessica was looking for a navy blue sweater that she sent out to be dry cleaned weeks ago. She was going to pair it with her red pants, if she ever located it. The red pants were critical. They were stretchy and could be pushed up above her knees so she could have her legs massaged during her pedicure. She had her mind set on wearing them with the navy sweater.

It was difficult to find because her closet was so full; all of her clothes were stuffed tightly together. Adopting a new approach, she started removing all of the clothes in dry cleaning bags and laying them flat on her bed.

She noticed for the first time that one of the bags had a handwritten note stapled to the top of the plastic. She tore the note away from the plastic to read it. It said: Yellow writing on the back of the shirt cannot be removed.

"What the hell?" she said out loud, reaching for another Kleenex and blowing her nose.

She removed the white blouse from the bag to examine it, but didn't see any writing or anything yellow. She held it up to the light coming from her window and still saw nothing.

"What are they talking about?"

She was about to throw the shirt back down on her bed when she caught just the faintest glimpse of neon yellow. She studied it closer. It was more perceptible now that the shirt was farther away from the sunlight. Bending the material from right to left, she made out the words "Snooty Drunk."

"What?! That was not on my shirt when I sent it out to be cleaned!"

She fumed, angry that someone had ruined her shirt, a wardrobe staple; a white silky blouse that could be paired with just about everything.

I'm calling the cleaners right now. They are going to reimburse me for this shirt. Better yet, they're going to find and buy me the exact one to replace this. And they are going to find out which of their employees did this and have them fired. Whoever it is must be jealous. Obviously he or she has a problem with doing my laundry. Well now they'll have the chance to find out because they're going to need a new job. No way are they going to get away with this.

She yanked a receipt off another cleaning bag, anticipating it would have the dry cleaning company's phone number on it.

That shirt fit me perfectly. I can't believe this. The nerve of some people.

She was unfolding a crumpled receipt when her phone signaled that she had a text. It was from Eli and Kate Newman-Shultz.

"Please meet us in our apartment for a few moments. We need to discuss an incident that took place in the dorm."

"Fifteen minutes," she texted back.

The text caused her to temporarily forget about calling the dry cleaners. She would have to find the navy blue sweater later. If she wasn't the dorm president, she wouldn't have to deal with Kate and Eli and whatever issue they were going to bring to her attention. She had enough to deal with without taking on other people's problems. She could effortlessly compile a list of things she couldn't stand about Kate and Eli, which she did while she chose a different outfit to wear so she could meet with them.

I can't stand the way they look and dress, which includes Eli's flowing Hindu or whatever pants and Kate's hideous thick leather sandals that she wears all of the time. Their stupid hyphenated last names. Their constant fighting that everyone can hear. I would hate to be them. Who lives in a dorm once they're married?

Twenty minutes later she knocked on the door to their apartment and they asked her to take a seat. Jessica looked around.

Okay, I'll have a seat on this really nice stool that you probably found on the side of a road. The apartment is as awful as they are, it's a perfect fit. IKEA bookcases and tables. A futon for a couch! Some sort of African rug hanging on the wall opposite an Andy Warhol poster. I can imagine them in here smoking pot and dancing around, when Kate's not busy screaming.

Kate began speaking, with words she had clearly rehearsed.

"Hello, Jessica. Thank you for coming."

"Hello, Kate. Hello, Eli." Jessica could barely stand to be near them.

"Someone, and we're not able to tell you who, so please don't ask, reported a racist incident that we need to talk to you about." Kate's face twitched slightly, like she was making an effort to control her emotions. As if she was trying to keep calm because she had exciting news she was bursting to share.

Jessica wanted Kate to get to the point so they could finish up. She wasn't feeling well and it was depressing to be in their dumpy apartment. But she knew she didn't have a choice, it was her responsibility as the dorm president to help sort out other peoples' issues.

"What happened?" Jessica asked, wondering who it was she would need to speak to next. Kate was looking at her with what appeared to be condescension. Jessica didn't think she could bear another moment in Kate's presence.

Kate spoke slowly and clearly.

"Apparently you said you saw a black man in the parking lot, and you think he might be the person who stole your car. You claimed he was suspicious, but you didn't have any evidence of suspicious behavior. So, you see, if you assume someone did something just because of the color of their skin, you are discriminating. And some of your dorm mates were offended."

"What? This is about me?"

Jessica was completely floored. She tried to register what she heard, but she was caught off guard to the point that she said nothing for several seconds. Kate and Eli continued to stare at her, waiting for a response.

"Are you serious?!" Jessica stood up once she had recovered. She began shouting directly into Kate's smug looking face.

"First of all, I was the one whose car was stolen, and vandalized, and left somewhere out in the boondocks! I feel like I was completely violated! And this is what you want to talk to me about?!"

Jessica was just getting started, her anger grew, her face got flushed, her heartbeat increased. It was the moment she had been waiting for all semester. Finally she had an excuse to tell Kate off. She was really going to enjoy this.

"Secondly, I did not say that, at any time, so I don't know where you're getting your information, but it's NOT correct."

She turned to leave, but then abruptly turned back to them because she wasn't finished.

"And even if I did say it, have you ever heard of the first amendment?!"

She paused; concerned for just a second that she was so angry she might have confused amendments. "Freedom of speech? Is this not a college campus? Are we supposed to censor all our thoughts because we might offend someone?"

She imagined her dark eyes like daggers piercing through the Newman-Shultzs, but inside she was thrilled because she had remembered hearing an attorney on television discussing the first amendment in the context of offensive statements and now it was completely applicable to the situation. She stepped even closer to Eli and Kate. They looked perplexed and hadn't said a word.

"You really should have thought about this first," Jessica continued, pointing an accusing, perfectly manicured finger at each of them in turn, speaking quieter now but with a scary intensity, and loving every second of it. "If you can't figure out who the real victim is here, maybe this job is just too hard for you."

With all the intensity she could muster, she shifted her fierce gaze from Kate to Eli and then back to Kate, who remained speechless. Kate was not accustomed to anyone yelling at her, she was the one who did all the yelling around her apartment. The meeting had not gone the way she had imagined, and Jessica had just threatened them. Eli said nothing.

Jessica turned and left, head held high, slamming the door behind her. Somehow Megan's "tip" about Madison seeing a guy in the parking lot had been convoluted so that the words were attributed to Jessica. It was massively unfair!

"Whatever! Why is the world so f—ing against me right now?!" she hollered as she stormed by the surprised woman at the front desk, leaving a most interesting impression on yet another person.

CHAPTER ᴛWENTY-ᴛHREE

Ethan and Brooke waited inside his warm Jeep for the bus from Waterbury to arrive carrying Brooke's sister. They kept the engine on to keep the heat running. Amanda had texted Brooke recently and according to the bus driver, they were close to their destination. Ethan flipped through satellite radio stations, searching for a specific song. Brooke looked out the window and tried to come up with ideas for things to do with Amanda. The moonlit sky was cloudless, and, as usual, it was cold. The bus station was a lonely place exposed by greenish lights perched above a corrugated metal awning. Its emptiness was interrupted only by the infrequent arrival of buses. A few other cars were waiting. Three yellow taxi cabs sat in anticipation of someone needing a ride. Two of them were lit from within by the drivers who were reading. The third driver was taking a nap. Everything was quiet with the exception of the music coming from the radio. Brooke tried her best to block out its noise.

The bus arrived ten minutes early. Ethan turned off the Jeep and they got out, moving closer to the bus once the first passengers came off. Ethan recognized Amanda instantly because she was a younger version of Brooke. She had the same straight blonde hair, crystal clear complexion, and long dark lashes. Her coltish, jean clad legs stretched down from a light blue winter jacket. She descended the stairs and looked around curiously. Then she spotted them and waved her hand with excitement.

"Amanda!" Brooke called out.

She strode toward them, all smiles.

"How was your trip?" Brooke asked her.

"It was good. Well, it was boring. But it went pretty fast" She shrugged her shoulders up and down twice as she spoke. She was proud to have taken the bus to New Hampshire by herself.

"This is Ethan, my friend."

"Her boyfriend," added Ethan with a smile, extending his hand to shake. He was sure Brooke would have mentioned him to her family by now, wouldn't she?

Amanda seemed suddenly shy and innocent as she hesitated, reaching first with her left hand, then quickly replacing it with her right before shaking, giving a slight nod of her head at the same time, as if she had figured it out.

"Let's get your suitcase. Is that all you have? Are you hungry? If we hurry we can catch the tail end of dinner at my dorm." Brooke started guiding Amanda toward the car. Brooke and Ethan had already had a conversation about dinner. He wanted to take them to the most elegant restaurant in town. Brooke had insisted that Amanda would have a more interesting experience eating in the dining hall.

"Cool!" Amanda exclaimed from the middle of the back seat, referencing the car, particularly its glowing map in the center of the dashboard. She looked happily from side to side, then settled on looking out the front window from the space between the two front seats.

Ethan drove slowly through the town before entering Everett, pointing out everything along the way. While Amanda took it all in, enjoying the ride, Brooke called home and talked to her father, letting him know that Amanda was safe and sound.

"Is that where you buy your food?" Amanda asked about the small grocery store. "Is that where you exercise?" she asked when they passed a dance studio.

"The gym where I work is down that street right there." Brooke pointed. "The school has a gym as well."

"Is this your first time at Everett?" Ethan asked. He was surprised when she said yes, but he told himself that it was Brooke's first semester here and perhaps her sisters had busy schedules of their own.

"We're about to enter the campus of the finest school in the country," Ethan announced as they approached the impressive iron gates with a giant E on the top.

He stopped in front of South Vernon so Brooke could take Amanda's suitcase up to her room. He parked his car and then jogged swiftly back to Brooke's dorm through the cold to meet them in the dining hall. As they moved through the buffet line together, Amanda seemed to take everything in with her eyes.

"We can have whatever we want?" she asked for the second time.

"Anything," Brooke told her.

The student checking IDs at the door of the dining room had not charged a guest fee for Amanda. Brooke was grateful because after scanning the salad bar and all the hot foods, Amanda selected two small pickles and two round dinner rolls. At the dessert table she added to her tray a piece of chocolate cake, two chocolate chip cookies and a cup of Jell-O with whipped cream. Each time she picked up a dessert she looked at Brooke, expecting to be reprimanded. Brooke just smiled and nodded at her.

"This place reminds me of Hogwarts," Amanda declared as they carried their trays to a table. Ethan and Brooke laughed. She was absolutely right–dark oak paneling lined the bottom half of the walls, medieval looking coat of arm plaques decorated the top, giant iron chandeliers, ornate carvings embellishing the window frames, all of it contributed to a wizard-like formality.

Amanda had truly enjoyed her desserts. She finished off the second cookie while looking around, taking cues on how to act from the students at the other tables

"What do you have planned for tomorrow?" Ethan asked after he and Brooke returned with second helpings.

"I'm not sure yet. I was thinking we could walk around campus, have lunch. There's a men's soccer game at two o'clock. We could go to that. But first I have to teach a class at ten. You can come with me or hang out in my room until I get back, or go to the library and read a book," Brooke told Amanda, between bites of her own cookie.

"Or you can hang out with me while Brooke teaches. I can take you around," Ethan offered. He had two young cousins that lived on the West Coast that he hardly ever saw. His limited time with them represented his only experience with children. But Amanda seemed pleasant and easy going. And she was Brooke's sister. He still knew so little about Brooke. This might be his opportunity to learn more.

"That's what I would rather do, if it's okay with you Brooke." Amanda seemed to enjoy Ethan's company and Ethan seemed eager to entertain her, so Brooke agreed.

"Of course it is," Brooke said, as she looked at Ethan. Again she wondered why he would offer. There seemed to be nothing in it for him. "I'll meet up with you both as soon as I'm done teaching."

"Okay, I'll come up with an excellent plan for tomorrow," Ethan announced. "Would anyone like another round of dessert?"

***

Ethan arrived at South Vernon to meet Amanda the next morning so Brooke could teach her cardio sculpt class.

"How was your first night sleeping at Everett?" he asked.

"It was good. It was fun." She was already well-fortified from a bowl of frosted flakes.

Ethan quickly realized he needed to ask more specific questions if he wanted more detailed answers.

"Ready for the museum?"

Ethan had carefully considered what he would have enjoyed doing on campus had he been twelve. Then he called his mother and asked for her opinion. Diane Altman was on the board of directors for Everett's museum. She knew they had a visiting exhibit on animal habitats. She thought it would be perfect for a child.

Ethan named each of the buildings they passed on the way to the museum. Amanda listened and nodded, smiling the whole time, at one point stopping to watch two gray squirrels that were chasing each other. They tumbled over one another as if in combat and then one broke away and scrambled up a giant sycamore tree, the other a few feet behind in pursuit. The first squirrel advanced out along a giant tree branch, moving without hesitation even as the branch became increasingly thinner. It was almost to the end and the chosen branch was sagging down with the weight of the squirrels. It quickly turned to face the pursuer and then they were so close their front feet were touching and they began to share a walnut.

"I thought they were fighting at first!" Amanda said, relief in her voice. She was excited about everything.

"Do you have a pet at home?" Ethan asked.

The squirrel antics had reminded him of one of the many things he didn't know about Brooke. The Altmans had a golden retriever named Jib. His mother brought him home as a puppy, a Christmas surprise the winter before Ethan started high school. Jib was treated like a family member. He had a monogrammed bed and coats, designer collars, and several jars on the kitchen counter that contained his favorite treats. Every time Ethan's mother called she told him that Jib missed him. Anyone listening in would be sure that Jib was a third sibling, although oddly named after a triangular headsail. The last few times his mother had mentioned Jib, Ethan had wondered if Brooke had a family pet, but then forgotten to ask her when he had a chance.

"We don't have any pets." Amanda sighed, clearly dismayed about the fact. "We had a dog when I was a little, but something happened to it. I guess it died. Then we had hamsters, a bunch of hamsters, and a rabbit, but they all kept disappearing. We don't even know how they got out of their cages. It was really strange. They just disappeared one by one. Sydney and I cried like crazy every time it happened and my Dad would get us a new one. Then my mother finally said that was enough and so we haven't had any pets for like years."

So, now he knew Brooke didn't have a pet. It was a start. He was content to learn about Brooke all day, and Amanda was a wealth of unfiltered information.

After the museum tour, which was a huge success, Ethan planned to stop at the student center food court and the school store. He thought he was doing a great job sharing Everett's history with Amanda as they walked from place to place.

"This is the student center. We get our mail and packages downstairs, there's also a store down there. People go upstairs to eat or just hang out."

Amanda followed Ethan inside where they circled the food court so she could see all they had to offer. Several students waved to Ethan. He waved back, hoping someone would ask who he was with. He didn't know why, but he was pleased to be playing tour guide to Amanda because she was Brooke's sister.

A large lighted "Refreshment Center" sign hung across the entrance to the self-service food court. There were several different offerings. Summit Sustenance offered pre-made sandwiches and salads, baked goods and coffees. Crevasse Cuisine had hamburgers, chicken tenders and French fries. Avalanche Frozen Yogurt allowed its customers to make their own frozen yogurt creations. Like many of the establishments in town, all of the food shops in the student center had a mountain reference in their name. No one knew if it was because they were in the mountains of New Hampshire, or perhaps because someone from food service marketing once confused the name "Everett" with "Everest."

"Avalanche Frozen yogurt…they even have frozen yogurt! And cotton candy flavor–that's my favorite."

"Do you want one? I'll get one, too." If he knew nothing else about kids, he remembered that it was always more fun to eat dessert with someone, especially when you were twelve.

They each filled a bowl with yogurt, sprinkles, hot fudge. Amanda tossed gummy bears and cookie dough balls into her mixture. Ethan paid, and then Amanda followed him to two empty chairs against the right wall, just outside the food court. She dropped her glove on the way and Ethan scooped it up and held it for her. From their location they could see just about everything happening in the lounge area. Sitting with Amanda, Ethan looked around the student center as if seeing it for the first time through her eyes. He felt protective and responsible for Amanda's well-being and was alert for any inappropriate behavior or language from students, something he would have been immune to had he been alone.

Don't even think about saying something R-rated out loud, he thought as he noticed two guys commenting on the derriere of the girl walking in front of them.

"So do you think I'll get to meet the rest of your family soon?" Ethan asked hopefully, between bites of his yogurt concoction, although he knew Amanda wouldn't know the answer to his question.

"I don't know, I guess." Amanda laughed.

"Tell me about them," he prompted.

"Well, they're just my family." She paused with her spoon in the air and thought for a few seconds. "There's a lot of yelling...not my Dad really but like my sister and I and like my Mom." Amanda laughed and then was thoughtful for a few seconds while she considered what sort of knowledge she had to share with him. Then she smiled with inspiration, tossing her blond hair behind her shoulder. "And the rest of my family is like totally crazy."

"Totally crazy how?" Ethan asked. It crossed his mind that he might possibly be betraying Brooke's confidence by asking, but of course, he was curious.

"Well, I have this one aunt who is like so weird. She lives like a few miles away and still I don't think I've seen her in like years. Not even for Christmas or the holidays. She's my dad's sister, and I guess she's just really strange and my mom says she never gets haircuts." Amanda pondered this for a second, wearing a mischievous grin, and then continued, "And then my mom's younger brother is a policeman who was in the war in Iraq and has all these anger management issues. Everyone says he has movie star good looks. He came to our house last Thanksgiving and then left and then came back in again and was like freaking out because his Taser was missing. He said someone must have taken it from his police car while he was at our house. He was yelling at my mom because he was going to have to tell his boss, as if it was my mom's fault, and my mom was like freaking out because he was totally ruining the day," Amanda finished explaining, almost breathless.

Ethan tried to imagine the scene. Whether he found it comical or frightening depended on how he pictured Amanda's uncle.

"Did he eventually find his Taser?"

"No. He didn't. He still thinks someone stole it from his police car while he was at our house. And my mom is angry about him thinking that. Oh. My cousin just got suspended from school for doing drugs. My mom never wanted us to hang around with him ever. He's like fifteen anyway. He's on my dad's side of our family, too, but he has a different mom, not the weird aunt I told you about first."

Ethan was interested in hearing about Amanda's parents, but not necessarily about the extent of dysfunction in her extended family. Amanda was laughing hysterically since it was first time she had thought about her family in this context and then provided details out loud. She realized she had plenty of information to share with Ethan.

"And I know your mother has a career, right?" Ethan cut in and prompted her so she wouldn't tell him about another strange cousin.

"What? Yeah, she's like really into her job. She's really serious about it. She's like at work all the time, and then she comes home and tells my dad like every single thing that happened at work that day and what everyone said and everything." Amanda rolled her eyes. "It's so boring to hear. And Brooke's not crazy. You know that, right? She's just super, super smart."

"I know," he said. "That's what I like so much about her."

Amanda grinned. It was nice being with Ethan, her sister's boyfriend.

Ethan's yogurt was long gone, and Amanda was finished with hers, although it looked like most of it was still in the cup, gummy bears floating in a rainbow of melted muck.

Ethan threw the cups in the trash and said "this way," gesturing toward the stairs that would take them down to the campus bookstore. Amanda paused at the top of the stairs. A tall stack of newspapers in a metal display stand caught her eye.

"Everett College Newspaper," she read. "Is this something I can take?"

"Yes. Those papers are free. The newspaper staff is eternally grateful to everyone that takes one."

"I write for the newspaper for my school." She scanned through the article headings, comparing them to those in her own school paper. Some of the Everett stories had an angry tone, or were about recent crimes. She didn't see anything along the lines of "Mr. Smith the Band Instructor is a Great Teacher," a feature story she had written for her school's most recent paper. She could appreciate the shift in sophistication. Still, she was proud of her Mr. Smith story.

"Oh. This article says a car was stolen from the campus parking lot."

"Oh yea. Brooke and I know the person that owns that car." He pointed to the picture of Jessica that accompanied the article. She was smiling confidently, her hair looking like she had just come from a salon.

"Was she freaking out? Because she looks happy, she doesn't look like she's upset about having her car stolen."

"I'm sure she was freaking out," Ethan laughed, "but that's not the image she wants to project. I'd like to read that article, too."

Stolen Car Recovered, Vandalized

A recent make blue Volvo S80 parked in the northern corner of the west student parking area was reported stolen on November 23rd. The crime took place sometime between November 20th and November 23rd. Everett security officers held a campus-wide search for the car and then reported the theft to the police. The car was found off campus on Stonewall Road by an Everett professor four days later. All of the windows and lights had sustained heavy damage. No items from inside the car were reported missing. Police believe at least two people were involved in the crime, since the vehicle was abandoned several miles from campus and two sets of shoe prints were found at the scene.

"Having my car and personal belongings stolen was emotionally devastating and a huge inconvenience," stated Junior Jessica Carroll, the owner of the vehicle and the president of the South Vernon dormitory. "I'm glad it was recovered, although it

required extensive repairs. This type of senseless, criminal behavior is inexcusable."

"Occasionally a car will be broken into," said Bob Finnegan, from campus security. "However, in my six years with Everett, this is the first unauthorized vehicle removal from campus."

Most cases of theft from cars occur when the vehicle is left unlocked. To help deter crime, make sure to lock your car at all times. Do not leave valuables in your car and do not leave spare keys in sight or anywhere on the vehicle. Make sure to report any on-campus crimes to campus security by calling 603-321-4690.

Ethan's phone buzzed when they finished reading the article. It was Brooke saying she was back on campus and wondering where to meet them.

"I told her to meet us at the campus bookstore. She should be there in ten minutes or less. Let's go down."

Ethan led Amanda through the school store to the ladies' apparel section, recognizable by the telltale pink mixed in with the traditional forest green.

"You need an Everett sweatshirt to make your visit official. Let's pick one out. It's on me," Ethan said.

Amanda carefully checked out every single rack before she chose the most classic sweatshirt of the bunch. On the front it was Everett's Latin motto on a small banner in the upper corner, *Promontorium et Praestare*, to peak and to surpass, and a giant E on the back.

"Excellent pick," Ethan said as he took it from her and approached the cashier. The balding man looked up from reading the newspaper to assist them. Amanda thanked Ethan repeatedly as they waited for the transaction to take place. She was so happy about having the new sweatshirt that she took it out of the bag and hugged it to her chest. Ethan laughed, remembering Brooke making the same exact gesture when he presented her with the gift from his mother.

When Ethan was in high school he had toured dozens of colleges with his parents in order to narrow down his choices. He had bought a sweatshirt at almost every single one, with the exception of the few schools that he had ruled out immediately. It was just a given that he would leave with a souvenir from every school. That's what he thought people did. He didn't remember being this excited about any of them. Of course, he was a few years older then. Amanda's reaction was so endearing that he wanted to tell her to go back and pick out something else, two things even, maybe a cap and some of the plaid pajama pants. But then Brooke was standing in front of them and Amanda was showing her the new sweatshirt and breathlessly explaining that they had frozen yogurt and went to the museum. Brooke smiled at Amanda and then smiled at Ethan with gratitude. Ethan felt like he did well.

CHAPTER TWENTY-FOUR

It was the last day of the semester. Jessica was leaving for New Jersey in the morning. Her Volvo was recently repaired and returned to her. One exam remained for her to take, microeconomics. Everett's honor code allowed for final exams to be self-scheduled so that students could take them in the order they preferred. Microeconomics was her most challenging course, so she had left it for last, and she was not prepared. While studying through most of the night, and seeing a good bit of the exam material for the first time, she discovered that she was still missing a few days of notes from when she was in bed nursing her cold. It would take a miracle for her to pass the exam.

And she was not well. Was she jittery and edgy from lack of sleep, or could it be from the extra ephedrine she had been taking to help her study? There was no way to be sure. She had recently developed insomnia and hadn't slept more than a few hours in what seemed like ages. She was incredibly tired during the day, relying on extra caffeine in order to function, but then she couldn't fall asleep at night no matter how hard she tried.

The past few weeks had been hell. So many things seemed to be going wrong, one after another. She probably shouldn't have angrily confronted Brittany and Megan in the hall, where others had overheard her. She had demanded to know why the Newman-Shultzs had accused her of racism. After all, it was Megan who encouraged her to report the suspicious-looking man who happened to have dark-skin. Jessica had barely acknowledged Megan's suggestion. Megan was the one who should have endured the unbearable session with Kate and Eli. Unfortunately, Jessica had caused a public stir by yelling at Megan out in the open, and the more people that knew about it, the more solidly the whole incident and the word "racist" had become associated with Jessica. It was incredibly unfair on so many levels.

And now she could barely focus. She just needed to get through the afternoon, get home to New Jersey, and then she could catch up on sleep for the next six weeks of the winter vacation. Her family was going to Florida for Christmas to be with her grandparents, since her Nana and Papa could no longer travel up the coast for the holidays. She was looking forward to relaxing with them. They treated her like a princess.

A study break seemed like a good idea. She pushed the power button on the television remote control. The Channel Seven Eyewitness Storm casters, Connie and Tim, were speaking with an abundance of enthusiasm about the huge storm that was brewing.

"Storm-force winds out at sea and upper level disturbances from Canada will be coming together to create this enhanced storm system. We're expecting incredible snowfall! This could be a historic weekend in terms of accumulation! Three feet expected across New England! Blizzard warnings will be going into effect over the next twenty-four hours. We're talking about a tremendous storm. And we will be covering it live for you over the next three days."

People were already talking about the big storm that was coming. While Jessica listened to the news she began to empty out her refrigerator. She was deciding what to do about the moldy orange in the back that she didn't want to touch when she heard a tentative knock on her door.

"Jess?"

It was Robert. She was relieved to hear his voice. "Come in."

"Are you almost ready to go home?" he asked.

"I'm getting there. I told you I have one more exam to take. Are you still leaving tomorrow? Are you worried about the storm?"

While Jessica was in Florida, Robert would be with his family in Aruba.

"I was thinking about leaving this afternoon instead. My parents think we should get earlier flights. They said Chase has to fly in from the West Coast this weekend and his flight will probably be cancelled and we'll have to leave without him anyway. I guess it could be days before he..." Robert stopped talking mid-sentence. At some point Jessica had stopped discarding food from her refrigerator and started glaring at him. Her furrowed brow and clenched fists told him he was in trouble.

"Why is Chase flying in? Is Chase going with you to Aruba?"

Robert didn't answer right away and that told Jessica everything she needed to know. He should never have mentioned that his sister was taking her fiancé along on their family vacation. There was nothing he could say that would help him now. He was about to experience the infamous wrath of Jessica.

"You didn't tell me your sister was taking her boyfriend!" she shrieked. Her irritability had reached a new high over the past few days. And now this. Robert had not invited Jessica to Aruba. It was just too much for her to handle. She had a container of expired fat free sugar free yogurt in her hand. She sent it sailing across the room toward Robert. It would have hit him squarely in the face had he not caught it before it made contact.

"Please calm down and stop yelling," Robert said calmly, attempting to diffuse the situation. The door to her room was ajar and someone was hurrying past. Robert walked backward to close it, all the while facing Jessica lest she hurl something else at him.

"That's just fantastic...that makes me feel so, so, important!" she continued in a lowered voice with just the perfect amount of practiced biting sarcasm.

"He's not her boyfriend, Jessica. He's her fiancé. There's a difference."

"I don't care...he's not her husband, is he? Did you even consider asking me? Did you?" She was yelling again. Loud. A little frightening even.

He knew better than to tell the truth, which was that he had most definitely considered it and decided he would enjoy the trip more without having Jessica with them. She seemed out of control. And, despite frequently taking those diet pills, her entire body was a bit puffy and bloated. Her eyes were red-rimmed, making her appear unstable. Robert was uncomfortable in her presence.

"Get out!" Jessica yelled, and Robert left willingly.

Jessica slumped down heavily on her bed, taking deep breaths. She raised a trembling hand to her head and then set it down on her lap. She felt unsteady, frustrated and angry. She had not handled that situation well at all. She didn't even want to go to Aruba with his family; she was excited to see her grandparents. She only wanted to have been asked. She shook her head. She had no intention of feeling sorry for herself. She was just going through a stressful phase. It would be over soon. She needed to pull it together and get through her last exam. She would take an extra ephedrine pill. That would help her focus. The super energy caffeine drinks were making her too wired, too anxious. She needed to cut down on those, and she would be able to do that starting tomorrow. She turned to look at her television.

"That's right, Connie, we're just in the pre-stages of this system that is definitely coming. Right now we're concerned about the wind and possible power outages. The winds are going to be vicious. We could have sixty- or seventy-mile-per-hour winds; that's hurricane force. We're talking about an incredible storm coming. It's going to slam the North East. Road crews are already getting ready because once that snow starts falling it's going to be continuous. Stay tuned, with our storm impact chart, we're going to show you just how bad we expect Storm Connor to be."

Jessica looked out the window. There was a dusting of snow on the bushes and trees outside the dorm. It looked beautiful and peaceful. The approaching storm would soon cover everything in a picturesque blanket of snow. She made a brave attempt to rise above her misery. She loved this time of year, the way it looked. She loved layering her beautiful and luxurious winter clothes. She had recently bought a fantastic new winter coat. She had so many pretty scarves to wear.

I will get through this day and then everything will be fine.

CHAPTER TWENTY-FIVE

Brooke knew that the next few hours could alter her entire life plan. She brushed large snowflakes off her shoulders as she entered the Preston Bates Lecture Hall through a side door. It was the largest lecture room on campus and the logical place for students to meet before each exam. The beautiful interior held a spacious stage bordered by immense forest green velvet curtains. Elevated rows of seats and balconies could accommodate two thousand people. Popular introductory courses as well as small concerts and theater performances were held there. At the front of the room next to a polished wood lectern, Sheila Davidson sat, back straight, legs crossed, behind a row of boxes. In front of each box was a placard labeled with all of Everett's majors: African Studies, Anthropology, Astronomy, Art, Biology, Chemistry, in alphabetical order, all the way to Women's Studies. Inside the boxes were the exams for each course in that major. When the Bisaillon Library tower bells rang to indicate it was one o'clock, students could come up and find their exam.

There were still a few minutes before the last exam commenced. Brooke continued into the auditorium, scanning across the seats. The first rows were fully occupied. As excited as students were about starting winter break, most had tried to spread their exams over as many days as possible, so the last offering was one of the fullest and Brooke had left chemistry for last. Her performance on the exam was critical. She had to ace it. Valedictorian. Summa cum laude. Highest Honors Thesis. Straight As. There was no other option.

At the end of the fourth row, Brooke noticed Jessica, who she had not seen in at least three weeks. The incident with the car was nothing personal. Brooke hadn't given a thought to Jessica in a long time. It looked like Jessica was staring right at her. Jessica looked unusually tired and disheveled, but then again, so did most everyone around her. Exam week was especially grueling for the highly motivated students at Everett. Too much caffeine, too little sleep, too much pressure, lots of stress.

Brooke acknowledged Jessica with a nod. Jessica's foggy, dilated eyes seemed to look right through her without seeing. Brooke brushed off the possible reproach without further reflection. She didn't care if Jessica didn't see her or if she was purposefully ignoring her. The Inorganic Chemistry final was Brooke's only concern right now.

Sheila stood up and explained the exam process for the final time.

"Hello, Everett students, and congratulations on making it to your last exam of the semester. In just a few minutes you will find your exam, as I know all of you have done at least three times now over the past week. They are categorized by major and then by class. Take as many exam booklets as you need." Sheila walked in front of the lectern smiling as she addressed the auditorium.

"Designated test taking rooms are marked with a sign on their door. If the room doesn't have a sign, it's not an exam room. Do not use cell phones, laptops, or any other electronic devices while you are in the room. Once you are finished with your exam you can leave the room, quietly please, and come back here to return your completed exam booklets and your exam copy. Exams must be returned by four, at the end of the allotted three hours."

Sheila paused before making the final required announcement that always made her feel uncomfortable.

"All of you have signed Everett's honor code contract and are expected to be familiar with its terms. You and every member of the Everett community are honor bound to abstain from cheating, plagiarizing, misrepresentation, stealing, and lying. Failure to comply with the honor code's terms during the exams and in all other endeavors is grounds for dismissal from the college. Failure to report a violation of the honor code is also grounds for dismissal."

With the formalities out of the way, Sheila leaned back against the table, brushing up against the Mathematics exam box, and crossed her arms across her mid-section.

"We have just another minute, so I want to wish all of you a wonderful winter break with your families," she said with a genuine smile, switching back to a more conversational tone. "I hope everyone is able to travel safely as planned before the storm hits. I know there are already flights being cancelled. Three feet of snow is the latest I heard we're expecting, starting late tonight…"

The church bell interrupted her mid-sentence. Students were out of their seats and heading toward the exam boxes before its vibrations cleared the air. The only thing separating all of them from the bliss of a five-week vacation and a carefree mind was the next three hours.

Brooke remained seated while students rose from their seats, lined up to get their exams and then filed out of the lecture hall.

"I'm going to miss your exercise classes. Can't wait for you to come back," Sheila said to Brooke as she approached the table, one of the very last students to do so. Sheila believed that it was students like Brooke who made Everett such an incredible place for everyone.

"Thanks," Brooke smiled. "I'm sure it will go by fast. I hope you enjoy your vacation…or, if you take one."

"Yes, I'll just be home decorating for Christmas and then entertaining family."

"Oh good," Brooke said.

"I just want to tell you that honestly I would prefer to leave out those final reminders about the Everett honor code. The mere act of saying it out loud diminishes what the code represents. A mutual confidence is required for the code to be meaningful. People act with honesty and integrity when trusted to do so. It's what makes Everett such an amazing institution."

"Of course," Brooke answered, she didn't care how Sheila felt about the honor code, yet she was amazed at the irony of Sheila's words considering what was about to happen. "I have to go."

"Of course. I'm so sorry to be talking to you when you need to focus on your exam. Good luck."

Brooke opened the section of exams under "Inorganic Chemistry II" and took out the test packet. She grabbed three exam booklets from the table and left the auditorium.

A few seconds later, she was alone, headed down a hallway lined with student art. She followed it through an overpass connecting the lecture hall to the three-storied academic building with the designated test taking rooms. Ahead of her, the last of the students pulled mahogany doors closed with bronze doorknobs. Everyone had settled in to hopefully prove how well they had mastered their subject. Brooke glanced behind her and then ducked into the ladies' room without being seen.

Inside the empty bathroom, she entered one of the stalls, locking the door behind her. She silently concealed the exam papers and booklets into her backpack. One of the signs advertising her exercise class was taped to the back of the door.

"Are you ready to change your life one muscle at a time?" it asked.

After using the facilities, she washed and dried her hands with paper towels, turning off the water with the paper towel in her hand to avoid germs. She cautiously went back out into the hallway. Instead of selecting one of the designated exam rooms, she marched down the empty corridor and exited the building through a side door.

Brooke made a beeline for her dorm amidst the swirling snow, ran up the front stairs, said a hurried hello to the young lady at the front desk and finally entered her own dorm room. She gently closed and locked her door, dropping her coat on the floor and stepping out of her boots as she moved toward her desk. She excitedly fired up her laptop, which seemed to be waiting conspiratorially along with all her chemistry books and papers.

"Holy Crap!" she said softly as she scanned through the exam questions. "Holy Crap!"

Nothing directly resembled the information in her notes; she was sure of this because her notes were ingrained in her memory. Did she have the right exam? Flipping back to page one, she confirmed that it was indeed Ms. MacIntyre's fall semester exam for Inorganic Chemistry II.

Frantically, she paged through her book looking for information that applied to the exam questions in front of her. Finding nothing, she turned to the internet and began typing in the key aspects of the questions, one by one. Finding the information she needed, she quickly assimilated the concepts, scrunching up her forehead as she fervently concentrated to assemble the correct answers. She was positive that much of the material had never been introduced in class. It was crazy. Ms. MacIntrye was possibly the worst professor she had ever known.

At three forty-five she had finished rechecking her exam for the second time, confident in her chemical configurations and perspective drawings. Marveling at the difficulty of the exam, she wondered how anyone else would achieve a half-decent grade. Surely it would be complete guesswork for her classmates, particularly if they gave a damn about the honor code. She returned everything to her backpack and then redressed in the coat and gloves that were still on the floor. Before leaving the room, she sat down on her bed, stretching her arms and back as she retraced her steps in her mind to make sure she wasn't forgetting anything. She ate two chocolate chip granola bars and a large cookie and drank a bottle of water. After a third check on the time, she headed back to the Preston Bates Lecture Hall.

Outside, the snow was still falling lightly, playfully being swirled around in the frigid air by the light wind, a teaser of what was soon to come. Brooke had just lifted her hood up over her head to protect her ears when she heard someone calling her name.

"Brooke! Hey!"

It was Ethan, walking with Robert in the direction of Ethan's dorm. Both were bundled in North Face winter coats, with hats and gloves, but she could recognize Ethan's build anywhere.

"No…not now," she said to herself.

With less than ten minutes to get back to the exam room, she couldn't stop to talk to them. Picking up speed, she kept walking, but turned to wave and blow Ethan a kiss. Robert pretended to catch it and feigned surprise and appreciation, while Ethan gave her a questioning look as to why she wasn't stopping.

Brooke laughed in their direction. As long as she kept smiling at them, it should be okay. She started to jog toward the lecture hall, away from Ethan and Robert.

***

Robert watched wistfully as Brooke's lithe body moved away from them. Brooke was amazingly uncomplicated for a woman. Not to mention beautiful, intelligent, and unpretentious. She seemed perfect. Robert was the one who had seen her first. What if he had introduced himself to her that day in the library, instead of watching Ethan make his move? Ethan was a lucky guy.

Robert had been thinking about Brooke almost incessantly. He was also upset with himself for wanting her, now there was no denying that was the case, because his best friend was madly in love with her. Bros before hos (his mother would not be pleased with that term). If only Brooke had a clone.

"I need to make a clean break with Jessica," he confessed.

"Really? You want to end things with her?" Ethan asked.

Robert didn't want to get into his reasons. He was not going to say anything negative about her. After all, he had dated her for long enough. She had changed or he had changed, or maybe he just couldn't see her personality clearly until now. He was tired of her snobbery and it particularly irked him when she insulted Brooke, which she did on a regular basis. Jessica's bad moods and demands were spiraling out of control and he had been avoiding her as much as possible. If only he hadn't stopped by her room today. What had he been thinking earlier when he mentioned that his sister's fiancé was going on vacation with his family? He was already nervous

226

before he knocked on her door, apprehensive that he would say the wrong thing, which was interesting because Jessica was the one who made outrageous comments on a regular basis and yet wasn't the least bit concerned about offending him or anyone else. That last encounter was when he knew for sure that he didn't want to deal with her anymore. He would be better off seeing someone more down to earth, someone who could make him more a "man of the people." Someone like Brooke.

"This would be the perfect time to end things, with both of us leaving for break, but I don't think I can tell her right now. She's been overly dramatic and I don't want to upset her." This was partly true, but honestly he was dreading her reaction far more than any emotional turmoil he might cause her.

Ethan didn't say anything disparaging; it was not his nature. More importantly, Robert could change his mind and then it would be really awkward if Ethan had voiced his true opinion of Jessica. He simply nodded, but his grin indicated that it was about time Robert had come to his senses.

***

Brooke repeated her earlier sequence of movements in reverse, entering through the side door of the academic building and walking straight to the bathroom. She came out of the bathroom carrying the exam booklets against her chest, traveled to the Preston-Bates lecture hall and then placed them in the appropriate boxes. She saw no one she recognized. Sheila was gone. In her place, an older woman in a flowing sweater with glasses around her neck smiled at each student and thanked them as they left. Brooke was glad that chemistry course was now officially a thing of the past, but it was frustrating that she had no longer had control over the outcome of her grade. The only proactive activity left was to pray for an A. But she didn't pray, she only worried, so her effective role in the process was complete.

Brooke remembered Ethan. She didn't want him wondering why she had not stopped to say hello. She had plenty of time before she had to teach at Resolution Fitness so she went directly to his dorm to see if he was there.

***

Just minutes earlier Jessica had also handed in her exam, after finally conceding to a three-hour saga of last ditch effort bullshit. Thank God she would never have to calculate the variable costs of production again. It was a huge relief that the semester was over. As she walked through Middleton Hall and across the snow-covered quads, she vowed that next semester she would go to all of her classes and do all of her assignments and never get so far behind again. She decided to cut down on caffeine and the ephedrine so that she could return to sleeping well at night. She promised herself she would start taking walks. She decided the best way to kick-off her Florida vacation would be to visit the spa near her grandparents' house. She would get a hot stone massage, a mud wrap, a manicure and pedicure. Just what she needed to emerge skinny, polished, buffed and better than new. Despite the jittery feeling coursing through her body, she felt hopeful that she would soon feel better. Imagining the luxurious sensation of a daily massage really helped her mood. In her mind she had seized the opportunity for a new healthy start.

As she rewrapped her scarf so that it completely covered her neck and protected her from the cold snow, she remembered her fight with Robert and decided it was time to make amends. She would find him now so that he could apologize to her and invite her to Aruba. She had no intention of saying yes. She wanted to go to Florida. She needed to decline his invitation in order to teach him a lesson about not taking her for granted. But on the way up the stone steps to Robert's dorm, she began to imagine sitting on the beach in Aruba while a tanned and muscular local delivered piña coladas to her cabana. She would get a much deeper tan in Aruba and it would be so much warmer than Florida. They had plenty of spas there as well. It was tempting. Perhaps she could fly to Aruba after a week in Florida.

She knocked on Robert's door and called his name while she removed her coat and gloves. He didn't answer. After waiting a few seconds, she knocked again rapidly and called his name more loudly.

"Robert. It's Jessica. Are you in there?"

She knocked again, called his name and waited two seconds.

"Robert. We need to talk." Her voice became increasingly irritated. It drove her crazy if he wasn't around when she needed him.

***

Ethan heard Jessica in the hallway. He was familiar with the sequence of events that would unfurl if Robert wasn't where Jessica expected him to be. First she would knock, then call, then bang on his door while yelling his name. Inevitably she would end up at Ethan's room to find out if he knew where Robert was and what he was doing and why he didn't answer his phone.

Ethan understood that Robert didn't want to deal with Jessica right now. He didn't blame him for that. If he were in Robert's shoes, he would grab a beer and barricade himself in his closet until he was sure Jessica was gone. He stepped out of his room. What were friends for if not crap like this?

"Robert's not here," he said in a particularly kind voice, unable to look Jessica in the eye because he was lying.

"We had a little argument and I really need to talk to him," Jessica explained. "Where is he? Do you know where he went?"

Ethan looked up and saw Brooke walking toward them. Seeing her completely brightened his mood. He couldn't help but smile, knowing she was there to see him.

"Hey, don't take it personally," he said. "My girlfriend came out of her dorm not twenty minutes ago. She saw me and then starting running in the opposite direction. That's exactly what happened."

He tried to look stern, but a grin formed and Brooke could tell he was joking. "But apparently she missed me and couldn't stay away. What were you running to anyway? Were you doing something you shouldn't have been doing?"

Ethan wasn't concerned about Brooke's earlier behavior, only curious as to why she had not stopped to say hello. He was just trying to lighten the uncomfortable gloom Jessica had created and to change the subject from Robert's whereabouts to anything else.

Jessica seemed desperate, but maybe he was imagining it just because he knew something she didn't know, that Robert was purposefully avoiding her, and felt slightly sorry for her.

***

Listening carefully to Ethan's words, Brooke was mentally begging him to be quiet.

"So, are you going to tell us where you were going in such a hurry?" Ethan teased.

He needs to shut up about seeing me coming out of my dorm. If Jessica puts two and two together, she would know that I should have been in the same place as her twenty minutes ago, a designated exam room, not coming out of my dorm. Unless... unless she never even saw me in the lecture hall before the exam. And, it's feasible that I could have finished the exam early, handed it in, come back to my dorm to get something and then left again quickly. I probably have nothing to worry about. But then, why is she glaring at me? She must know. Oh shit. She knows.

Brooke studied Jessica for clues to her state of mind and what she saw was not reassuring. Jessica looked openly hostile. A swell of urgency rose below Brooke's composed features. She was convinced that Jessica knew she had cheated.

***

Ethan sensed some strong tension. Maybe it was a hormone thing. Jessica was glaring at Brooke, it was clear to him that Jessica was trying to intimidate his girlfriend, but Brooke was staring back with a fierce intensity, as if studying her. Jessica wasn't showing any signs of leaving and Ethan wanted her out of there so he didn't have to keep making excuses for Robert. The only thing he could think of to do was to offer everyone a drink.

"How about a Captain Morgan and Coke then?" he suggested to Jessica, nodding his head in encouragement. "To celebrate the end of the semester. I even have diet Coke. Maybe even something cute to stir it with." He thought that would cheer her up and then she could leave in a good mood.

He headed into his room to make the drink for Jessica.

"I know you won't want to have a drink before your class, but I won't stop you if you change your mind," he said to Brooke as he bent down to open his refrigerator and grab a diet Coke. "Did you hear that the Governor of Massachusetts issued a driving ban from ten P.M. tonight until ten P.M. tomorrow?"

Ethan's television had been tuned to the weather channel all day so he could listen to the storm hype. He had planned to go skiing tomorrow morning with some friends before returning to Rhode Island. It might be the most amazing soft powder he had ever experienced, or, if the forecasters were correct, it would be such a forceful blizzard that the slopes would actually have to close. He was also hanging around in order to have one more night with Brooke before they both left for winter break. He had invited her to his house several times and she had said non-committedly that she would call him when she got home and they would work out the days. He knew by now it was best to be patient with her, but he was worried that if she didn't agree to some definite dates soon his mother would be calling her directly to extend her own invitation. Brooke had not invited him to her house in Connecticut, but he wasn't going to let that bother him. Much.

"You know those weather guys can barely contain their excitement because their audience went from a few thousand viewers to everyone on the East Coast just for the next few days. Listen to them."

Ethan turned up the volume, guiding their attention to the television.

"There is no way that New England is not going to have a white Christmas this year! Storm Connor will deliver an expected thirty inches of snow across the area. The winds are going to pick up and they aren't expected to settle down for a couple of days here. It's going to be a major impact event. Thousands of flights are going to be cancelled. We'll have meteorologists on the ground and meteorologists in house to keep you posted every step of the way."

"And that is the result of global warming people!" Tom Andres exclaimed. He was passing by and heard the news report. Tom had done an internship in Washington D.C. with the Democratic

Committee on Environmental Concerns last summer. He got them coffee, typed their minutes, researched what they told him to find, and handed out hardcopies. He also listened and learned intently, capturing every nuance in the meetings. He tucked his head inside Ethan's room to show off his knowledge.

"Global warming is the opposite of having a blizzard," Jessica shot back, momentarily distracted from her troubles by the opportunity to correct someone.

"Not so, my dear. That is the common misconception. It all comes down to atmospheric physics. The warmer the atmosphere, the more moisture it can hold. Then, when the temperature is cold enough for snow, there is way more precipitation to dump. Less overall snowfall with each year, but more massive blizzards. Oh yea—I heard they found your car trashed somewhere out in the boonies."

"You heard right," Jessica sighed.

Brooke looked down at her feet at the mention of the Volvo. She didn't know exactly what she was going to do about her current situation, but she would figure it out. And it had to be soon. There was no chance of allowing Jessica to ruin everything for her.

CHAPTER TWENTY-SIX

Sarah was more than ready to go home. With hundreds of flights being cancelled in anticipation of the storm, she had been checking the status of her flight every thirty minutes for the past few hours. She did not want to get all the way out to the airport and then have to turn around and come back. On what would have been her final check before she headed out, she heard what she had been expecting all along.

"Flight 452 from Boston-Manchester airport to Raleigh is cancelled. You can try and rebook for Sunday."

She called her parents to let them know about the delay and said she would keep them posted. Then she proceeded to unpack some of her bags. It could be a few days. What on earth would she do? Most people had already left campus in anticipation of the storm.

For the first time this year she had more time than she knew what to do with. There was no homework, no hours scheduled at the front desk, no soccer practice. She was supposed to be maintaining a specific training schedule for soccer on her own during the break. Which meant she should probably go for a run now because, if the weather forecasters were correct, and they seemed completely positive this go around, she wouldn't be able to run outside for quite some time after today. She preferred running outside to running on the track any day. Maybe she could call Brooke and they could do a long run. Brooke was still here, Sarah was certain, because she said she had to teach a class tonight before she could leave for vacation.

She suddenly recalled her previous promises to take one of Brooke's exercise classes before the end of the semester. She would go to Brooke's class tonight! She was so glad to have remembered. The class was in half an hour, there was still time. She quickly threw on a t-shirt and some running pants, and then a sweatshirt. Then she second guessed her choice of outfits, perhaps everyone else would be wearing some special yoga type clothes. Whenever she did yoga with her soccer team, her shirt rode up and exposed her stomach every time she did a forward fold. That wasn't going to happen tonight, she would be better prepared. Pulling the sweatshirt and t-shirt back off over her head, she found a more fitted top from her dresser and put that on instead. She grabbed her phone and called Brooke, hoping she hadn't left for class yet so that she could ride with her. If Sarah had to take the bus all the way there, then forget it. Yes, she promised, but she had to be reasonable. Besides, she would probably arrive too late if she took the bus.

***

Jessica had left a bunch of messages for Robert and he still hadn't responded. She had two drinks with Ethan to celebrate the semester's end. *Endured* two drinks was a more accurate description because Brooke was hanging around like a clueless, useless loser and staring at her. Perhaps Brooke was finally trying to pick up clues on how to dress. Jessica hadn't noticed Brooke in the auditorium earlier. As far as Jessica knew, she hadn't seen Brooke in weeks, and she wanted to keep it that way.

Why doesn't she just disappear? She doesn't deserve Ethan. She's a nobody. What kind of psycho just exercises or studies every minute of the day? And Robert obviously finds her attractive, too; he's mentioned it a few times. How can they possibly like her?

There was no point in hanging out in Ethan's room any longer so she left the Hatfield dorm and headed back to South Vernon. She had planned to leave for winter break in the late morning. She thought she would be spending her last night with Robert, but now she didn't even know if he was still on campus.

He has some nerve if he left without saying goodbye to me! Why isn't he returning my calls?

234

Inside her room Jessica turned on the television and opened a suitcase to pack. Tired and lonely, but also on edge and just not well, she half listened to the growing excitement and information about Storm Connor. The storm coverage was on every major channel. Unsure if it would help her or make her feel worse, she brewed an espresso while periodically checking her messages, anxious to hear from Robert. She received a group text from Brittany telling everyone goodbye and Happy Holidays. Brittany had also been planning to stay through the weekend but her message said she managed to get an earlier flight out to the West Coast so she could leave before the storm hit.

"My boots!"

Brittany had failed to return the brown heeled dress boots that she borrowed a few weeks ago. Jessica flew across the hall in her socks and knocked on Brittany's door. When no one answered, Jessica rattled the handle and found it locked.

Just like Robert. Is everyone purposefully avoiding me? she asked with irritation, although she didn't seriously think that could ever happen to her.

"Brittany." She tapped her knuckles impatiently against the wood. "Brittany!" she yelled more loudly.

Meghan came out in the hall from the next room.

"Oh, hi Jessica. You're still here, too?"

"Has Brittany left? I will be furious if she left without giving my boots back."

"She just left like a minute ago. You just missed her. I think she's going to get her car and move it closer to the dorm because she has a lot of stuff to take to the airport, but I'm not sure. She had a bunch of suitcases with her when she left so she might not be coming back. You can probably still catch her before she leaves. If you hurry."

Jessica started dialing Brittany's number to stop her. No answer and the call went to voicemail.

"Brittany! It's Jessica. Do not leave campus yet," she shouted into the phone. "Do not leave campus. I need my brown Cole Haan boots! Why is all of this happening to me? Ahhhh!" The last

235

exclamations were not intended to be part of Brittany's voicemail, but were included because she was screaming them before she hung up.

I'll bet she's not answering because she's got them in her suitcase, Jessica thought, her temper flaring.

With determination she rushed back to her room and tossed her phone on her bed. She grabbed her fleece-lined boots and shoved her feet inside forcefully, then stormed out of her room without taking the time to gather a coat or to stop and lock her door.

I will get those boots back if it's the last thing I do!

No one saw her run down the hall, down the stairs, out the front door and into the initial stage of the storm, wearing only her thin fuchsia colored sweater over a white camisole. Once outside she was immediately sorry she didn't take the extra few seconds to grab a coat. The sky was unusually dark already and it was colder than she remembered from even an hour ago. The snow was being tossed around every which way by the swirling wind. A feeling of vulnerability overcame her when she realized that in her haste she had also left her phone behind.

Her plan was to catch Brittany getting into her car before she left, get her boots and then have Brittany drive her back to the dorm. Huffing and puffing, she made her way as fast as she could across the grass toward the student parking lot. Running felt terrible and unnatural, and provided a temporary distraction from the cold. Her sexy lace lingerie was no sports bra and she was uncomfortable. As she got closer to the parking area, she started scanning for any signs of a vehicle about to leave. She gasped as she slowed from a jog to a walk to catch her breath. Each intake of the sharp, cold air seared her lungs. Unable to suppress a cough, she produced a coarse barking sound that helped to clear her chest but hurt like hell.

Not a second too late, when she was almost across the street, she saw the shadow of a dark SUV coming straight at her with its headlights off.

"Idiot! Turn your lights on!" she yelled between hacking coughs.

***

Brooke was just pulling out of the parking lot on her way to teach at Resolution Fitness. Her thoughts were so consumed with Jessica, and the obstacle she presented, that she forgot to turn on the Jeep's headlights.

There might be nothing to worry about, but if I'm wrong I could be expelled from school. I'm certain she would report me. She's never seemed to like me. And I have no idea why, I've never done anything to her. Well, I did mess up her car, but she doesn't know that. I need to take care of Jessica tonight. The more time that goes by, the greater the chance of her exposing me, and that's not going to happen. Of course it would be her word against mine, but I can't take the chance.

Her thoughts circled around and around again.

Mr. Wilhelm practically idolized me, and yet I wasn't willing to take a chance with him. Jessica doesn't even like me. I'm not leaving Everett. I belong here. I need to solve this problem as soon as I get back from the gym.

Almost too late she saw a dim figure starting to cross the road. It was then, as she slammed on the brakes that she realized the Jeep's headlights were off. A flick of a lever illuminated the space on the road directly in front of her and the figure was revealed to be none other than Jessica, her lips forming the word "Idiot" while large snowflakes fell on and around her. Brooke was initially surprised, and then amazed as it dawned on her that things always had a way of working out. A golden opportunity had presented itself and she was going to pounce on it. Without hesitation, she rolled down the passenger side window and leaned across the seat to get Jessica's attention.

"Jessica!" Brooke yelled. "Get in! I need your help with something."

***

Jessica recognized Brooke's voice first, and then the Jeep. She realized with a deep irritation that Brooke had issued more of a demand than a request.

Well, what do you know? Brooke is the idiot who almost ran me over. Who does she think she is driving Ethan's SUV like she owns

237

it! I can't stand this girl. I hope Ethan comes to his senses over the break. What the hell does she want anyway? If Brittany leaves and I don't get my boots back because of Brooke that will just be it!

Jessica continued to look around, frantically searching for Brittany's car in the darkening night.

"Get in!" Brooke yelled again through the open window.

The wind was cutting through Jessica's thin sweater as if she was completely naked. Now that she had stopped trying to run, she was so cold it seriously hurt. She rewrapped her arms around her chest in a futile effort to keep in some of her body heat.

I can't believe I'm out here looking for a car and freezing, again! Well maybe Brooke practically running me over is a good thing. She can finally put herself to good use and drive me around the parking lot until I find Brittany and at least I'll be out of the cold.

Jessica opened the passenger door and lifted herself up and into the front seat. The heat was welcoming. She slammed the door, looked down at her hands, and placed them between her jean clad legs to warm them up. Out of her peripheral vision, she noticed Brooke taking something out of her gym bag. She started to turn toward her. Brooke was grinning.

What the hell is she doing with that creepy smile on her face?

That was Jessica's last conscious thought.

***

Brooke pulled the trigger on her Taser. She directed twenty seconds worth of electricity into Jessica's muscle fibers. The currents incapacitated her, overwhelming her nervous system. Jessica's body contracted uncontrollably, violently, as her startled eyes locked with Brooke's. Her mouth opened, producing an incoherent noise. Giddy with excitement, Brooke released the Taser and redirected her focus to the road. Jessica slumped over, her eyes closed, and her head made a *thunk*! as it hit the passenger-side window. Brooke reached her arm over, felt the Taser make contact with Jessica's chest area, and pulled the trigger again, all the while keeping her eyes on the road. She maintained pressure on the stun gun's lever for what seemed like an impossibly long time, which she counted. She watched with fascination out of the corner of her eye, as much as possible while driving, as Jessica's body visibly tensed all over and then collapsed again.

She put the Taser down and reached into her bag again, feeling around until her fingers located the smooth steel of her thermos. She knew it was there, more than half full of chloroform, but just had to make sure. She would use it when they parked at the gym, until then, the stun gun was taking care of everything just fine. She turned up the frequency of the windshield wipers because the snow hitting her windshield was making it hard to see. Brooke's cell phone rang but she chose to ignore it; she already had enough going on inside the car. Jessica was insufficiently dressed for the weather. What was she doing in the parking lot without a coat and gloves? It was almost surreal that Jessica had walked right out in front of her. It was an incredible opportunity. And she was so glad she had the Taser.

Brooke felt completely elated and excited. But because Jessica had appeared so unexpectedly, she didn't have a well thought out plan. Yet. She had been dying to use the Taser on a person ever since she took it from her uncle's police cruiser, but didn't know when she would have the chance. She wished Jessica was more muscular. Did anyone have less muscle tone than Jessica? But because of Brooke's cheating dilemma, Jessica was the one person she most needed to disappear. She wanted to pull over and examine her but, unfortunately, she didn't have time without being late to teach her class. There was nothing worse than an instructor who waltzed in late with a whole room of people waiting on her. It was just rude and unprofessional.

Jessica had not stirred, but at the first stoplight on Ash Street, Brooke tased her again to make sure she stayed unconscious a bit longer, watching in fascination as her muscles contracted involuntarily and then became visibly rigid. When the electricity stopped flowing, her body settled heavily back against the door. The weight of her head was supported against the car window; her chin had fallen forward, almost to her shoulder. Brooke looked quickly around the outside of the car, but there were no other cars nearby. It would be hard for anyone to see what was happening anyway because of the Jeep's tinted windows and the heavily falling snow. Brooke turned back to Jessica to study her body and palpate the muscles in her neck and arms. Jessica's flesh felt soft, yielding under the pressure of Brooke's fingers. She appeared to be unconscious. Then the light turned green and Brooke had to accelerate. Her cell phone rang again, and again she ignored it.

She leaned toward Jessica and put her fingers on her neck to feel for a pulse. She was curious about Jessica's heart rate, expecting it to be extremely subdued, but to her surprise, she felt nothing. She repositioned her fingers and pressed harder, then lightly, moving to several spots on Jessica's neck. Nothing. She released her fingers and tried again, looking into the rearview mirror to ensure there were no cars waiting behind her. She stared at Jessica in amazement.

What the hell happened?

Brooke had extensively researched the effects of the Taser since she first obtained it last Thanksgiving. Everything she had learned indicated that it would be highly unusual for someone to die from it, even if it was used repeatedly within a short timeframe. It took 0.1 amps of electricity to stop a heart and a stun gun couldn't deliver that much. She knew it could set off irregular heart rhythms, which could be life threatening, but there had to be a significant underlying condition, like high concentrations of stimulants in the blood. The only cases on record where a relatively young person had died involved addicts, with systems full of cocaine, crystal meth, or other strong stimulants. She didn't think Jessica was using those kinds of drugs. Almost every time Brooke had seen Jessica, she had a coffee or energy drink in hand, unless she was having an alcoholic beverage, but Brooke didn't think that alone would be enough to contribute to her death.

Did she have a cold recently? Decongestants contained ephedrine, which could also cause heart problems, but only when taken long term, so that didn't seem likely either. She remembered Jessica's glassy eyes and dilated pupils from earlier. She must have been taking something. Brooke was amazed, and incredibly curious as to what had contributed to Jessica's fatal arrhythmia. She would need to take a sample of myocardial cells from Jessica's heart to view under a microscope. She expected the contours of the cells' nuclei to be stretched and narrowed because of the electricity, but it would be fun to confirm. That was one thing to look forward to.

Brooke experienced a split second of panic as she recalled the final moments of various animals. Their bodies convulsed and then released just about everything with a disturbing eruption of sound and odors.

Oh please, not in Ethan's car. How would I deal with the mess?

Brooke quickly leaned to her right and slid her fingers under Jessica's thighs, moving them over and around the passenger seat. The leather was only damp from melting snowflakes and she smelled nothing unpleasant. She sighed with relief that Ethan's car had been spared, and then with regret that Jessica was already dead. It had been too sudden. It was the second time she had caused something like this to happen and then essentially missed it. She marveled at the coincidence. Her first undertaking had also been ridiculously easy and had accomplished a remarkably similar goal, eliminating the only person who could mar her perfect school record.

***

That same night that Mr. Wilhelm had found her operating on a live cat, Brooke had snuck back into the lab in the cover of darkness. Cedarhurst was not high profile enough to have surveillance cameras around the academic buildings and logging in to her father's computer had provided her with the necessary entrance codes.

She went to Mr. Wilhelm's office, the same place she would be meeting him in just a few hours, and found his "Science!" mug, cleaned and ready to be filled with his next brew. She placed a few colorless, odorless drops of her own chemical concoction into the bottom. Her extra-curricular experiments in the chemistry labs paying off in an unexpected way. Then she went back to her room and slept.

241

She arrived ahead of time for their meeting the next morning, feeling anxious and excited. She could hardly wait to see what would happen. But Mr. Wilhelm had arrived even earlier than usual and the only surprise for her that morning was finding him already slumped over, face on his desk, shocked eyes wide open, and his "Science!" mug half empty. At seventy years old a heart attack was not all that suspicious, particularly in a relatively sedentary person.

It was Brooke that had called 911. It was Brooke that everyone worried about. How horrible for her to have walked in on such an unfortunate and tragic scene. What an unexpected and terrible shock! It was no wonder that she felt the need to transfer and have a fresh start. How many times had her father referred to the incident as "unfortunate timing" on her part? Little did he know how accurate that was, but for an entirely different reason. She had missed watching Mr. Wilhelm die by mere minutes.

Her plan had been genius, especially with the limited amount of time she had to put it together, but it had done nothing to satiate her burning desire to watch death occur or to get her hands inside a human body. She could not wait to be a surgeon and operate. There would always be at least two fascinating outcomes, active involvement in perpetuating life, or witness to death. She had missed the opportunity to be a careful observer of death, again, but she reminded herself that there were plenty of other things she could do.

This was meant to be, she thought, glancing at Jessica's body with renewed confidence, *my very own cadaver*. She had a bone saw and dissecting tools in her closet, but wouldn't be able to get them until after her class.

Brooke turned off Ash Street and traveled the last three blocks to the gym's parking lot. She parked the Jeep in an unlit area as far from the other cars as possible, it's where the employees were supposed to park anyway even though they never did when it was cold. She was relatively secluded there; the closest car was across the lot. She turned off the engine and glanced around. People were coming to the gym despite the weather, or maybe because they knew the storm was coming and the gym might be closed tomorrow and possibly even the day after that. She watched as a car arrived and its driver went running toward the gym, head down. No one was going to see her.

Now she could give Jessica her full attention, but she didn't have much time. She checked for a pulse again, this time putting her hand up underneath Jessica's shirt against her bare skin right under the silky line of her lace bra. She felt nothing. She put her hand and then her ear in front of Jessica's mouth to listen and feel for signs of breathing. There were no signs of life. She checked the clock on the Jeep's console, looked out the front windshield to keep watch, and formed a plan.

Okay, step one, here goes, she said to prepare herself.

From inside the car, Brooke tugged and lifted and yanked Jessica's body across and then through the center of the seats, using all the muscles she had developed from hundreds of workouts to heave and wrench her into the back of the car. She grasped her sweater and shirt, her arm, her shoulder. She pushed against her back and lifted her torso. It was an ungraceful process and it was hard for her to believe how heavy Jessica seemed. The muscles in Brooke's shoulders and neck strained with the effort. She had to twist from the waist, using only her upper body strength to get the job done. She was used to challenging her muscles, but until now it had always been without compromising her form, not the anything goes type of effort she was currently executing. However, in less than a minute, Jessica's body lay in a heap on the floor behind the passenger seat. Her lower half tumbled on top of her head into a position that would never occur if she were alive.

Brooke got out of the car and opened the back door. The wind lifted and tossed her ponytail into the air. She hurriedly unfolded Ethan's stadium blanket and spread it over Jessica's body. She pulled the edges of the blanket down around her and checked to make sure that she was completely covered on every side. She moved quickly because Brooke was always early, she was never late, and she had to get her class started in a few minutes.

CHAPTER TWENTY-SEVEN

"Hi!" Brooke greeted Jacob, one of the fitness trainers, as she came out of the cold and into the gym. Jack gestured hello, returning her huge smile with one of his own. He was just finishing up a workout with one of his regular clients.

"We might have to cancel our session tomorrow," he said to the solid-looking man who was gulping down a bottle of water. "I'll shoot you an email if the gym has to close. We'll know by tonight and if I was a betting man, I'd bet we're going to have to close. It's supposed to be a hell of a blizzard."

Brooke heard him and wondered if her parents would be able to come and pick her up this weekend as planned, or if they would be delayed by the storm.

Her first stop was the employee room to punch her time card. Then she hustled to the fitness studio. The room was full of flushed faces, some caused by the outside cold and some from warming up on cardio machines; they were all happy to see her. Coats and scarves and boots lined the perimeter of the room in small discarded piles. Brooke knew she had a good following based on the number of people that came out for her class even with the storm approaching.

"Are you going to be here over the winter vacation?" someone asked her as she hooked a microphone on to her shirt. They knew that she was a student at Everett and that most of the students took off for winter break.

"This is my last class for the next three weeks. I'll be back after New Year's day."

She repeated this statement again to the class after turning on her microphone so that everyone could hear. "There's going to be a reduced class schedule during that time. You can call the Exercise Hotline to find out the times and the teachers. Now let's get started." Brooke smiled, she was happiest when she was exercising. And when she had something special to look forward to.

An energetic beat started to play and she led the class through warm up exercises consisting of squats, lunges, and large flowing movements.

"We're going to start by isolating the gluteal muscles with a bridge series. Lie down on your backs. Move your hand weights to your side where you can reach them. First set with knees in parallel. Starting with a Kegel, connect your lower abs and imprint your spine to the floor, press your ribcage down. Now contract your glutes. Remember that what you're keeping still, your stabilizing muscles, is as important as what you're moving. First set..." She was just about to start counting when she happened to look toward the entrance; she raised her eyebrows and her face registered surprise at who was standing there.

It was Sarah—she was looking around for an open space. She saw Brooke looking at her, grinned and waved her hand. She silently mouthed the words "I'm here!" and then after looking around again, put down a mat and got into position on her back. A young woman begrudgingly moved over a few feet on the floor to accommodate the additional body. Brooke was really happy she had come. She quickly changed her plan for the class to incorporate work that would be most beneficial to Sarah, who already had very tight glutes and hamstrings.

After class, there were a bunch of people wanting to thank Brooke, ask her questions or to wish her a "Happy Holiday." Brooke glanced over the crowd a few times in order to smile apologetically to Sarah, who she knew was waiting patiently for her.

"You made it. I'm so glad you came," Brooke exclaimed when Sarah was finally one of the last people in the room.

"Yes! Oh my gosh. That was really good. I could totally feel it. My arms were killing me. And I learned so much. I loved how you explained exactly which muscles were firing and how they were all connected."

"Oh good. Probably not your typical soccer workout, right?"

"No, it wasn't. Very different, and very good. Just what I needed."

Brooke was glad that Sarah appreciated her class.

"So my flight got cancelled and I realized I finally had a chance to try your class. It was totally last minute. I tried to call you for a ride, so just ignore like three missed calls from me. Someone was leaving right when I was calling you so they ended up dropping me off here. But I need to get a ride back with you. Is that okay? You have Ethan's car, right? "

"Absolutely. Yes."

"Good! I did not want to take that bus anywhere tonight."

"I'm so, so thrilled that you came." She gave Sarah a quick hug. She was happy, but she also realized that things had just become a bit more complicated, considering Jessica's lifeless form lay heaped in Ethan's car.

"I just have to punch out my time card."

Brooke was feeling ecstatically happy. Jessica's body presented an unlimited educational opportunity. She was looking forward to it so much that she partly wanted to put it off and savor the anticipation.

"Can you go out? For some reason I always crave hot chocolate after a workout in the winter, but I can never get it because I have to rush back to the dorm. There's no rush tonight. I have time. Do you want to go?"

"Sure. I have nothing planned for the next two days. I would love to go. I wonder if the storm has gotten worse."

"Probably. Okay, I'll be right back, just have to punch out, and then I'll meet you in the locker room to get changed. I'm going to take a quick shower. I'm not stepping outside all sweaty tonight!"

"How about The Perk House?" Sarah asked ten minutes later as they walked briskly to the Jeep,

"Anywhere is fine. I just want to do something different and celebrate a little. Exams are over! Yay! No more chemistry class from hell!"

Their boots lifted tufts of fluffy snow off the ground with each step. The snow was falling in thicker heavier flakes and the wind had picked up noticeably. The Jeep looked lonely with no other cars parked nearby. Brooke clicked the key fob twice so that both her door and Sarah's door unlocked.

"Why are you parked so far away?"

"The employees are supposed to park here, but it looks like I'm the only one following the rules."

Sarah laughed and quickly closed her door, shivered, and then wiped the snow off her face with her gloved hand, which was also wet and didn't help much. She turned and saw what looked like a huge mound of blankets in the back seat.

"I'd like to be wearing a blanket right now," she said.

"Don't touch them, they're really dirty," Brooke said calmly.

Please don't touch it, Sarah. Please, please just turn around.

"Can you turn the radio on, Sarah? I want to hear the latest on the storm."

Brooke started the car, and a blast of cold air hit them before it turned warm. She turned on the headlights, the windshield wipers, the defoggers and then the seat warmers. She turned to look out the back window as she reversed, simultaneously blocking Sarah's view of the back seat area. As Sarah familiarized herself with the stereo system, Brooke peered behind the passenger seat so that she would know exactly what Sarah had seen. It looked exactly like Sarah had described it, a mound of blankets. Brooke turned back around as the news came on.

"This is going to be a weather event for the history books. The heaviest accumulation is expected to start very soon. A blizzard watch is now in effect for portions of Massachusetts, Rhode Island, Connecticut, New Hampshire, and Vermont. This could paralyze this region of the country for days. Widespread power outages are possible."

"No," moaned Sarah. "Why couldn't New England have waited to have its blizzard tomorrow night so I could be in North Carolina wearing shorts?!"

"Shorts? It's that warm?"

"My brother wears shorts year round. He doesn't even own pants," Sarah informed her.

"Can you imagine if the power went out at Everett? The dorms would be so creepy in total darkness."

"They probably have generators or something, don't you think?" Sarah asked.

"I have no idea."

The Perk House served specialty coffee drinks and desserts all day; beer, wine, and appetizers in the evenings. The upstairs had armchairs and couches for lounging and studying, and an abundance of outlets for charging laptops. Some students spent entire days here instead of in the library. The café was always busy, even on the last day of the semester with a major storm brewing. It was a short drive from the gym, and Brooke was grateful to find a spot out front that didn't require parallel parking.

Once inside, Brooke took out her phone, pulled off one glove with her teeth, and hit the contact button.

"I have to get a pair of those gloves with the pads on the fingers so I can work my phone. I need to give Ethan a call. It will only take a second."

"Ethan is still here? Oh…of course he's still here. You have his car."

"He was going to stay and ski this weekend with some friends. He said if they can get to the ski slopes it will be amazing, but who knows how difficult it will be to drive tomorrow. One second," – then, to Ethan– "Hi. I'm going to get a hot chocolate with a friend and then I'll be back after that. It's exciting to be out with the storm coming. Just wanted to let you know." Then she laughed. "Yes, it's Sarah. I'll see you soon."

She hung up and turned to Sarah.

"He was joking that my friend better be the type that wears a sports bra. Let's go."

"I have to say I'm intrigued by your relationship." Sarah offered tentatively. "He seems crazy about you. Don't you like him?"

"Sure. I like him. What's not to like?" Brooke answered.

The end of the semester combined with the approaching blizzard had created an excitement that Sarah and Brooke could almost feel inside the Perk House. Hot drinks and alcohol were more desirable with the snow falling. Brooke ordered a hot chocolate with a warm cinnamon chip scone. Sarah asked for the same and then they waited for a table to open up. After a short wait, a couple vacated a table adjacent to the giant window in the front of the store and Brooke and Sarah took their seats. A nearby fireplace emanated heat and a comforting glow and only a pane of glass separated them and the cozy interior from the outside elements.

"I love seeing the snowflakes under the street lights. It's so pretty. See how they look when they pass through the light? Magical," Brooke commented. "It feels like Christmas Eve for some reason. Like we're waiting for something big to happen because of the storm."

"I would be half way to Raleigh by now if my flight hadn't been cancelled. I'm disappointed, but this is pretty. I'll try and appreciate it," Sarah declared.

"So your flight got cancelled last minute?"

"Yes. I rebooked for Sunday, hopefully that won't get cancelled, too. What a pain. My grandmother bought this plane ticket for me as an early Christmas present because I told them last month that I wasn't coming home. The soccer team has to be back two days after Christmas anyway. Last year I drove home with a freshman from Raleigh. I didn't know him. He just posted on the ride board that he was going and I gave him gas money. Let's just say he was socially awkward. It was the longest, most uncomfortable ride ever, and I said I wasn't doing it again; I was going to stay here for Christmas. I told them they could come here. So my grandmother bought me the plane ticket. Not working out too well for me yet."

A mammoth truck with a snow plow passed by outside the window. The whoosh of its engine, the sound of its heavy metal plow on the cement and its slowly spinning light were somehow lulling. Brooke and Sarah watch as it pushed a growing mountain of snow down the street, past Ethan's car, and then angled its load off to the side into an empty lot.

"Oh my gosh." Brooke started laughing, she was relaxed. "I just remembered something. I have to tell you about this party I went to when I was in high school." She took a sip of her drink before she continued. "I was at a party with about fifteen other people from my school. No parents were home, obviously. It started snowing while we were there, hard, or maybe it was already snowing. Anyway, the whole time we were at the party we could see these yellow lights spinning around and around outside on the road, a ways from the house. People kept saying 'They're really plowing those roads well tonight!' I can't tell you how many times one of us at the party commented on all the plowing, because it was sort of far from the house and we couldn't see it well. We were having a great time inside. Well, the first person to leave the house went outside about midnight, then came rushing back in and yelled 'All our cars are gone!'" Brooke had to laugh. "We thought the tow trucks were snow plows and for hours we basically watched as all our cars were towed, one by one, while we were like 'they're really plowing your street so well...duh.' It was hysterical, not at first, but later, once we had our cars back."

"Why did they tow your cars anyway?"

"Oh...because you're not allowed to park on the side of the road when it's snowing hard. The plows can't get through."

"That makes sense. That must have been funny...after. I can't believe you didn't know what was happening. How was it that none of you knew what was going on right under your noses?"

"I don't know." Brooke thought for a second. "I guess that's how it is when you have a preconceived notion about something, or someone. You can't see beyond what you think you know. You only see what you want to see, until you have no choice but to face the truth."

"Yes," Sarah said. "That's a good point. And sometimes the truth hurts, right?"

"It definitely hurt when we had each had to pay to get our parents' cars back from the towing place."

A television in the upper corner of the seating area was tuned to local news. A perfectly groomed woman with voluminous blonde hair was commenting enthusiastically on the storm from inside the studio.

"The weather conditions are lining up just as we expected and will deteriorate rapidly. Winds coming down from Canada may be in excess of fifty miles per hour. Visibility is going to be very tough. The Governor of Massachusetts has implemented a driving ban from ten tonight until ten P.M. tomorrow. All of Interstate 95 from Rhode Island into New Hampshire will close to all but essential traffic. This will allow the trucks to get out on the streets and do their jobs, get the roads cleared. Train and bus routes will also be cancelled across New England. This is going to be a huge storm, and a historic one for this time of year. Let's turn to Tony in Manchester, bringing you the latest out on the streets."

The picture on the screen changed to show a guy outside with a bright yellow ski jacket and hat, snowflakes whipping around his head.

"Here in New Hampshire we're already feeling those winds, up to twenty miles per hour, but it's going to get much worse. You can see it's snowing here." Tony gestured behind him so that the audience could fully appreciate that it was indeed snowing. "It's been snowing lightly for a few hours, but that will change very quickly. The snowfall will increase dramatically and the winds could reach sixty miles an hour, maybe more. It's going to be a blizzard. If you aren't already home, you need to get there and stay there. We'll keep you posted as Storm Connor arrives. Lindsey...back to you."

Sarah tilted her cup back to savor the last drops of warm, sugary liquid.

"It's so cozy in here. But we should go, Ethan is waiting for you," Sarah reminded her.

"Okay," Brooke agreed. She was oddly relaxed and excited about the prospect of dissecting Jessica's body. She just needed to figure out where to take it. She couldn't very well throw Jessica over her shoulder and head into to her dorm room. Just as she was about to rise, her phone rang. It was a number she didn't recognize.

"Just a sec, I'm going to answer this. I'm not sure who it is, but it's local."

"Hello."

"Hello. Is this Brooke Walton?"

"Yes. May I help you?"

"This is Professor Fred Herbert. I'm the head of the Academic Review board. How are you this evening?"

"I'm fine. Thanks." But suddenly Brooke wasn't so fine anymore. She could sense her heart rate rising. She didn't know a Professor Herbert, and she had a few good reasons to be very concerned about his call. Had Jessica called him already? Was she about to be expelled?

"Brooke, are you familiar with the Peak of Everett award?"

"No. I don't think I've heard of it." She was confused. It didn't sound like anything related to cheating, or stealing, or Jessica's dead body being in Ethan's car.

"It's a great honor. Everett's faculty picks one person from the entire student body who will receive the award each semester. The student we choose exemplifies the best that our College has to offer in spirit, leadership, and integrity, and, of course, academic achievements."

"Oh."

"And I have the privilege of calling you to say that you were chosen to receive the award this semester."

"Oh. Wow. That's amazing. Thank you so much."

"No, thank you. Your professors unanimously agreed to bestow you with this designation. You'll receive it at a ceremony when you return after break, and then it will be announced again at the commencement exercises in the spring. It's a huge honor, Brooke, and from what I understand, it is well deserved."

"Thank you. I don't know what to say."

"My pleasure. Enjoy your holiday, and I look forward to meeting you in person when school resumes."

Brooke looked up at Sarah, who was watching her intently, a questioning look on her face.

"What was that about?"

"I guess I won an award for school. That was a nice surprise."

"What sort of award? The Peak of Everett award? No way! Was it The Peak award?"

Brooke nodded yes.

"Oh my God! That's amazing! I'm so proud of you." Sarah jumped up from the table and gave Brooke an enthusiastic hug. "You have no idea what a big deal it is, Brooke! Usually it's like foreign students who have perfect grades and speak five languages and get invited to the White House because they're heading up global anti-famine campaigns, crazy serious stuff like that. I'm so impressed! Good for you!"

Sarah was positively beaming at Brooke. Her excitement was contagious, and Brooke felt incredibly happy.

"You have to do a search and find out who the past recipients were. There are Nobel Prize winners! I'm so proud of you! This is fantastic!"

"Thanks. Thanks a lot."

It was looking like Jessica hadn't had enough time to ruin Brooke's life after all.

CHAPTER TWENTY-EIGHT

The wind snatched at their clothes and pelted them with snow as they walked hurriedly to the Jeep. The plows had already pushed a short wall of snow next to it.

Brooke unknowingly held her breath as they got in, worried that Sarah would look in the back seat again. The worst case scenario Brooke could imagine was that Sarah would grab for the blanket, dirty or not, because it was so cold. No explanation would suffice if that happened and she saw Jessica's body. Actually, that wasn't true. Brooke could pretend to be shocked and horrified and the blame would fall on Ethan. After all, it was his car. She could easily make it his problem by arranging a few things so that he would look undeniably guilty. But that wasn't the easiest solution. She still had the Taser, and the chloroform, so no worries, although Sarah was strong. She hoped there would only be one dead body at the end of the night because Sarah was her favorite running partner.

Sarah leaned forward and started wiping condensation from the inside of the windows. Then she fiddled with the dashboard controls, helping Brooke to find the front defrost button. Brooke had to put the windshield wipers on high speed in order to see. As they pulled away from the curb, listening to warnings about the imminent blizzard, Sarah started feeling anxious about getting back to the dorm. She never looked in the back of the car; she was too concerned about what was going on outside the front windows. She gazed at the road intently, as if her concentration would help them get back safely.

Back on campus, Brooke made the turn toward South Vernon to drop Sarah off instead of turning toward the parking lot. She pulled the car as close to the front of the dorm as possible and shifted into neutral.

"You're not dropping me off. I'll come with you to park the car, don't be silly," Sarah insisted.

"I'm not going in. I'm going right to Ethan's dorm; it's closer to the parking lot. I'll be fine. Don't worry. I'm so, so glad you came to my class! I'll see you tomorrow? Now get out. Go!"

Sarah shook her head at Brooke's stubbornness. She felt a little guilty about being dropped off when Brooke still had to park and walk through the storm, but Brooke was insisting and had refused to leave until Sarah got out.

"Okay. Congratulations again! And I loved your class. Hurry, okay? I can't believe how strong the wind is blowing!" Sarah got out quickly, slammed the door, and rushed up the stairs with her head down.

Brooke drove away, exhaling loudly through her mouth and feeling some of the tension in her shoulders release. She was grateful that a potential disaster had been averted. Now she needed a place to be alone, and it couldn't wait. If the storm passed, Ethan would be taking his car to go skiing. She had to get Jessica out and take her somewhere.

The snow was falling with more weight and frequency, as if being dumped from the sky. The storm had strengthened even since they left The Perk House. Brooke flicked on the high beams as she passed a small group of people in front of the dorm. It was hard to see, but she could tell they were having a snowball fight. Not everyone had the sense to go inside and she wished they did because she needed to find privacy.

She continued past the dormitories and the academic buildings, past the basketball arena, around the fitness complex, behind the tennis courts and the pond. Everything looked different in the deepening untouched snow. Finally she found the maintenance building. It was dark and quiet. Desolate. No one would be out for a walk or exploring the campus tonight. But then it occurred to her that the maintenance building housed the shovels and plows, and what if the grounds crew got calls to come back to campus to clear the interior roads? After what happened at Cedarhurst, she wasn't about to take the risk. With frustration she realized that she had perhaps chosen the worst place to go. She needed a remote location where she had no chance of being disturbed. The memory of her Mountain Day picnic with Ethan gave her an idea.

The gravel road was undistinguishable from the land around it because of the snow cover, but eventually she was able to identify where it filled the space between the trees. Brooke drove slowly down the gravel road, perched on the edge of her seat, through the giant stone wall that marked Everett's remote back exit. It was truly spooky on Stonewall Road. The windshield wipers struggled to keep her view clear, just long enough for the headlights to illuminate the crazily falling snow. She drove less than ten miles an hour while the Jeep lurched in and out of ditches, heading farther away from the campus. If she went any faster she wouldn't be able to see. According to the dashboard thermometer, it was ten degrees outside and, with the wind chill factor, would feel much colder.

Twenty minutes elapsed, at this cautious speed it felt like she had traveled a greater distance than the last time she was there. The road was unmarked by other vehicles, its borders completely hidden under a covering of whiteness. Nothing was recognizable. The snow slashed horizontally at her window. The storm was out of control and still increasing in intensity. She made one turn and leaned further forward, squinting for signs of the bridge's iron railings because she knew she had to be close now. The Jeep was barely moving when the steel side frame of the bridge appeared, looming just mere yards ahead of her. Instead of being centered with the bridge, she was to its left, which meant she had been driving several yards off the side of the road.

By the time she reached the bridge, she fully realized that the storm had destroyed any hope of experimentation. Self-preservation was a much stronger motivator than intellectual curiosity. She needed to get rid of Jessica's body and get herself to safety.

She straightened the Jeep and drove to the center of the bridge, judging by the arch of the steel railings. She put the car in park and sat still another moment, feeling anxious about emerging into the raging storm. She hated that she had no other options regarding Jessica, but the weather was too fierce to go on with her original plans.

Ice-cold air smacked her face as soon as she opened her door, burning her exposed skin. The snow whipped around her eyes, temporarily blinding her. She left the car engine running while she got out, slammed her door shut and went around the car to open the back door. She was humbled and terrified by the powerful storm as it overwhelmed her senses. It was incredibly cold, loud, and frightening. The weather conditions had changed so quickly. How was it possible?

Snow flew into the car, coating the back seat and floor. She attempted to pull the stadium blanket off of Jessica's body with one firm yank, but it was stuck. She shoved Jessica over to the right with one foot and pulled the blanket out from where it was caught underneath her hip. With the blanket lifted, Jessica looked like a complete mess. Brooke gazed down as she braced herself against the car to stay upright, feeling torn about what she was about to do. The temptation to take Jessica somewhere warm and well-lit and slowly cut into her was unbearable, but she had no ideas. The wind was howling, she could barely see and she could barely stand up. Keeping her eyes open against the onslaught of snow was near impossible; she had to squint to protect her vision. There were so many things she wanted to learn first-hand on a human cadaver, and now she had to forgo all of them! It was the storm's fault. And she hadn't planned for any of this. The weather conditions had worsened so quickly that it seemed imperative to get back to the dorm.

She tossed the blanket onto the back seat where another coating of white immediately assembled on its folds. She pulled Jessica up by the arms, squatted down, tucked her shoulders into Jessica's chest and pulled again. Jessica's sweater snagged on something and her whole body was suddenly jerked back out of Brooke's grasp.

Okay, deep breath, pretend you're in a cross-fit class and this is the next multi-functional move. Get it together, you can do this.

She released the snag by tugging Jessica to the side. She straightened up and was able to pull Jessica partway out. She leaned backward and lifted, but Jessica's head hit the top of the door frame and was knocked off of Brooke's shoulders. Jessica body collapsed in an unwieldy heap, half in and half out of the car, her brown hair splayed across her face and over the snow covered ground. The door of the Jeep, at the mercy of the wind, slammed into Brooke and knocked her forward. Her legs pressed against Jessica's body and stabilized her, but not before her own head hit the edge of the doorframe.

Brooke reached up to touch her forehead, it would be badly bruised, but she couldn't feel it because the exposed skin on her face and neck were already aching from the cold. She gathered her determination and started again. This time she succeeded in dragging most of Jessica out of the car. Crouching down low, she hoisted her body up and over her shoulder. In this position Jessica's body was partly shielding Brooke from the assaulting snow. The car door was blowing backward against its hinges now. She tried to kick it closed, but was unsuccessful and almost lost her balance again. Forgetting about the door, she hurried toward the side of the bridge, her legs straining to carry Jessica's weight. With all her strength, she flung Jessica's body against the steel railing, aiming to get most of her across the top. Jessica's face was turned toward the sky. The snow was coating her features, making her eyebrows look thick and grey. Her loose hair was tangled and blew out and away from her head like Medusa.

Quickly, Brooke pressed Jessica's torso against the railing so that she wouldn't slide down while she boosted her upwards, hands lifting from under the back of Jessica's thighs. She moved Jessica upward until more than half of her weight was on the opposite side of the railing. Brooke released her, stepped back, and watched with the wind wailing around her as Jessica tumbled out of sight and down to the creek below. The falling snow and blowing drifts contributed to near whiteout conditions and Brooke couldn't see to the bottom. It was a long way down. She remembered that giant boulders protruded from the water. A *whack!* reverberated as Jessica's body made contact below, barely discernible from the howling cacophony of the storm.

Brooke staggered back to the car, difficult in the wind even without the burden of carrying a lifeless body. The wind was a giant vacuum attempting to suck her clothes away from every angle. After opening the front door and jumping inside, she struggled to pull it closed again. Shuddering, she shook her head in disbelief at the unexpected ferocity of the storm. It was a shock to her system and now superseded the disappointment she felt at having to dispose of Jessica so quickly. It took a minute to calm her nerves using deep breathing, inhaling through one nostril and exhaling out the other. The water dripping down her face didn't register because she was numb from the cold. She put the Jeep in reverse and slowly, carefully backed off the bridge, using all of her mirrors and the back-up camera, none of which proved helpful. Wary about hitting the sides of the bridge, she debated getting out of the car to ascertain her location, but she didn't think she could bear to even open the door again.

She was terrified about getting in an accident and having to explain what she was doing out there, if she didn't die from exposure first. The car dropped gently down, indicating she was off the bridge and on to solid ground. She backed up another twenty yards or so in order to turn around. She made several small forward and reverse movements with the car, turning a bit with each one, because she wasn't sure how much space she had available on the road. She felt the tension in her shoulders release a bit once the car was facing forward again. The snow was falling so fast that her tire tracks from less than five minutes ago were almost obliterated.

Brooke could not believe what she was experiencing. She grew up in Connecticut, but she had never been outside in a blizzard before. She had never seen anything like it. It reminded her of a horror movie she watched about a white-out in Antarctica, and things did not end well for any of its characters. She made out the end of the tree line marking the turn back onto Stonewall Road and told herself that she would make it if she kept calm.

Since Stonewall Road was lined by fields, it was again impossible for her to tell if she was on the road or heading out into the middle of nowhere. She felt panic rising. She stopped the car completely, unsure of which direction to head. With no clues, she started moving forward slowly, just taking a guess as to the correct direction. Through the constant movement of the storm she spied something solid and still. A crumbling stone wall just a few feet to her left. It should have been many yards away if she was traveling on the road. She jerked the car toward the right just before she hit the wall. She stayed close and parallel to the stones, using them as a guide to keep her on the road.

CRACK!

A large tree branch hit the front windshield, startling Brooke and causing her to let out an involuntary scream. The branch bounced forward and was crushed by the car, leaving her nerves completely shaken. The tension in her body was so pronounced that her forearms were tight and sore, locked in rigid positions. She removed each hand from the steering wheel and shook it out, attempting to relieve the tightness. Her trembling hands reached toward the radio controls as she decided that hearing someone else's voice might help her stay focused and calm. It was tuned to a news station out of Boston.

"We are already receiving reports of accidents–cars going off the road because they can't see in this snow. Stay inside, and definitely stay off the roads. It's dangerous outside, you don't want to be trapped. We've already had ten inches of snow and it's falling heavily and it will continue to do so into tomorrow. This storm has created a very dangerous situation. We have very strong winds, coastal flooding. Almost two hundred thousand customers without power already. Hurricane force winds are taking down trees and power lines. This is going to be a historic event, one for the record books."

Brooke listened to continuous storm commentary while she inched along in the Jeep for thirty nerve wracking minutes. Sticks and branches continued to fly around and at her.

She had plenty of time to think about Jessica and what would happen to her body over the next few weeks, but she didn't because she was too stressed about the driving conditions to concentrate on anything but getting back safely. She almost cried when she finally reached the giant stonewall entrance, and then the gravel road that returned her to Everett. She stopped the car behind the maintenance building, as close to its brick walls as she could manage. The building provided protection from the storm on one side and she felt relatively safe for the first time in over an hour.

The wind had ushered snow into the car while the door was open. The entire back seat was soaking wet and even the front seats and the dashboard were dripping. Brooke climbed through to the back seat and wiped down every surface with the stadium blanket. She would tell Ethan it fell out of the car at the gym. Or better yet, she should wash it herself to get rid of any traces of Jessica.

Her clothes were drenched as she scooted back into the front seat. She turned the radio off and for a full minute she sat and breathed, taking stock of the situation as the wind whipped about carrying with it every small thing that wasn't tied down. She wondered if Tony from the weather station was still standing outside in his bright yellow ski jacket so that everyone could see how hard the snow was falling. She imagined the newscaster saying "You can see that Tony's eyelashes are frozen together and he has frostbite on his ears because it's really coming down now."

Brooke laughed. She wasn't back indoors yet, but she felt safe, relieved and exhausted. What an ordeal! In comparison, she hadn't needed to dispose of Mr. Wilhelm or Bradley, who wasn't actually dead, but he might as well have been. She had simply walked away. Killing Jessica had been a tremendous effort, as if Jessica had been high-maintenance until the bitter end.

Brooke unzipped her coat pocket to remove her phone and discovered that Ethan had called and texted her several times during the past hour. She called him and he picked up before the first ring was complete.

"Where are you? It's not okay to be driving in this weather! It's really dangerous right now." Ethan's voice was serious and assertive. Once his television announced that the full force of the blizzard had arrived, he had become an insanely worried wreck waiting on Brooke.

"I know. It's incredible. Unbelievable! One minute it was just windy and snowing and then it was a blizzard! It sort of ruined my plans, but I think it will prove to be a gift in the long run."

"What plans did you have?"

"Just something I'd been thinking about doing for a long time. Never mind. I have some exciting news. I won something and I bet you know all about it so you can fill me in. I'll tell you when I get there."

CHAPTER TWENTY-NINE

It took days before anyone concluded that something unforeseen had happened to Jessica. She was simply gone. "What do *you* think happened to Jessica Carroll?" became a terrific topic of conversation across campus when everyone returned from winter break. Was it an accidental death, suicide, or foul play? The information that was gathered over the subsequent months seemed to point to one of the first two options, a mysterious tragedy of her own making, one that had been building up over the course of the semester and had manifested itself in many significant forms.

Her parents were initially irritated at what they assumed was a lack of consideration. They figured her original plans to return home had been altered by Storm Connor, but then two entire days passed without hearing from her. Power was out all over New England, so it was possible that she had been unable to charge her phone. They were worried, and they had to delay their plans to fly to Florida. Since they couldn't get hold of Jessica, Foster gave Rebeka the task of tracking down Robert Mending and a few of her other friends. All of them had left campus by then and assumed she had as well, and no, they had not heard from her since they left school.

"Isn't it unusual to go a few days without speaking to your girlfriend?" Robert was asked. He said that it was, but admitted that she was angry because he had not asked her to accompany his family to Aruba. Due to their argument, he wasn't expecting to hear from her.

The Carrolls became extremely concerned and called campus security. Jim and Bob checked her room, which was unlocked. Some of her belongings were packed and her refrigerator was empty, its contents rotting in her trash can. They found an assortment of high-end liquor, enough energy drinks to keep a family awake for a month, empty prescription pill bottles that had not been prescribed to her, along with two types of anti-depressants that had. Several essential items were inside the room: her phone, a winter coat, her wallet, and credit cards, which seemed to indicate that she had never left the dorm or if she did, she wasn't planning to return because she was headed to a place where none of those things were necessary. Security called the Carrolls to report what they had found. The Carrolls called the police, and, soon after, their own private detectives.

The police worked closely with campus officials, updating the president and vice president of the college several times a day. Everett's attorneys reviewed all of the college's official statements on the matter before they were publicly aired so as to minimize any chances of potential litigation. There was solid evidence that Jessica had been alive and well on December 16th. She took, and spectacularly failed, a microeconomics exam that afternoon. South Vernon residents were interviewed over the phone around the country and even on four other continents, in an effort to determine who had seen her last. Of note, Maria Chow saw her arguing with Robert Mending in the late morning hours as she happened by Jessica's room.

"She was totally out of control. I could hear her screaming from the end of the hallway because her door was open. She threw something at him just as I walked by. It looked like a baseball. Hurled it right at him. I heard him pleading with her to be quiet and then he shut the door."

Megan O'Rourke was determined to be the last person who had seen Jessica that day. A distinction of which she was proud.

"I saw Jessica on the last night of exams. She was completely furious at Brittany Harris, because Brittany had borrowed her brown Cole Haan dress boots and was leaving for break without returning them. Jessica was really angry all the time though, so that's not unusual by itself. The last I saw she was going to find Brittany before she left campus so she could get her boots. But then Brittany came back to say goodbye to me and I said 'Did you see Jessica because she wants her boots back' and Brittany said she didn't see her but that she had already left the boots inside Jessica's room. Did you know about her car, that it was stolen and vandalized a few weeks ago?"

Every person the police interviewed told them about Jessica's car being stolen, as if the police would have missed the report with that information.

Brittany told the investigators that Jessica had left her a message about getting her boots back at six P.M. At the end of the message Jessica yelled, "Why is all of this happening to me? Ahhh!"

"I don't know what was happening to Jessica. Maybe someone else accidentally forgot to return something of hers, before they remembered and brought them back."

Brittany had not deleted the recording—it was *that* interesting—and so the police were able to hear it for themselves. Brittany was in the parking lot when she received the voicemail and she had come all the way back to the dorm to return the boots. She also denied that she was the one supplying Jessica with unlimited ephedrine pills.

The police asked every dorm resident they questioned if Jessica had any known enemies. Almost everyone said that "some people" thought Jessica was a snob, and maybe a racist, but there was no one that came to mind who would have particularly wanted to harm her.

The detectives easily uncovered Jessica's penchant for prescription pills, that she was a "lush" and a caffeine addict. The dorm's head-resident, Kate Newman–Schultz, was positive that Jessica did cocaine or meth, which would explain why she seemed "like an escaped lunatic, really edgy and practically insane" when they had to meet with her about "an issue." The police had to press about the nature of the "issue" only to discover that it was the racial incident they had already heard so much about from other students.

Near the beginning of the investigation, the police received a call from the dry cleaning service employed by Everett College. They wanted the police to know that Jessica Carroll, the missing girl who was all over the local news, had left them an irate message just a week before her disappearance. They had deleted it, but not before everyone that worked at the business had listened to it. They had no trouble recalling what was said. She had accused them of writing messages on her shirt with invisible ink. Specifically, the words "Snooty Drunk." She first wanted to make it clear that she was barely even a social drinker, and then implied that they did it out of jealousy because their lot in life was to do laundry for people like her. She insisted that someone be fired and she wanted a new shirt. At the time they found the message to be blatantly discriminating but also highly amusing because the owner of the store was an Everett grad and his oldest son was currently a freshman there. In light of the current situation, they felt terrible about playing the message repeatedly and having a laugh at her expense. They should have been more sensitive, the young woman was disturbed and had needed help.

Suicide was the most likely possibility. Jessica took anti-depressants, and had been for many years. There was no way to know if she had been taking them recently as prescribed. Her English professor said she was struggling and had handed in a peculiar paper exploring the mental health and suicides of some female authors, which may have been telling. An examination of her college transcript offered plenty of reasons why she might have been feeling like a failure at a school like Everett, where the students tended to be intensely competitive in regard to academic success. A further review of her admission application and her high school transcript unearthed an awkward situation for Everett's admissions department, and a bigger mystery, possibly to be dealt with at a later time. Mainly, why on earth was she accepted there in the first place?

Jessica's professors explored the connection between her disappearance and the theft of her car. During one especially dynamic brainstorming session in the Administrative Building, they discussed the logistics of a scenario where she had staged the theft and vandalism on her own, possibly for attention. Leaving it alone, cracked, and damaged and miles from campus could have been her way of reaching out for help, metaphorically and subliminally.

There were many outgoing calls from Jessica's phone leading up until six fifteen that evening, most of them to Robert and Brittany. Fortunately for Robert, who would have lined up to be a prime suspect, if there had been evidence or suspicion of an actual crime, he was on his way home to Greenwich and had stopped to get gas, proving his location, before Jessica was last seen in the halls of her dorm. He knew she was having a tough semester, she wasn't sleeping, and she was increasingly irritable, but she was so supremely confident about everything that he never once considered her in need of help. He felt guilty about whatever happened because maybe if he had stayed Jessica would at least be around to get the care she apparently needed. He had not realized the magnitude of whatever it was she was going through.

Ethan also felt terrible about Jessica's unexplained disappearance, even though he had never liked her and had considered her akin to the Wicked Witch of the West. But now, the word around campus was that she was more of a train wreck. He was upset with Robert for not making that more clear. On the last day that anyone had seen Jessica, Ethan had provided her two stiff drinks in an effort to calm her down and get rid of her, two drinks more than she apparently needed. He would have played that whole scene out differently if he had known Jessica was so unstable she wasn't going to make it through the day, although his priority would still have been to protect Brooke from Jessica's snobbery.

The Carrolls questioned if Campus Security should have explored the initial vehicle theft incident further. Might that have prevented this subsequent event? Were they even remotely related? Was it possible that the people who had stolen her car had anything to do with her going missing? The only clues that had been found with the car were two pairs of small footprints, sneakers and boots, so that line of thinking went nowhere. Foster Carroll felt enormously guilty that he hadn't given the theft or Jessica much of his attention when it occurred.

What made all of this even more devastating for the Carroll family was that their nephew Bradley now existed in an irreversible coma, the result of a violent and unexplained attack during a fraternity party. Detectives found no commonalities between the incidents other than heavy drug and alcohol use. Bradley's blood alcohol level had been through the roof. It was possible that Harvard fraternities would go the same route as Everett's and disappear so as to prevent further tragedies.

Brooke was never interviewed by the police. Why would she be? She lived in the same dorm as Jessica, but on separate floors. Other than Robert and Ethan, they were not in the same circle of friends and had almost nothing in common. If they had interviewed Brooke, she would have said that she had, coincidentally, watched Jessica efficiently down a few drinks in Ethan's room after their last exam. She left to teach a class at Resolution Fitness in front of more than forty people, at almost the same time as Megan said she saw Jessica go after Brittany and the boots. After that, Brooke went to The Perk House with a friend, and then spent her last night of the semester with her boyfriend. Her parents drove to campus the next day, a trip that took three times longer than usual because of the road conditions, and took her home.

The police had to stop their searches by Christmas. They were hampered by too many obstacles—the storm, the Christmas holiday (there was almost no one around to interview in person), and zero evidence of any crime. There wasn't much that could be done. It snowed and snowed and snowed, breaking all the records. Everything was covered with mountains of fresh snow making it impossible to find clues or tracks. The Carrolls arranged for the best avalanche search dogs in Alaska to come to Everett. The dogs searched for days, covering every inch of campus including all the way out to the remote opening on the edge of Stonewall Road. By then Jessica had been missing for over a week, and since she was miles away from campus, the dogs found no trace of what they were supposed to find.

Armed with an extensive and thorough profile on Jessica Carroll, the police detectives conceded that she most likely got too drunk or high celebrating the end of the semester, passed out somewhere and succumbed to hypothermia. Or, a combination of mental instability and the drugs she was taking caused her to wander off, again resulting in a bad ending, which may or may not have been intentional, because of the freezing temperatures and the unprecedented blizzard. Or, she might have known exactly what she was doing when she went somewhere private and secluded to end her life. There were lots of possible explanations, and the least likely, based on what they knew, was that Jessica had been the victim of foul play. It was never suggested by anyone that she had been gleefully killed and disposed of by another female student, an alarmingly beautiful psychotic perfectionist who didn't want to take the chance that she had been caught cheating, and that it had absolutely nothing to do with the condition of Jessica's mental and physical deterioration over the course of the semester. They never guessed that Jessica's only mistakes had been confidently glaring at Brooke and being in the wrong place at the right time. They expected to find Jessica's body somewhere near campus once the snow melted, if Foster Carroll's privately hired detectives didn't find it first.

Brooke received the prestigious Peak of Everett Award and the only A on Ms. MacIntyre's chemistry final. Her perfect GPA remains intact and she's working on her applications to medical school. Her first choice is Rothaker, because it's the top med school in the country. She continues to run out to the bridge when she has the chance. She's waiting for the snow to melt because she knows that what is lying beneath by the creek will fascinate her. Just like the cauliflower cat.

The End

The book ended, but the story isn't over. The sequel begins with Brooke's first day at Rothaker, where she is a first-year medical student. You can tell that she's even more confident by the way that she talks about what happened to Jessica. I've added a little romance to make it more fun and you can't help but root for one of the new main characters.

ROTHAKER

Brooke is thrilled to be starting her first year of medical school. She is stunning, brilliant and exceedingly ambitious. Despite the unsettling activities of her past, she's vowed not to do anything that might jeopardize her future. She's totally focused, although she's also interested in uncovering the dark secrets that haunt her new classmate, Xander Cross.

Medical school is demanding, and expensive, but manageable until one of her lab partners becomes concerned with Brooke's behavior and the situation turns serious. The closer she gets to becoming a surgeon, the more she has to lose, and she will do whatever it takes to make sure nothing and no one stops her from achieving her goals. Just one mistake could destroy it all.

ABOUT THE AUTHOR

Jenifer Ruff is the author of dark thrillers, *Everett* and *Rothaker*. She grew up in Northampton, MA and earned science degrees from Mount Holyoke College and Yale University. After graduate school at Yale, Jenifer worked as a health care management consultant for Kaiser Permanente, Anderson Consulting and PriceWaterhouseCoopers. She has been an avid reader and an exercise devotee for as long as she can remember. She is also a certified exercise instructor who has taught classes for many years. Jenifer now lives in Charlotte, North Carolina with her husband and children. When not exercising or writing, she manages the activities of her three active sons. For more about Jenifer and upcoming books see jenruff.com.